I0672618

Eiffel Spirit

By

Anita Robertson

DEEP READ PRESS
LAFAYETTE, TENNESSEE
www.deepreadpress.com

First Deep Read Press edition

ISBN: 978-1-954989-01-6
Cover Design by: Kim Gammon
Edited by: Shena Newberry Wilder
Published by
DEEP READ PRESS
LAFAYETTE, TENNESSEE
www.deepreadpress.com

Dedicated to the spirit of someone I hold very dear and whom I miss with all my heart.

Un

Fading

*T*HE Legend lived and I am here to testify to his existence. Some will say stories of the Eiffel Spirit were only imaginary. I am here to say that not only were they real, but they are forever engraved in the history of Paris. Lives were lost at the foot of the Tower. Young women were cast down and abandoned from the iconic structure. The city was paralyzed with fear.

Sworn to secrecy, I have kept his story from becoming public knowledge. In order to protect the memory of the only woman he had ever loved, he made me promise to keep his secret. There was only one caveat. I would be allowed to reveal the details of his semi-mythical existence only after his death.

I am Natalie Bertrand. I was with him on the night he died, and I remember every detail of that still and eerie night. It was as if we were the only people who existed. The Rue des Rosiers had never been so quiet. I found myself listening intently for a sound that would reassure me that the world had not ended.

Suddenly, a cool breeze swept through the window. The wind picked up, slapping the old shutters against the house as if it came on purpose to escort his soul from this earthly realm. Creating their own rhythm, the shutters seemed to be tapping out a fond adieu.

I sat close beside him. My rocking body soon took on the beat of the shutters. I swayed back and forth for what seemed like an eternity. As the moon glided by the window, I witnessed the whiteness of his thin skin, paler than even his ordinary countenance. Still, I held his hand, thinking I could forestall the reality of what was happening by not moving from that spot. While I stroked his cold hand, I found myself wishing that I had the power to infuse him once again with life, all the while knowing no such power existed within me.

Finally, as the light of day no longer offered me the safety of the night's seclusion, I summoned the courage to fully gaze upon him. His long gray locks were splayed upon the pillow. I gasped when I beheld his face, unprepared to see that his eyes were still open. I held my breath as I looked into them. Although the light was extinguished, they still maintained their deep blue-green tint. I remember thinking that they were the color of the Seine as it ran though the city he loved. With trembling fingers, I closed his eyelids, sighing as I realized they would not observe the light of this new day.

It was then that the torrent let loose from my own eyes. It began to pour rain outside at the same moment. Even the heavens were crying for the loss of the enigmatic Eiffel Spirit.

No longer would I learn from his patient suffering. No longer would I endure the constant concern for his safety and his health. No longer would Paris look for him in every crevice as the population embellished the details of a life, they would never fully understand.

But now, The Spirit needs to be exonerated. His life was full of purpose and I believe that I must reveal the details now that I am free to do so.

Our lives had always been intertwined. As a bridge to telling his story, I must weave in the details of my own, for it is the only way to divulge the details of the Eiffel Spirit's existence. And I must begin from the first moment that I became aware of his existence.

Deux

The Cape

I awoke to the sweet scent of the linden trees curling like smoke through the small slit that was the only window in my bed chamber. A child of seven, I had not yet realized the space that I called my room was a closet that my mother converted to suit my very few needs. It never occurred to me because I seldom spent any time in the confines of our rented apartment on the Rue de Rosiers.

I stood upon my cot so that I could observe the view of the avenue through the high window on an early spring morning. Other scents soon pervaded the air. I closed my eyes and pictured Madame Fournier's croissants and baguettes turning a golden brown in the bakery ovens below our apartment.

The crisp scent of coolness from the water in the Seine could also be detected. All the components of this aromatic bouquet called to me. I felt as though a force was pulling me toward nature. I simply could not stay inside with the fresh air and spring blooms waiting such a short distance away. I was drawn to the outdoors, like a moth to a flame.

As I tiptoed out the door of the apartment, I reached for the red cape that my mother made for me to keep the morning chill at bay. Although I was never cold at that age, I did this to please her in case she woke and saw that I was gone. I was never aware of the temperature or in any way uncomfortable as a child unless it was from the feeling of being confined. I was always in pursuit of freedom. I rejoiced as my bare feet flew through Eiffel Park and I became one with the glorious spring morning.

I did not know that he was watching me.

My cape had become my wings. Laughing, I ducked in and out among the blooming expanse of the massive lindens. Spring flowers were poking through the green grass as nature healed the injuries that the park suffered during the winter snows. I gave in to the temptation of picking a small bouquet. Humming to myself I continued to spread my red cape out behind me as I danced to the tune that I sang to myself. I must have looked like one possessed with an unquenchable desire to fly.

He watched as my long chestnut hair tangled itself around my face. Impatiently, I pushed it away from my eyes, so I could catch a glimpse of where I was running. He heard my soft giggles and observed the choreography of the dance that I created in my utter joy.

As I approached the tower while twirling about, I stopped short when I observed the pale specter posed there behind its golden footing.

Although scared, I was at once enthralled by the look of him. At first, I thought the still figure might be a statue, perhaps added temporarily to the base of the Eiffel for some art exhibit. I must have appeared to be part of an exhibit myself as I stood there frozen in my tracks.

Time stood still.

Vaguely, I heard my mother's voice calling my name. The sound was muffled as if I were in a tunnel or a fog-like state of unreality. My heart was focused on the creature who studied me with such intensity that I felt my own strength being drawn into his being. It was as if my young soul was being sucked toward this mystical force. Then, with the swiftness of a light breeze he was gone, and my mother's voice became clear and demanding behind me in the park.

I was still emerging from the trance created by his presence. The feeling I was left with was not unpleasant. Although, as I emerged from this dreamlike state, I was slightly surprised to find myself in front of the tower rather than in my cot surrounded by my coverlets. The past few moments had resulted in a surreal and strange feeling.

At that moment, I realized the encounter had not been a dream. The vision of the pale creature had been real. I looked all around me for the being who had caused my heart to stop. But there was no trace of him. I was aware that I would remember this morning for the rest of my life.

From the corner of my eye, I saw my mother approaching and knew at once that she was disturbed by what she saw. She began scolding me as soon as she was near. She was distressed when she saw my bare feet and noticed that my shoulders were only loosely wrapped in the thin red cape. She practically spat her words at me.

"How do you think I feel seeing my child looking like a street urchin in the Eiffel Tower Park? This is a public place, Natalie, and there you are with your hair in knots and no slippers on your feet. Hurry now before anyone sees us." It was a scolding I had heard countless times before and knew I would hear again.

Her verbal jabs continued. "How could I be such a thoughtless child causing her such worry? Didn't I know it was dangerous for a child to roam around the city alone?"

Before grabbing my hand to drag me home, she put one hand on each side of my bright red cheeks warming them up with her own body heat. As she led me toward the bakery, with an alarming amount of speed, I felt a slight twinge of guilt for causing her such worry and potential embarrassment.

My mind kept conjuring images of the strange apparition I had seen and although my mother kept up with an endless number of reprimands, I barely discerned the words.

Neither of us noticed as my cape slipped from my shoulders and was caught in the updraft.

Madame Fournier looked up from the bakery counter as we entered, but my mother sheltered me toward her body and rushed me upstairs to our apartment. There were to be no good morning pleasantries that day.

I was certain that I would run off again in the early morning hours another day. I would simply have to feel the delight of turning in circles as I spread imaginary wings.

And I would not be able to resist the chance to see him again. He was already haunting me.

Trois

Screams

*I*T would be quite a while before our next encounter, although I looked for him many times.

My mother began to watch me like a hawk, and though I knew she was protecting me, I felt as though I was being kept in a cage. I heard her tell Madame Fournier that if she did not keep an eye on me, I would wind up in a heap someday on the lawn of the tower park, or perhaps be snatched by a band of gypsies.

Madame had laughed at this comment and to my mother's chagrin she said that I probably would not mind at all being part of a gypsy caravan. She said that she was sure it would suit my nature very well.

When I was exceptionally lucky, I was able to convince my mother to have a picnic at the tower park. On those glorious days, we bought a few slices of ham from the butcher down the street, and of course beseeched Madame Fournier for a fresh baguette. Mother would tuck a bottle of wine in the basket, and a thermos of water for me.

Those outings were as good for my mother as for me, though she would never admit that the fresh air and the voices of other people injected our day with some life-giving energy. I think she was aware that I had ulterior motives for being in the park. She watched as I stared off into the distance more than once. However, since I always had a vivid imagination and few friends, she refrained from asking me a lot of questions when I drifted off in my own little world. She knew how much I hated being cooped up indoors and by giving in to the occasional outing, she felt as if she was making it up to me.

She told me that if she accompanied me on these small excursions, she did not have to be afraid of what kind of trouble I might get into. Sometimes, she brought a book of poetry and read out loud to me. Those were very special days.

All of that changed when I reached the age of eleven. Activities surrounding the tower became sinister that year.

It began the night of April 23, when the stillness of the pre-dawn hours was shattered by high pitched screams from the second landing of the tower.

The screams awoke many of us in the apartments near the Eiffel Park.

I found out later that several people sat straight up in their beds frozen with fear.

The screams were followed by sirens. Lights were turned on down the avenue as we all drew near to our windows trying to catch a glimpse of something. Without venturing out that night, as scared as we were, we hoped to observe a clue of what might be happening in the park.

My mother appeared at the door to my little room and told me to get back under the covers. She tucked me in and tried to appear calm, but could tell that any feelings she had of security were shattered by the screams and the sirens.

She kissed my forehead and returned to her own bed. The kiss was unexpected since she rarely showed her feelings and never revealed an emotional response.

When I closed my eyes I envisioned an image of the being I encountered years before at the Eiffel Park. I wondered if that specter had been the source of the night's chaos.

I pulled the covers over my head and hid there until the sun lit up my room.

Quatre

Aftermath

*T*HE streets were abuzz with gossip the morning after the night-shattering screams. I made myself invisible by hiding in the corner of the boulangerie downstairs. I knew I would hear the story in the early part of the day when neighbors congregated to get their baguettes and croissants.

A body had been found at the foot of the tower nearest the strand of linden trees. It was a young woman with long, black hair. She was found there completely naked except that her body had been covered by what they were saying looked like a lace bridal veil.

She had not yet been identified.

The police had kept most of the people back from the scene, but Pierre de Crois had breeched the barriers and was now holding court in the bakery as he captivated the locals with the details.

There was no blood on the body, he reported. In fact, he was eerily surprised to see that the girl looked like she was only sleeping and might stand up and walk away at any moment. Monsieur de Crois proclaimed that she was quite beautiful, and her death was a waste of her youth and potential. He relished in being the center of attention as he wove the story of the young girl's demise, and although his audience seemed to be in awe, I wondered how much of what he said was embellished for the sake of drama.

He was even more delighted as some of the patrons offered him coffee and pastries so that he would stay longer to answer their questions. One thing was certain. Until the incident was fully investigated, the park would be closed to the public and for tonight there would be an imposed curfew in the entire area.

Shoving the last morsel of pastry into his mouth, Monsieur de Crois looked around at the eager group, paused and made the announcement that law enforcement would begin the curfew that evening at 8:00.

One by one the customers dispersed.

My mother had not shown up to hear the tale told at the bakery. She was probably already sipping her cognac.

Five weeks later another body was found near the foot of the tower, this time it was a young tourist from Belgium. I returned from school that afternoon to find my mother whispering in our doorway with Madame Foulette, who sold lacework in the shop next door.

Mother motioned for me to pass on by and the conversation ceased until I was out of earshot. But it did not matter. Several of my classmates were aware of what had happened and news of the girl's death was scribbled on notes that were passed around in class during the entire school day.

Yvonne Demarco particularly enjoyed her status during the process. Everyone was soon made aware that her father, who served on the local police force, was called to the scene at daybreak and was one of the first to view the victim.

I read one of the notes Yvonne wrote when it was passed over the shoulder of the student who sat in front of me. She had punctuated the words by drawing a crude picture of a body lying on the ground. She had sketched what looked like a veil on the deceased girl's head. For effect, she used a red colored pencil to depict a trail of blood dripping down the side of the Eiffel Tower, covering the victim and staining the ground. I was appalled at the drawing and at the same time impressed with Yvonne's artistic talent.

Still, if my mother thought she was protecting me from the details of the latest crime she would have been surprised to learn that the staff and students at my school were just as mesmerized by the mysterious events as were the rest of the city's residents. It seemed that gossip was the life-breath of the inhabitants.

It was customary for me to dash downstairs to the boulangerie as soon as I finished dressing every morning. After a brief glance in the hall mirror, checking that my school uniform was not in some degree of disarray, I scurried downstairs to bring my mother our daily baguette. It was a typical breakfast in those days with a strong cup of black coffee.

My mother broke with tradition after the murders began occurring with more regularity. Instead of waiting for me to perform our morning ritual, she began rising earlier. She told Madame Fournier that she wanted to stand next to her as she opened the shop door each day. She had become so anxious by the events at the tower that she was having trouble sleeping.

She told me that she needed to know every morning if there had been more foul play during the night. She said she was too nervous to stay in bed while I retrieved our bread and coffee. She even began to share some of the local gossip with me when I sat down with her for breakfast at one of bakery's small tables. I was astounded that my mother was treating me like an adult, sharing the details of what she had heard. Suddenly, I was being informed of things she never would have mentioned to me before.

It was the first time I heard the name, "Eiffel Spirit."

Parisians had coined this phrase for the murderer in the tower, who apparently delighted in slaughtering young women and had a knack for hiding himself somewhere in the park or within the tower itself. The police were frustrated at the lack of clues surrounding the murder scene.

Although Madame Fournier and the other shopkeepers were concerned about the crimes, they were more worried about the effect of the incidents on local tourism. They reported to all within earshot that fewer visitors were congregating at the tower for photographs. No one was making reservations for the restaurants within the tower and there were fewer shoppers on the surrounding streets.

My mother said that the ripple effect had already begun, throughout the city. Shopping had even come to a standstill on the Champs-Elysees and there were fewer reservations being made at the local brasseries. I was not sure if my mother was upset with the merchants for making their business losses seem to be more important than the deaths of the young victims, or if she was mad at the tourists themselves for not showing up in their usual numbers.

As I have gotten older, I have discovered that most major news events reach a crescendo and then fade away as they are pushed further back into the past. This was the case of the alleged murders at the tower. The second victim was finally identified. Her picture appeared in the newspaper and her family was barraged by reporters asking for every detail of her life.

For a time, the local population held its collective breath in fearful anticipation. But the criminal activity seemed to end abruptly, leaving everyone wondering why.

After two years, the stories of the victims had grown to legendary proportions. So many added details from the imaginations of the populace that even those of us who knew the original circumstances wondered if they might be true.

The tower became even more of a tourist attraction as people came to see the site of the crimes. Stories were even invented about sightings of the now famous "Eiffel Spirit." The mysterious killer, dubbed madman, serial killer, social misfit, seemed to have disappeared, and the news, like all old news had become distorted.

I heard several versions of the facts as time passed. Some said that there had been at least a dozen murders. Others reported that the victims had been found violated, or that they had been killed for their jewelry. One line of conjecture reported that the victims had gold fillings removed. I overheard a group of the teachers at the academy whispering that they heard the girls had been cut open and their hearts removed. I believe this was my favorite contrived piece of gossip during those days.

The Eiffel Tower, even more of an icon was now considered to be the spot where the city held its darkest secrets.

Cinq

Origins

MY mother told me several times that we were not poor when my father was alive. She said that he delighted in buying gifts for me when I was a baby and that she would often see him standing by the side of my crib just watching me sleep.

"The sun rose and set on you, Cherie. If you had not already captured my heart, I might have been jealous of your father's affection for you."

"Why did you live in such cramped quarters, Maman?"

"We were young and in love, believe me we could have lived under a rock and been happy. Besides, your father loved the view of the tower from this apartment. He said that he always wanted to have the tower in his sight and that he had promised himself he always would."

By the time Father died, close to my fourth birthday, my parents were contemplating a move into their own space, although living here, and being near their good friend Madame Fournier had been totally acceptable.

My mother became even more attached to me after my father was gone. She would climb into my small cot at night to put her arms around me, I believe it helped to sustain her in her grief.

My bedtime stories were reminiscences of their days together, falling in love, getting married and then sharing that love with me. I think that she told me the stories more for the purpose of reliving the events herself, rather than to soothe me to sleep.

It was important to her that I become educated, believing that this would be my salvation and my deliverance from poverty as I matured. She insisted that I learn several languages when I was little. She taught me herself since she had mastered them with such ease. She was a firm believer that children grasped new languages so much faster than adults. She tutored me in Spanish and Italian.

She said that my aptitude for learning languages was due in part to my infatuation with music. She believed that the intonations of the romantic languages were musical in themselves and therefore easy to absorb by someone with what she called an "ear" for the notes.

I read many books as a child, mostly because I had few friends. I would have enjoyed playing with other children more often, but when I was old enough to go to the public school, I realized that we lived right on the border of the school district and there were only a few students who lived nearby. I only saw my few acquaintances during the school day.

It never bothered me though because of my independent spirit and I'm not sure if a friend could have kept up with my energy level or been able to tolerate my stubborn nature.

Once widowed, my mother had extraordinarily little for us to live on. We were fortunate that Madame Fournier was such a good friend. I have often wondered if she made my mother pay the rent at all. If she was able to keep up that obligation when my father died, I am fairly sure that it fell by the wayside as she slipped further and further into the bottle.

Six

Changes

*A*s I approached my teen years my mother began to age rapidly. She cried often, sometimes moaning to me about how much she missed my father. On other occasions she would rant and rave about how she was always doing without the finer things of life because she had to spend all her money on me. And then there were days I would come home from school to find her asleep with her bedroom curtains drawn and every crack covered where light might seep in. I discovered quite early that on those days it was better to leave her completely alone. It felt as though from that point on she was no longer interested in raising a child, it was as if she had thrown me away with yesterday's fish guts. There were no qualms on her behalf in this abandonment. I learned to fend for myself very quickly.

Madame Fournier began saving me the stale bread leftover at the end of the day and occasionally sent her son, Philippe up to my apartment with small pieces of cheese or a bit of sausage from their own evening meal. What I did not learn until years later was that the boy shared part of his own food with me too, even from our young ages, he was already interested in impressing me.

To my surprise, Madame Fournier took me aside one rainy evening to tell me what was wrong with my mother. She explained that at a certain age woman experience what she called a change of life. It seemed she wanted to shroud the whole thing in mystery by leaving out some crucial aspects of my mother's suffering. But as I learned later, Madame Fournier was simply too modest to look me in the face and explain the workings of the female body.

Tactfully, she got the point across that my mother was not well and it was since she was a woman who was getting older, who was changing inside in areas concerning her female organs. However, she omitted the fact that my mother would probably have been better off if she had not relied so heavily on the medicinal aspects of her brandy. As a naive young woman, I had no way of knowing that drinking could devastate many aspects of a person's life and that this addiction had already played a key role in my mother's relationships, one of which affected the very core of my own life.

On the morning of December 29, I awoke from what had been a vivid dream. I was a child again, twirling in my girlish ways and doing my own choreographed dance around the Eiffel Tower. In the dream I was waiting for something or someone and laughing in anticipation of the encounter to come. And then "he" was standing there. The Spirit I had seen that fateful day. In the dream his features were clear. My subconscious created an ominous creature which immediately incited fear.

Paler than the sheets on my bed, he stood about five feet ten inches. Thin, but not frail, he was somehow formidable and self-assured. He lifted his arm and held his hand out to me and even though I was afraid I found myself dancing toward him. It was then that I abruptly curtailed my gleeful dance to look directly into the eyes of the being. I glided toward him as if floating, no longer subject to the laws of gravity.

As I reached my hand toward his, he slowly revealed a smile that I will never forget. His entire countenance morphed into an angelic form. Suddenly, I was filled with a feeling of being loved. Not just loved, but cherished. His smile was comforting and warm and I was filled with the realization that I had waited for this moment all my life. Right before our fingers touched, I awoke with an intake of breath and sat straight up on my cot breathing unevenly, still feeling his presence. Realizing that the encounter had been a dream, I was relieved that I had not really been in contact with the mysterious Spirit.

Then, I saw something on the corner of the bed that had not been there the night before. It was a bright flash of red and I was momentarily paralyzed before summoning the strength to investigate what it was. When I picked up the flimsy object, I immediately recognized it, even though I had not seen it for years. Slowly I brought the bright red fabric closer toward me and hugged it to my breast.

It was my childhood cape. The one that I was wearing when I flew through the park on the day I first saw him. It was lost that day and had not been seen since.

How had it arrived and been placed there on my cot? My heart raced slightly as I held the garment close. Did he perhaps deliver it here to my bed? More importantly, had I only dreamt of the encounter with the "Eiffel Spirit" or was the dream inspired by an actual visit?

Sometimes our experiences are shrouded in the cold light of day when they become overshadowed by a traumatic occurrence. On the morning that the cape appeared, reality merged with fantasy, presenting an enigma that alluded me.

I was in my final year of compulsory schooling and eager for it to end. I yearned to be recognized as the adult I felt I was. I no longer wanted to be condescended to and could not wait to discard the school uniform which designated my youth.

On this cold, December morning, I knocked on mother's bedroom door before dashing out to school, as was my usual custom. Some mornings she called to me to come in. Most of the time there would just be a raspy voice on the other side of the door that told me to be safe and to come straight home after school.

It was not completely unusual for there to be no response at all. Today was like that, but today I was filled with a sense of foreboding, so when there was no reply to my knock, I quietly turned the brass doorknob and tiptoed inside to kiss my mother goodbye. For a very brief second, I stood by the side of the bed and just stared as I watched her sleep. I glanced at the nightstand that held several bottles of various medicines and the ever-present bottle of cognac.

I wanted to be angry with my mother for what I considered to be a waste of her life. I knew that the neighbors all talked about her drinking habits and reclusive ways, but I always felt sorry for her. There was a sadness about her and even at my young age I knew that it was only when she escaped into the bottle that her pain became bearable.

I kissed her slightly on her cheek and then stood back abruptly to look at her again.

Suddenly, my knees collapsed beneath me and I landed hard on the floor beside her bed. She left the world the way she wanted to, in complete silence, numbed by the effect of the pills and the comforting taste of liquid gold.

The coroner ruled her death an accidental overdose and I made the decision to accept this although my heart told me my mother died of unquenchable sadness. Later, I came to the realization that his decision to describe mother's death as accidental on the death certificate was not based on compassion.

The coroner's secretary was Madame Fournier's sister. Madame Fournier became my self-appointed guardian during the years of my mother's gradual demise. She was concerned for my welfare and was wise enough to see the path that my mother was on. She took the precaution of insisting that my mother sign up for a meager life insurance benefit a few years before she died so that I would not be left penniless. It was imperative that the death certificate leave no room for a self-inflicted demise.

Madame Fournier also assumed the responsibility to see that my mother was buried with dignity. She arranged a small service and tended to the actual burial, although it was in a pauper's grave. She and I and young Philippe were the only people who stood by as the pine box was lowered into the dark wet earth. The rain turned from a slight drizzle to a hard and fast downpour.

The world seemed to stand still as the cheap coffin came to rest below the ground and I will never forget the sound of the shoveled dirt as it contacted the pitiful container. I tried to pray but forgot the words that I had learned as a small child. I was slowly accepting my new state as an orphan and at that moment prayer did not seem to me to be useful in any way.

Silently we walked home together. Madame Fournier steered me toward the bakery and made us each an extraordinarily strong cup of coffee which we shared in her small sitting area behind the shop. It was then that she told me of my meager inheritance and outlined a couple of plans she thought I should consider for my future.

Patiently, she told me that she was reluctant to discuss real world issues with me during my mourning period, but she felt responsible to offer me guidance and wanted me to know that I was not alone.

She told me not to be concerned for the immediate future. She said I was more than welcome to stay in the apartment and help in the bakery, but that she wanted me to give serious thought to expanding my horizons. She said she would help me find a job in one of the shops on the avenue. Here, she paused while I came to the realization that my schooling was now a thing of the past. Even with her reassurances, I knew that Madame was not in a financial position to support me. Circumstances would dictate that I find a way to support myself. Gently, she made it known that it was time for me to grow up.

"You are an intelligent girl, Natalie," she said as she looked into my eyes. Her own eyes were still swollen from crying at my mother's grave. "You love to read, and you know different languages. I have always felt that you would be successful when it was time for you to make your way in the world. Please understand that I want you to take your time to consider all options. I am not sending you out on the street and plan to patiently wait while you investigate what is available. In the meantime, I will help in any way that I can."

"I love you Madame," I said. My voice was exceedingly small that day as the pain of heartbreak was so fresh. I would find out what steps I needed to take next.

But first, I needed to sleep.

Sept

Plans

*D*ESPITE feeling completely exhausted I could not turn off the thoughts that spun through my brain. I climbed the stairs to my small apartment carrying the sack of bread and cheese Madame had provided for my evening meal.

I wondered if I could cope with the burden of responsibility that I now shouldered. The weight of recent developments could be compared to the traffic of carriages and pedestrians on the bridge during market day. Sometimes it creaks under the weight and threatens to collapse. I wondered if one more worry might cause me to collapse.

I sat for hours staring out the window as the sun went down and the stars began to populate the dark black sky. The rain had stopped but there was a cold wind blowing through Paris that evening. The tower was lit as usual, emitting a golden glow over the linden trees and the rest of the park below. I was hypnotized by the glowing structure, once sturdy yet, eerily mysterious.

Was the Spirit there tonight? Would he ever make his presence known to me again? For now, I was truly alone in the world and I wanted so much to be loved.

As the next few weeks sped by, I seemed to become more and more enveloped by the sadness that began with my mother's death and was compounded by my fruitless search for a job as well as a place to live. I envisioned myself living in the same apartment, helping Madame Fournier at the bakery and growing old there, unable to break free from the circumstances that life had dealt me. I knocked on doors and answered advertisements to no avail, until finally on a cloudy mid-week morning, my persistence paid off.

A family living in the 4th Arrondissement, on the wealthy side of the river, was in immediate need of an au pair to attend to their five-year-old girl and they were offering room and board to the successful job candidate. I was determined that would be me.

I arrived at 6 am dressed smartly in one of my mother's starched white blouses and a black skirt that I had to pin to make fit around my small waist. Madame Fournier leant me her black wool coat and bought me some new shoes which had absolutely no style at all. No one could look more matronly and serious than I did in that early dawn, even at my young age.

The butler looked me over from head to toe before admitting me to the drawing room where I waited for the lady of the house. As I perched on the edge of the settee, I was aware of the utter silence of this household. The ticking of the grandfather clock was the only sound I heard for the ten minutes that I waited, until I finally heard approaching footsteps. I stood stiffly when Madame Marshand entered the room. Surprisingly, she reached out her hand to shake mine as she approached and smiled sweetly, then she motioned for me to sit down.

I knew at once that I liked this woman and was pleased that she was younger than I thought she would be. I surmised Madame Marshand was probably in her mid-twenties, which would mean that her child had most likely been born when she was barely out of her teens, close to my age now.

She read the letter of reference from Madame Fournier and smiled as she refolded the paper to hand it back to me. The butler appeared out of nowhere, as if on cue, with a tray of tea and the daintiest little croissants I'd ever seen.

Madame Marshand engaged me in conversation, and I found myself talking easily to her about being on my own since my mother's recent death. I also disclosed my love of books and told her that I loved to write poetry and take long walks in the park. There was something about this woman that made it easy for me to reveal myself and I was enjoying the relaxed atmosphere she created that morning.

Finally, she declared it was time for me to meet Celeste. I followed her upstairs to the nursery where the child was playing on the floor of the room with a dollhouse full of furniture. She got up immediately and ran right into her mother's arms. It was obvious that this mother and daughter relationship was based on affection. Madame Marshand introduced me to Celeste, who turned to smile at me right away and invited me to join her on the floor to play with the dollhouse.

Madame stood to the side observing my interactions with her daughter for several minutes before asking me to join her again in the parlor. "I'll just be a moment with Mademoiselle Natalie, my dear" she said.

She told the girl that she would be back to help her get dressed shortly as she kissed her on the cheek. Happily, the child resumed to her solitary play time.

Downstairs again, Madame Marshand asked if I thought I would like to have the job now that I had met her daughter and spent a little time in the house. The way she phrased her question it seemed as though I had been the one doing the interviewing and that the decision was up to me. I answered quickly saying that I thought Celeste was a sweet girl and that I had very much enjoyed our encounter. I told her it would be my pleasure to be of service to her household as an au pair.

I began to feel a sense of profound relief envelop my entire nervous system. The doubts and questions that I had been pondering for the previous month were more disquieting than I had let myself fully contemplate. Now that an answer was at hand, I felt lighter than I had in a long time.

Madame Marshand led me to the library and knocked softly on the heavy oak door before we both entered her husband's sanctuary. Monsieur Marshand rose when we entered. His wife introduced me as the new au pair and he said it was nice to meet me, although I was certain he hardly looked at me. I felt as though we had interrupted some kind of important business here in what was obviously his workspace and was relieved when Madame Marshand motioned for me to follow her out, gently closing the door behind us.

The butler was told to show me my accommodations in what would be my new home. Madame Marshand told me that it would be most convenient if I could move my belongings into my space within the next day or two. She said it would be helpful if I could begin my position in the household on the following Monday morning. It was becoming increasingly difficult to keep myself from jumping for joy at this announcement, but somehow, I maintained an air of dignity as I told her that was most acceptable.

The room that was designated as my bedroom was bigger than the apartment my mother and I shared. It contained a full-size bed, a nightstand and a washstand, and even a small bookcase where I was told I could store my own books. There was a large armoire which I knew I would never fill with clothes. The room was accessible through the side door to the hallway that contained a water closet that I would share with the cook.

I smoothed the lovely floral bedspread with my hand and observed a vase of flowers beautifully arranged on the nightstand. I was more than thrilled and felt that the entire opportunity was almost too good to be true.

I almost danced my way back to tell Madame Fournier the good news. In fact, when I reached the Tower Park, I did do a couple of twirls, as I had done when I was a little girl. It had been about that long since I had been this happy and I was once again carefree and light-hearted.

Without my knowledge, the same entity who was present during my childhood encounter at the park, was watching me now. But, although I had thought of him often over the years, the Eiffel Spirit was completely dismissed from my thoughts on that magical day. My new life was beginning, and my heart was light.

Huit

Celeste

CELESTE endeared herself to me within my first week of being her caretaker. Not only did she delight in having me all to herself at playtime in the nursery, but she also sat in rapt attention when I read books to her or otherwise engaged her in short educational exercises.

We made use of the globe in the family's library to pursue some considerably basic geography lessons and I began tutoring her in simple mathematic formulas as well. Her young mind was like a sponge soaking up whatever knowledge I imparted. At first, I wondered about the aptitude of a child who was so young, but when I referred to Celeste as being only five years old, she was quick to point out that she was, five and a half. She beguiled me from the start with her wit and intelligence.

Madame Marshand left the two of us to ourselves on most days, only periodically checking into the nursery to evaluate how the child's day was going. Celeste was quick to brief her mother about what we had been studying and I could tell that Madame Marshand was pleased to hear about the instructions I was giving her.

A five-year-old child cannot spend an entire day in a school-like setting, however. I made sure that we allowed time to play. We enjoyed sitting on the floor of the nursery together playing with her well-loved dolls, dollhouse, and other toys. Celeste particularly enjoyed it when I crouched down behind her small dresser and put on a puppet show for her using a pair of my stockings on which I had drawn funny faces.

She had an affinity for drawing and coloring pictures. I was impressed with what seemed to be a natural talent in her artwork. I enjoyed observing her interpretations as she described the meanings of her pictures. Her demeanor became quite serious as she explained her drawings and her aptitude seemed beyond her years.

Occasionally, we shared her drawings with the rest of the family at dinner time, so they could partake in something that gave her so much joy. I relished on her behalf the compliments her parents bestowed on her creations. It was obvious that her mother doted on her and that Celeste's happiness was of utmost importance. I sometimes felt that Monsieur was barely aware of his daughter's presence and only chimed in with a word of praise when he felt all eyes were on him waiting for interaction.

Celeste and I went for walks and packed up picnics for the park when the weather was fair. I was thrilled to find that my charge enjoyed being outside in nature and rambling through the open space of the Eiffel Park as much as I had at her age.

After I had been with the family for about eight months, I was reading Celeste a bedtime story at the end of a long day. As I read the book, I found that my mind was half occupied with thoughts of spending some time alone in my room before I went to sleep. Those moments alone at the end of each day had become a treasured time for me.

Celeste's voice broke my reverie and I had to ask her to repeat her question.

She was interested in knowing if I had seen the man at the Tower. I had not seen anyone at the park that afternoon except a couple of young mothers pushing prams and whiling away the time with each other, but as Celeste went on to describe the man, she had seen I felt a chill go down my spine.

"He was thin." She spoke. "And very pale." She stated that he was standing behind one of the pillars of the Tower for a long time during our picnic and she was surprised I had not seen him as well. When I asked her if he was smiling at her, she said that he was not.

As I tucked her blankets around her, she added that the man had motioned for her to come closer. She said he had scared her slightly. When I asked why she did not tell me about him when he beckoned to her, she replied that she was going to but when she turned back to look at him again, he had disappeared.

We would not be going to the Eiffel Park again for quite a while after that day due to a series of events that began that night.

Madame Marshand was disturbed when I met her in the dining room the next morning for breakfast. She asked Cook to serve Celeste her breakfast in the kitchen so that we could be alone as we sat at the table.

"There has been an incident at the Tower."
She whispered to me.

She further reported that the body of a
young woman was found there among the
linden trees in the early dawn. Police were
scouring the area for clues to the crime and the
park had been closed again as it had been years
ago when similar circumstances had occurred.

I did not tell her that Celeste and I had
picnicked there the day before and I most
certainly refrained from reporting the child's
sighting of the pale man who beckoned to her
from the shadows.

I did not tell anyone about that chain of
events mainly because I was afraid that I would
lose my position in the household if Madame
Marshand knew how close Celeste had been to
the Eiffel Spirit mere hours before the heinous
crime occurred. I would not be recreating the
incident in the future either and vowed to
myself that Celeste would never be exposed to
such danger again.

Memories from years ago arose not only in
me, but in the minds of many Parisians as the
investigation continued. It was easy for me to
conger the image of my mother standing in the
doorway of the Boulangerie discussing the
crimes with a passerby. I remembered being
particularly intrigued when I heard the gossip
about the wedding veils that were seen on the
victim's bodies.

The newspaper mentioned this gruesome
detail in the reports of the latest murders as
well, and I found it particularly distressing.
Young women were once again encouraged not
to venture forth alone in the city and warned to

avoid the Tower completely. Fear pervaded the thoughts of all who might be susceptible to whatever evil force was at large.

I wondered if this incident would eventually die down and be forgotten as was the case of the other alleged murders previously committed in the park. The incident did not remain isolated nor was it forgotten. Over the next month, two more young women were found dead.

I called on Madame Fournier on one of my days off to see if she had more information than I because of her proximity to the Tower. She did not have any more facts than I had read in the newspaper, but she did tell me that on more than one night during this warm summer, the windows of her apartment were left open and piercings screams split the silence of the still night. When this happened, she knew another body would soon be discovered.

She also reported to me that she had heard a loud evil laugh on the nights of the screams. No one else had reported the laughter to the authorities, so Madame confided in me that she refrained from telling anyone else about this sinister sound. She told me that she did not want to be subjected to the reporters who would certainly want to interrogate her about the laughter.

The "Eiffel Spirit" was awake.

Neuf

Routine

WALKING back to the Marshand home, I found myself thinking of the creature I had dreamt about on the night of my mother's passing. I had never discerned if the vision had been a dream or reality and was always full of wonder, especially since discovering the red cape that had mysteriously appeared at the foot of my bed.

But whether the vision was real or imagined, I recognized the entity as the same one I saw behind the foot of the Tower when I was seven years old. The vision of that specter, that I had mistaken for a statue, was firmly imprinted on my brain. I wrestled with what I had been told about the evil circumstances and the lingering fear precipitated by the assailant at the park on the one hand and the benign appearance of the spirit whose smile had once caused me to feel loved.

Although, it seemed obvious that the pale specter was involved in the crimes, I refrained from mentioning my personal encounter to anyone. The murders were the sole subject of local gossip and I did not want to expose myself to being questioned if it seemed I had pertinent information. My theories were only based on supposition and I did not have enough information to be of value.

Even so, my footsteps quickened as I walked past the Tower and I refrained from looking directly at the structure. I slowed to my usual pace only when I was a safe distance away. Only then did my breathing settle back to normal. I became acutely aware that my heart had been racing fiercely. If Madame Fournier's intention had been to instill me with fear when she told me the local gossip, she had been successful. I vowed not to return to the park until the mystery was solved and the perpetrator was behind bars.

Of course, that meant I had to disappoint Celeste the next time she pleaded for a picnic in the park. I convinced her that we could have a lovely afternoon walking along the Seine and stopping for a sorbet at one of the stands set up along the riverbank. Being the happy child that she was, I found it easy to turn this new adventure into her favorite outing. I did everything in my power to be sure she heard nothing about the events at the Eiffel Tower even though the conjured suppositions were on everyone's lips and whispered rumors were everywhere.

I steered her away from several groups of other au pairs with their charges that we met on our route along the river. I could tell what they were talking about by their worried faces and I found it shocking to see these other young women discussing the crimes in the company of the young people they were caring for.

I spared my employers of any knowledge of the type of gossip that was circulating. Neither did I broach the subject of the recent crimes with Madame or Monsieur Marshand even when Celeste was not present. The world I created for their daughter simply did not leave room for the dark or mysterious. Like Celeste herself, it was important that the mood be sunny and the laughter light and often. I was determined that she would grow up in a world far different from the one that I had, without any of the concerns that I endured daily. She was a bright, carefree child and I was determined to encourage these attributes.

Not only did I begin to care for Celeste like a big sister, but I was also beginning to treasure the person that I had become since I took up residence with the Marshand family. I had a delightful room of my own, ate wonderful meals on a regular basis and spent time with a child I had come to think of as a treasure. Celeste lit up when I entered the room. Even the time we spent in lessons was time we both enjoyed.

Each afternoon we appeared in the drawing room at our scheduled time for tea and I was made aware that Madame Marshand was quite taken with me and the relationship I was building with her daughter.

Celeste bubbled over with joy spending this hour each day with her mother. She loved to tell her about her latest studies and to relate stories of the excursions we took when we went out. I loved it too. It was fun to hear the child's interpretation of the encounters we had with street vendors, or what she had seen looking in the shop windows along the strand.

One morning we strolled past a pet shop with a toy poodle in the window. Celeste was determined that we were going to bring the dog home with us. It became my duty to pull her away from the vision of the puppy that she wanted and change the subject in order to interest her in an ice cream cart a short distance away.

During tea that afternoon, she pleaded with her mother about the dog, telling her that she wanted it more than anything else in the world. Madame Marshand laughed as her child rambled on and almost spilled her tea all over the tray. It was my belief that Madame was just humoring her daughter on, but by the end of the hour it seemed that Celeste had won the battle. As we headed back to the nursery, Madame Marshand pulled me aside and instructed me to go out the next day on my own to inquire what the store was charging for the small dog. She also wanted to know how much it would be to buy a bed and a leash of some sort for the animal. It seemed that once again the child would receive whatever her heart desired.

That evening as I brushed Celeste's long chestnut hair, I smiled in delight thinking about what an upcoming surprise for her might be. I was thrilled that Madame Marshand was apparently going to allow me to at least be involved with the potential granting of the child's wish.

I arose early the next morning. Cook had been made aware of my designated task, meeting me in the kitchen with a cup of coffee and a warm croissant before I headed out. I donned the cape and gloves that Madame Marshand gave me as protection against the cold weather. The cape had been Madame's the previous winter. She told me that the women in her social circle simply must update to the latest fashion each year or they would be the talk of the town.

I was more than happy to help save her from this embarrassment, and the cape fit me perfectly. No one, of my social status, had any idea of which style was represented in which year.

Dix

Ami

*T*HE pet store had just opened when I arrived and at first, I was upset to find that the small poodle was not in the window this morning, having been replaced by what appeared to be a liter of small black pups, adorably bumping into each other, since their eyes were not quite open yet. Happily, the poodle was easy to locate in a cage near the door, still sleeping and not ready to begin looking as cute as she had the day before when she won Celeste's heart.

I wound up in the queue behind an exceptionally large woman who was arguing endlessly with the salesperson behind the counter. I surmised from the discussion that the woman had bought a bird of some kind at the shop and that the bird had flown away. She was attempting to convince the shopkeeper that she should receive a refund. Of course, she was told that the store could not reimburse her for the lost bird and the clerk was trying as hard as she could to be polite about the refusal.

Even though it was nice to be in the warm shop instead of out in the cold, I wished that the discussion would come to an end, so I could make my inquiries about the poodle and head back home.

It was then that I noticed him. First, I felt that feeling of someone looking at me. The feeling was intense. I turned toward the shop window and then stood paralyzed with fear. Standing outside the shop was a figure dressed in a long-hooded cloak. It was impossible at first to see the face of the person, until he lifted his head a little more and then I knew it was him. The pale, almost transparent skin tones of the Eiffel Spirit were unmistakable. He stood transfixed just staring at me. And then, after what seemed like hours, he smiled, the way he had years ago. From my feet to the top of my head I recognized the glow his smile imparted. And once again I was filled with a feeling of love.

"Mademoiselle." I heard the call coming toward me, as if from miles away. "Mademoiselle." I heard it again. "Are you alright?" The voice asked. "Can I help you with something?"

As if emerging from a dream, I turned toward the clerk and realized where I was and what I was there for. Quickly, I glanced back toward the window. The phantom had disappeared.

"Did you see that man?" I asked the girl behind the counter.

Her look of incredulity assured me that she had no idea what I meant and by now she was looking at me as though I might be deranged. I changed the focus to my reason for being there in the first place and inquired about the dog. I was also shown the recommended bed for the size of the puppy and which bowls and leashes the clerk suggested. I made a written list containing all the pertinent information and thanked the clerk for her assistance. As requested by Madame, I inquired if the clerk could refrain from selling the little poodle until my employer was able to come pick her up.

She advised me that she would hold up any potential sales until Thursday of the week, at which time she would consider our interest invalid. I thanked her and reached in the cage to pat the dog on my way out of the pet shop.

As I walked back to the Marshand home I was continuously looking over my shoulder to see if I was being followed by the specter I had seen at the window. Perhaps there was something wrong with me. Perhaps these sightings, even though rare in my young life, were a sign that I had some type of mental disturbance. But whether real or imagined, I would not share the secret of these visions with anyone. I was convinced no one would believe me, and scared that they might look at me with the same sense of disbelief as the store clerk.

I presented Madame Marshand with the list of items and prices when I returned home. Madame wasted no time in approaching the door to her husband's office, closing it promptly behind her. I assumed the next phase of the project was to acquire Monsieur's approval for the purchase.

It was Celeste's birthday the following week. Madame Marshand told me they wanted to present the puppy as their gift to her at her birthday party. Preparations had already been underway for the occasion and I was aware that formal invitations had been sent to various acquaintances.

I was surprised that Monsieur Marshand attended the small affair. The party was held in the garden room in the back of the house. The room had been decorated with yards of pink ribbons. The tables were draped with floral cloths and the large punch bowl displayed an inviting beverage. The crowning glory in the center of the head table was Cook's creation of a three-layer cake covered in the palest of pink frosting, with small white flowers around the edges. The children in attendance were giddy in anticipation of eating the beautifully decorated confection.

I was pleased to present Celeste with the small gift I had purchased for her. I wanted to encourage her artistic endeavors, so I bought a small set of charcoal pencils and pastels and a pad of drawing paper. She was excited as she unwrapped the tissue paper and delighted with the gift. I was happy to receive a small hug from her as she thanked me. Already I was looking forward to seeing her draw in the days ahead thinking what a nice break it would be for the child during our regular study sessions.

But the highlight of the day, was the entrance by Monsieur Marshand with a white box that he presented to his daughter as she sat in the decorated birthday chair in the center of the room. He beamed as she pulled the ribbon off and set the tiny poodle free from the box. The butler quickly retrieved the pup and set her on the child's lap.

Celeste squealed with delight as she held the dog close to her chest. "Papa." She whispered to her father. "Merci, Merci. I will call her 'Ami.'"

From that day on, the puppy rarely left her side.

I tucked Celeste in on the night of her party. She was so tired, she welcomed going to sleep and did not even request a bedtime story. Madame Marshand allowed her to keep Ami next to her in bed that night, although Celeste had been told this was only because it was her first night in her new home. After that, the dog would be trained to sleep on a small bed next to the child's cot. Celeste promised her mother that she would help teach the dog to obey this rule, but tonight was special. I think the dog was as tired as the child, for they both were asleep within minutes, and I never saw a happier pair.

Onze

Jules

I was invited to join Madame and Monsieur Marshand in the parlor that evening after Celeste was asleep.

Monsieur Marshand's brother was to be a house guest for a week or so, and Madame wanted to formally introduce us, although I became aware of him earlier at the birthday party. He and Monsieur Marshand both rose as I entered the parlor and I was immediately self-conscious feeling a blush rising my neck to my cheeks.

With bowed head, I approached the intimate gathering as Madame Marshand introduced her brother-in-law. I believe this was one of only a few meetings I had attended since working in the home that Monsieur was present and seemed to be aware that I was there too. I did not consider mealtime as part of the equation, since he spoke so little at the dinner table and most of his comments were directed to his small daughter. I was a bit uneasy in his company. However, I found his brother charming at once.

"Jules." Madame Marshand began, "I'd like you to meet Natalie, Celeste's au pair. She is a wonder; we don't know what we would do without her." I looked up and was immediately entranced by the young man who reached out for my hand and pressed in lightly to his lips. "Delighted." He spoke.

We sat drinking tea and I felt my cheeks redden even more as Madame Marshand extolled my virtues for a few more minutes. She made quite a fuss describing all the things I had done since arriving at their home. She told Jules that her daughter had never been as happy as she was in my company. She went on to describe the education I was providing for the child and smiled at me as she told him about some of the outings that Celeste had described to her.

It was obvious to me that Jules was delighted to hear about his niece's happiness. His amusement was in direct proportion to the boredom experienced by his brother as the conversation continued.

Jules was quite easy on the eyes and I think I began that same evening to develop a crush on him. I was particularly drawn in by his habit of brushing his hair off his forehead, which disclosed a boyish type of charm. I began to fidget as I nervously hoped that someone would change the subject and that Madame would stop talking about me. Instead, I noticed Jules smiling in my direction, most likely amused by my discomfort.

"I am honored to make the acquaintance of one who has been entrusted with the care and education of our darling Celeste." He spoke. "She is a special child, dear to us all, Mademoiselle, and it seems, from my own observations at her birthday celebration, that my sister-in-law's faith in you was well-placed."

I wanted the encounter to end as soon as possible and prayed for a quick escape. My unease was clearly the result of my lack of instruction as to the way the members of high society behave. Thankfully, Jules rose shortly to announce the day had been a long one for him. He said that he had been up at the break of dawn to catch the train to Paris. He said he would see everyone at breakfast and headed up the stairs.

I stood up then and said I would also be retiring. I thanked Madame Marshand for including me for tea and for the introduction. Her husband appeared as relieved as I was that the uncomfortable situation was ending.

As I pulled the covers up on my bed, I found that I was eagerly anticipating breakfast the next morning and the opportunity to spend more time with Jules. I was sure that he did not consider me worthy of his time or conversation, but that did not matter, I simply wanted to see him again.

Celeste joined us in the dining room for breakfast, a rare occurrence occasioned by her uncle's visit. He was already enthralled with one of her stories as I entered the room, and neither of them seemed to notice me at first. When Jules did look up, he smiled at me and motioned for me to sit in the empty chair next to him. Cook brought my plate shortly thereafter and I spent the rest of the meal in the happy company of these two members of the mutual admiration society.

Jules suggested that he join Celeste and I on whatever outing I had planned for the day. When I asked Celeste what she thought we should do, and whether her uncle should accompany us, she squealed with glee. It was an echo of the squeal she emitted when the gift box revealed her precious puppy the day before.

After what appeared to be thoughtful deliberation, Celeste declared that we should go for a picnic, but not just any sort of picnic. She virtually demanded that we have a "dress-up" picnic wherein the three of us must wear our best Sunday frocks. Jules barely suppressed a laugh as she insisted that meant a suit and ascot for him.

When she looked at us with pleading in her eyes, I realized why her parents seldom told her "no." The child was just too adorable when she used her wiles to wrap the adults in her life around her little finger.

If I had not already learned that Celeste was a kind child, mostly good-natured and considerate of others, the use of her girlish charms might have been unnerving. Instead, I gave in to her, as I was sure her uncle would. I finished my breakfast as I tried to imagine which "Sunday frock" I should wear to the picnic. I had two dresses and Celeste had seen them both on numerous occasions.

The important thing to me was that Jules was going with us, and perhaps I might get to know him a little better.

We set out looking rather stylish for a regular Tuesday afternoon. Madame Marshand waved to us from the front door and I knew that she was pleased that Jules and I were off on a day of fun with her daughter. Celeste took charge of the leash that was attached to her precious Ami. The dog wound up getting so excited with the prospect of a walk that she ran in circles wrapping the leash around the child's legs more than once. All three of us laughed each time we stopped to untangle this impediment to the dog's freedom.

Jules was extremely patient with Celeste as he offered his assistance and it was obvious in the way he smiled at her, that she was a special presence in his life.

I wondered what passersby were thinking as they saw the three of us and the little puppy heading down the street dressed to perfection. Personally, I was hoping that they were thinking Jules and I were a couple. Obviously, we were too young for Celeste to have been our daughter, but it was my hope that we appeared as a couple out for a walk with our favorite niece on a lovely Spring morning.

Celeste looked at me from the corner of her eye as Jules directed us toward the Eiffel park for our picnic. We had not been there in a long time, at the request of Madame Marshand. I knew she would be upset if we did not inform Jules that the park was off limits.

As we drew nearer to the tree lined street, I saw that there were several other people at the park including the usual tourists overwhelmed as they gazed at the Eiffel Tower. A long queue had formed for the elevator to the top. I also observed several children playing with a ball on the grass under the linden trees, and more than one group of young mothers were standing around talking and laughing with each other as their children played.

Several artists had set up their easels on the lawn, spread out to capture on canvas the landmark Tower. During our many walks past the local galleries, I became aware that many of these paintings would soon be on sale and would sell quickly to tourists and locals alike.

"We should go somewhere else for our picnic." I finally said. Madame does not want us to spend time at the Eiffel Park." "But Mon Ami." Celeste exclaimed. "It is so nice to be here again, I have missed it. Please, let us picnic here."

While Celeste secured the puppy's leash to a nearby tree, I whispered to Jules a brief summary of the mysterious events that had occurred over the last few years here at the Tower.

"Madame is being protective of her child and does not want us to picnic here, she requested that we not even be in the vicinity. I do not want to encourage her anger. We really should find another place to spend the afternoon." I expected a completely different reaction on the part of Celeste's uncle. Ami was enjoying the shade of the tree where Celeste had secured her leash. The walk seemed to have tired the pup out. She stretched out and laid down to sleep.

As Celeste walked back toward us on the expansive lawn, Jules let out a mocking laugh, saying it sounded like the mystery of the Eiffel Spirit was perhaps concocted. He said that it seemed to him that the Eiffel Park was probably one of the safest places in the city of Paris. After all, the people were out in the open where they could be seen by so many others. What, he asked could happen with all these people around as witnesses? Besides, none of them seemed to be concerned with any consequences of potential villains hiding behind the Tower or the trees.

"Perhaps my sister-in-law is overreacting for the sake of her daughter. I applaud her concern for the most part, Mademoiselle Natalie, but I am here today, and I believe I am capable of protecting a small child, a dog and an au pair." Amusement was written all over his face.

Celeste looked at me and I sensed her concern as she overheard the tail end of our conversation. I nodded in her direction indicating to Jules that she could hear us speaking about whether the park was safe. I held my finger to my lips.

"Now, my dear niece." He said to her. "Who would even think to harm you or Mademoiselle Natalie with me here as your escort. I will rise to the heights of your own knight in shining armor should any threat come your way." With that he bent forward in a slight bow to Celeste and me and we both giggled in response.

"Now, help me spread out the blanket and let us investigate the contents of that lovely basket. I believe that Cook has packed us some very delectable treats which I am eager to devour. I think I worked up an appetite just toting the food here."

Douze

The Encounter

OUR delightful afternoon in the park was such a welcome change to our daily routine. Jules entertained both Celeste and I with stories and conversation that put me at ease regarding my previous concerns. It was wonderful spending time on the lawns where I played as a child and where I had memories of picnics with my mother in the days before she was ill. From where we sat, I could see Madame Fournier's bakery and I pictured her behind the counter catering to the demands of her regular customers. I hoped that she had hired someone to help her during the past couple of years and that since I was gone, she was not trying to handle the shop and the baking by herself.

Jules delighted Celeste with the story of his train excursion from Normandy to Paris. She asked for the details of the sleeping car and wanted to know what he had been served for lunch in the lavish dining car. Her uncle did not spare any details as he regaled her with the tale of his adventure, although I had the feeling that fiction and fact might have been mixed for her enjoyment.

"We have sat too long." I announced, "It is time that we give Ami some exercise. In fact, after consuming this sumptuous repast, I believe it would do us all some good to stretch our legs."

I encouraged Celeste to help me load the picnic basket with the remains of our meal in a neat manner, to show respect for Cook and the hard work she had gone to for us. Jules seemed impressed that I was giving Celeste lessons in consideration and thoughtfulness.

Again, my imagination conjured up the image of the three of us walking the dog through the park. Certainly, we were an attractive looking threesome, obviously from the bourgeois side of town. Earlier, I registered more than one look of admiration from the people we passed, and I must confess that my nose was slightly in the air as I relished the appreciation, happy to be playing this part. Preoccupied as I was, I was not prepared for the rapidity with which the events of the next few moments occurred.

Lost in my daydream, I was shocked into the present as Celeste screamed. She was near tears announcing loudly that Ami had pulled too hard on the leash and was now running free. With lightening quick reflexes, Jules answered by chasing the fluffy ball of white, but he was no match for the speed of the small dog. Ami was out of sight in mere seconds.

I stood there trying to calm Celeste assuring her that we would find her dog, as my heart pounded heavily. I found it hard to believe my own words. The two of us walked fast toward the Tower, in the opposite direction from where Jules had run when suddenly we heard the shrill squeal of an animal in pain. Celeste looked at me in horror and I knew that we were both picturing Amis lying injured somewhere on the lawn at the foot of the Tower.

It was then that we saw a figure clothed completely in black, his face covered with a red mask, running away from the scene toward the avenue of Madame Fournier's bakery. Celeste gasped in fright. Again, we heard the high-pitched squeal that sounded like a suffering creature. I sensed that we were getting closer to where the sound was coming from, both of us afraid of what we might find.

Suddenly, Jules was running toward us. He was gasping for breath and looked quite pale. I told him to catch his breath and to hold tightly to Celeste's hand. Assuming an air of authority, I said to wait right there on that spot while I investigated the sound that might be the lost puppy. Although I had not worn shoes intended for walking very fast on a field of grass, I was at the foot of the Tower in mere seconds.

I looked back to see that Jules and Celeste had stayed firmly put where I asked them to wait. Then, I took a few more steps forward, calling the puppy's name as I scanned the area. I heard the whimpering and prayed that it was Celeste's dog and that I was in time to save her.

I stood frozen when I saw him. The specter of my youth was standing behind the foot of the Tower. He smiled when he saw me, and then the most amazing thing happened.

He reached under his cloak and handed me the small puppy who began wagging her tail as soon as I took her into my arms. I petted Ami and whispered a comforting word to her as I looked her over for any sign of injury. She seemed to be perfectly fine. When I looked up, the pale being was gone.

Celeste ran toward me when she saw me holding Ami. Jules was close behind her breathing heavily. "I am so relieved that you found the dog." He spoke. "She was trying to outrun a cat." I lied.

I could think of no reason to inform Jules about the truth of Ami's rescue. Besides, I did not want to scare Celeste by revealing that I had seen the Spirit. I was afraid that if I did, she might conjure up the image of the phantom that I believed she had once seen for herself.

"Perhaps it was a mistake to picnic here at the Tower Park." Jules conceded as we walked home. I remained silent, but the look I gave him implied my agreement.

Madame Marshand was in the kitchen when we returned, going over the menu with Cook for the evening meal. I deposited the picnic basket on the counter and informed her that I was going to take Celeste upstairs for her afternoon nap.

Jules was in the study with his brother. I caught a glimpse of him as Celeste and I ascended the staircase. He looked past me as if I were not there. I wondered if our friendly exchanges were to be a thing of the past after our excursion to the park.

Was Jules embarrassed because there had been an incident during our picnic? Did he think I was blaming him for what potentially could have been the outcome had the puppy not been found?

Celeste was tugging at my dress as I drifted off into these thoughts about Jules. The child was already over her own emotional involvement in the incident and was anxious for me to read her a story and settle her down for a nap.

That is a marvelous thing about children, I thought. No matter what they experience, if it is not overly traumatic, once everything is back to normal, they tend to move on. Celeste exhibited that resilience by urging me to come up with a plan for what we would be doing after her nap. I was at once reassured that my actions in rescuing Ami had caused her no concern and only deepened her faith in my abilities. I admit that it was a relief for me not to dwell on the incident any longer. I finally relaxed as I sat in the comfortable chair by her bed with her favorite storybook.

Within minutes the child was asleep, Ami snuggled beside her. I leaned my head against the back of the chair and soon joined them in peaceful slumber.

At dinner that night the conversation was somewhat stilted. Jules and I gave each other several warning glances when Madame or Monsieur Marshand asked about our outing earlier in the day. Both of us were guarding our words and it seemed to fill the room with a cloud of hesitation that pervaded talk of all subjects of conversation that arose.

I kept telling myself that I was just imagining the magnitude of anxiety in the atmosphere but at the same time I could not wait for the meal to end so I could make an excuse to retire early to the sanctuary of my room.

Madame Marshand acknowledged that I must have worn myself out during the day and said she would tuck her daughter in herself that night. I was excused to have the evening to myself.

In my haste to leave the scene and spend no more time in Jules' company it did not dawn on me that I had not sworn the child to secrecy. I had an affinity for teaching her to tell the truth, but in this case that would come back to haunt me in a direct and perilous fashion.

Treize

Consequences

COOK delivered a meager breakfast to my room in the morning, which was an unheard-of break in the morning ritual. She knocked on my door at dawn, handed me the tray and looked down at the floor as she informed me that the mistress wanted to see me in the drawing room after I had eaten.

Although this was most unusual for several reasons, I was sure Madame was acting on the best interests of the household. Although I questioned the break in routine caused by this early summons, I assumed that her usual good judgment was in force.

Perhaps Monsieur Marshand was departing on an unexpected business trip this morning. As one of the leading defense attorneys in Paris, he was highly in demand and frequently needed to meet with defendants and other legal counsel away from the city.

Perhaps Madame needed a special errand that I needed to run early in the day. Or perhaps Jules was returning home early, and she thought I would like to wish him adieu.

Suddenly, I shuddered thinking that she needed to see me because Celeste had taken ill, and she was in need of my help in this early hour.

I dressed hastily as these thoughts ran through my head. I swallowed the coffee in gulps taking another bite of croissant, as I tied my boots and then opened the door of my room.

Madame Marshand was standing near the fireplace when I entered the drawing room. Jules was in the large chair sitting across from her and they both had an air of stern anticipation about them.

I entered the room and stood frozen on the oriental carpet, feeling as though my knees might give way and leave me lying on the multicolored threads.

It was then that I noticed Ami in a small basket at the feet of Madame Marshand.

She spoke. "Perhaps the dog was not a good idea." She said and then she paused. I looked over at Jules for some type of explanation, but it was not forthcoming. In a few minutes, Madame Marshand looked directly at me and continued what she had to say.

"I don't know if I am more upset with the fact that this dog ran away from the three of you yesterday at the park, causing distress for my daughter and concern for you and Jules as you searched for her, or if the disobedience of my orders is more distressing.

It was made quite clear to you, Natalie, that the Eiffel Park was off limits for my daughter, and yet you and my brother-in-law decided it should be the site of your picnic.

I am disappointed and unsure what to do in this situation. I have entertained the idea of getting rid of the dog, for one thing, although I am certain it would break Celeste's heart. I have also thought that perhaps I need to hire a new au pair, one who listens to the instructions that I issue, but again I hesitate on this route since it is Celeste who would suffer. I have brought you both in here this morning to see if you might have another solution to offer, or if you have anything to say for yourselves. Rules have been broken here, and I am struggling with deciding a just outcome."

Now, I was sure that I would faint. Madame Marshand's words cut through me like a sharp knife. Ever since coming into their employment I had tried to do everything right. I wanted so much to be an exemplary au pair, one who would be a treasured part of the household and one who would be with my charge until she was old enough to no longer need my care and protection. Now all of that was on the line. One afternoon, one decision that I was aware was wrong, and I would pay for it for the rest of my life. It was only because of my own weakness when confronting Jules at the park, that the situation had escalated to this terrible moment of truth.

I could not bring myself to say anything in my own defense. My throat ached with a dryness I had never felt before. Even though a prompt response may have been called for and may have eased my punishment, the words would just not come. I was already experiencing a self-reproach that had begun the day before when the Spirit of the Tower handed me back the lost puppy. I knew then that I had put Celeste in a terrible situation and regretted immediately that the park had been our destination. Now, I wished I had asked her not to tell her mother where we went yesterday, or about searching for her lost dog. Yet, my only comfort came from knowing my own integrity was not compromised asking the child to tell an untruth, or even not to tell the whole truth, even though it meant losing the job that I loved.

It felt as if hours had passed as I stood frozen in the drawing room. The tall grandfather clock seemed to be ticking at a slow tempo as I waited for what was to happen next. Even though the clock seemed to have almost stopped, I was sure that my heart had never beat so fast. Finally, it was Jules who spoke.

"It is my fault." He spoke. "It was I who insisted that the Tower Park was the ideal place to picnic, despite Natalie's repeated warnings that it was not considered safe. She even explained to me that you had forbidden Celeste from going there because of your concerns."

"I must ask sincerely that the punishment for this offense not fall to the au pair. What was she to do when I led the group in that direction? Surely, she is no match for me. She must have felt obliged to go along with what I said and did."

"I will return home, Monique, much earlier than I had planned to, so you need not worry that I will further corrupt your family. But I beg you not to do anything to this young lady because of my foolishness."

Madame Marshand looked at me. I held my breath in anticipation. This woman held my fate in her hands. "I will call for you in a little while." She said to me. "First I will confer with

Monsieur Marshand and we will let you know of our decision shortly. You may return to your room to wait."

With my future on a perilous and insecure course, I sat on my windowsill and stared out at the garden so beautifully groomed and laden with so many colorful blossoms.

I am not accustomed to praying regularly, but as I sat there that morning, I said a short prayer. As tears welled up in my eyes, I asked that some type of grace might prevent me from having to walk the cobbled streets again, knocking on doors, attempting to find employment and a new home. My dread multiplied as I contemplated this outcome, looking for a position, without having a letter of reference.

It had been so long since I had felt this pitiful insecurity. Over time, I had become a vital part of this family, treated with more respect than servants in many other households. I thought of this as my home, this room as my room, never questioning the fact that there would be breakfast in the morning, and supper in the evening. Now, I had reverted to those difficult days after my mother died. Once again, I felt alone and the old pain in my heart began to overwhelm me.

Time was frozen as I sat there contemplating my future. Was the mistake I made yesterday going to cost me the job of caring for Celeste? I knew it was wrong yesterday on our way to the Eiffel Park, but never dreamed that the consequences could be so severe.

Deep into my thoughts I did not hear the knock on my bedroom door.

"I have been knocking for a while." Cook said, as she stood framed in my doorway. "Madame wants to see you again in the drawing room." Her look was one of concern and I knew that the household staff was already informed of my dilemma. It never took long for the whispers to spread and surely someone had their ear pressed to the drawing room door during the encounter that had taken place that morning. Cook's somber expression added to my unease. As I walked toward the drawing room, I wondered if she and the other servants were already aware of Madame Marshand's decision. I was sure that the butler thought nothing of eavesdropping on his employer's conversations even when the drawing room doors were closed.

Jules was no longer in the drawing room and to my surprise, Monsieur Marshand had joined his wife there, instead. Their conversation came to a halt as I entered the room.

"Please sit." Madame Marshand instructed me.

The butler drew the doors closed and an eerie silence enveloped us all.

Monsieur Marshand rose from his chair near the fireplace and turned toward me.

During the time I had lived in this house there had been occasions when I was afraid of this man, finding him to be of a stern demeanor. But I had also witnessed his pleasant manner when speaking to his daughter and I had even seen him laugh more than once.

When he looked at me, he began with the usual stern expression, but then, to my surprise, he smiled at me.

"My brother, Jules, can be rebellious at times." He spoke. "After careful consideration of the events of your outing with him yesterday, we have made a decision about your standing in our household. Of course, we did consult Celeste regarding the incident with her puppy. As you know, my dear, my daughter is enamored with you, so the situation of your employment here is a delicate one. We must do what is right for the safety of our child, but we must also consider what losing you might do to her emotionally."

His words were floating in the air, never really within my full perception. I felt as if I were standing on the side of cliff as my destiny lingered in the air. Time stood still as I waited for the verdict that would tell me how this day would end.

Monsieur Marshand cleared his throat and continued.

"We have decided that you must stay, for Celeste's sake. But and I must warn you here, this will be the last and only pardon you will receive if ever the rules are broken again. My wife and I are to be obeyed in all things where Celeste is concerned. This time, I am laying a large percentage of the guilt from yesterday at the feet of my brother, who, it seems, cast all caution to the wind even when you made him aware that the park was off limits."

I did not know what I should do at that moment. I distinctly heard him say that I would be staying as Celeste's au pair, but the rest of the words never landed squarely on my ears. I remained in that fixed spot as if I were glued to the floor.

"Did you hear what Monsieur Marshand said, my dear?" Madame asked.

"Yes, and thank you both for not dismissing me." I said in a weak voice.

"Cook will bring your dinner to your room tonight. We have told Celeste that you have today off, so she will look forward to seeing you in the morning, as usual. That will be all for today." I mumbled my thanks again and made it back to my room just in time before I completely lost all the strength in my legs. I fell onto the bed and wept for joy.

Quatorze

The Spirit

THE Eiffel Spirit did his own musings as he hid in the shadows of the Eiffel Tower:

The masked one has again been the vehicle of havoc here at my beloved Tower. It seems that he delights in the ability to sweep in for short intervals destroying what the innocent park visitors hold dear. He loves to instill fear in people and to torment even the small animals who are enjoying the vast beauty and clean air of the Park.

Ah, but I am a swifter force and this time I was able to stifle his evil pursuit. I stretched out my arms and caught the falling pup before the damage was done.

I followed the girl the day she went to the shop for the dog. I knew that this pet belonged to the household where she lived, and I would see to it that the mademoiselle with the red cape did not suffer another distressful loss, if I could prevent it.

The Masked One had already run past the Tower. I am not sure if he was aware of my interference in his planned carnage. Surely, there were too many of his victims that I was unable to save. But, when I saw how happy the girl was after retrieving the dog and then handing it to the child, my own anguish was eased. I put aside the thoughts of the threats of his evil and morbid acts, at least for the moment.

I had not always been successful in out-thinking the red-masked villain. Many of his victims were mourned throughout Paris. Innocent girls had their young lives snuffed out. But my vow to protect the girl with the red cape would be kept even if I had to make the ultimate sacrifice in payment.

I had kept my promise to protect that girl. Even though it would mean that I wouldn't see her again, I prayed that she stays far away from the Eiffel Tower Park in the future.

For the moment, I knew that she was safe from the Masked One's snares. That night, even I was at peace.

Quinze

The Discovery

*T*HE next morning, I walked Celeste to school. I returned home with the idea that I would organize her bedroom. Things had been stashed lately without much rhyme or reason, and I wanted to put everything into its proper place.

I found hair ribbons in the drawer with her school stockings. Various art supplies were left on her dresser and on the surface of the small vanity where she sat when I brushed her hair. I had the distinct impression that this reflected Celeste's method of "cleaning" her room. It looked as though she had been hiding items in whatever space or drawer was handy when she was finished with them. As her au pair, I did not consider it my responsibility to teach her to be organized or even respectful of her possessions, by preaching at her. However, it was my hope that if things were made neat and were easier to find, the child might be inspired to keep them that way.

I was being paid by the Marshands for an entire day of work and the time that Celeste spent attending classes was time I could use to her benefit, perhaps even making it a learning experience of responsibility for what her parents had bestowed upon her.

During my childhood, I had only a small percentage of belongings compared to the child who lived in this wealthy home. I treasured all that I had and used my possessions with care and thoughtfulness. I believed that Celeste could learn this type of respect for the things she owned by subtly showing her easy ways to take care of them.

The drawer of her nightstand was particularly cluttered. I laughed as I pictured the adorable child, removing her loosely tied hair ribbons at night, her rings and other treasures and then opening the drawer to toss everything in the drawer at once.

The drawer appeared to be full of a month-long accumulation although I knew I had sorted it out slightly more than two weeks ago.

Shoved among some very sticky hair ribbons was the remains of a peppermint stick, left over from a party Celeste had attended. I also uncovered a crumpled drawing that looked as though it was meant to be tossed in the trash.

Although childishly fashioned, I was able to interpret who the figure in the crudely executed artwork represented. The person depicted was clothed in what looked to be a long cloak or cape. Some type of covering was drawn across the mouth and nose. I shuddered when I saw that Celeste had drawn an object on the bottom of the page that might have been a dog. The child had drawn a broad line through the mysterious person in the cape.

I held the picture for several minutes as I thought about the experience at the park with Ami and the Eiffel Spirit. Apparently, Celeste had seen more than I thought she had on that afternoon.

Feelings of guilt overpowered me as I reflected on the impact that the events had on the child. I should never have listened to Jules. I should have insisted that we should not go to the Tower Park. I would need to assure my dear Celeste that I would never let her be exposed to such a terrifying experience again. I clutched the picture in my hand, full of anger and something close to hatred for the entity that had caused her such distress. I wanted with all my heart to eradicate from Paris this evil force and to restore peace to those who were petrified, particularly Celeste Marshand.

Seize

The Gift

*A*s the next few months passed, I thought about Jules often. At supper, my employers often discussed his various travels. He had recently spent some time on the Isle of Crete in exploration of historic artifacts. Monsieur Marshand informed his wife that he thought his brother's pursuits were time spent in accordance with the lifestyle of the idle rich.

Monsieur's scowled when he spoke this way, blatantly indicating his disapproval of his brother's carefree adventures. More than once he mentioned to Madame that Jules needed to do something worthwhile with his life.

Personally, I was just relieved that the subject of the Eiffel Park excursion no longer seemed to be an issue where Jules was concerned. It appeared that the months that had passed worked like healing balm washing forgiveness over everyone involved in the horrific event.

More importantly, Celeste no longer seemed haunted by the vision of the specter and since we had completely avoided that area of the city ever since, there was no cause for her to be reminded of the trauma.

Madame Marshand spoke up on behalf of her brother-in-law. She told her husband, within my earshot that Jules was just sewing his wild oats and that she believed he would settle down after a while when he matured. She said that his exploration of ancient civilizations and histories was a better way to spend his time than in the pursuits which engaged many young Parisians of the day. She hinted at a dark side of the modern young people of the City and their activities.

She told her husband that others of Jules' age and social standing were enjoying a way of life that would prove to be a detriment to their reputations as well as a blow to their parents' expectations.

I was not exactly sure that I understood all her implications, but I was happy to hear her defend Jules in this way. My girlish infatuation with him had not diminished during his absence.

One afternoon when Celeste was napping, Madame Marshand asked me to join her briefly in the garden. I held my breath as I approached the bench where she sat, holding a freshly cut bouquet.

I searched my mind for any recent activity I might have engaged in that might bring about a reprimand. Madame Marshand smiled when she looked up, and I was relieved to see that this was to be a more pleasant interchange. She handed me a small package saying that the beautifully wrapped present was included in a box that Jules had sent to the family and which had arrived that morning from Greece. I was astounded that there was a gift for me, and I was speechless as I held it in my hand.

Observing the mixed emotions that were obviously on my face, Madame told me that tea would be served about a half hour late that afternoon, and if I would like, I could go spend a few minutes by myself until Cook summoned me.

I took the package with me to my room and sat on the window seat. Carefully, I peeled back the paper and untied the string that wrapped around the parcel. Inside was a small box made of marble with a gold plaque on the lid. My name was etched into the plaque in cursive letters. I ran my finger across the etching delighted to feel the indentation where the letters delicately spelled my name.

Then, I felt the smooth marble of the box itself. It was cool to the touch like the icicles that formed on frozen branches in winter. I marveled at the way it seemed to shine so white and pure there in the palm of my hand.

Only then did I think to remove the lid and I was happily surprised, for the box contained a necklace of such beauty as I had never seen before. I lifted it carefully as if it might break simply by being handled. I held the oval amulet in my hand. It was the most precious thing I had ever touched.

A small written note accompanied the piece which described the details.

A black, velvet ribbon was inserted into the circle of gold that was attached to the top of the pendant. The note said that this was for the purpose of tying the necklace around the wearer's neck. The breathtaking cameo had a pale blue background. Hand carved in relief over the blue background was a pure white stone. The carving was a delicate picture of a silhouette of a young girl in profile. I gasped when I saw the resemblance between the girl in the carving and myself.

Madame Marshand appeared in the doorway. "I was going to send Cook for you, but I thought you might show me what you received from Jules, if I asked nicely."

I held the necklace out to her.

"Well, this is most lovely." She spoke. "May I help you to put it on?"

I lifted my hair while she gently tied the black ribbon. The cameo came to rest on my throat.

During the remainder of the afternoon, I composed a thank you letter to Jules in my mind as I attended to Celeste and completed my chores. Jules had not forgotten his niece when he selected the souvenirs from his travels. Celeste also received a gift that afternoon. Jules penned a note to her, carefully printed, which Celeste was eager to read to me.

"Uncle Jules wrote, 'for my darling Celeste. The prettiest girl in Paris.'" She beamed. Then she handed me the little ring he sent to her.

"Look, it has these symbols carved into it." Celeste announced, proudly. "Uncle Jules wrote that the symbols are Greek for 'love.'" The child could not have been more thrilled.

That evening as I read her a bedtime story, I found that my hand reached for the cameo on my neck. I thought of Jules and I smiled.

Dix-sept

The New Age

*A*s the next couple of years passed there were few changes to our daily home life. We had an established routine. Living with a schedule was reassuring for me as it gave me a feeling of security. Monsieur and Madame were always kind to me, and I loved their child more than most au pairs might. Although I cared for her more than just a hired custodian, I was always aware that I was their servant and that there was a distinction between family affection and my tenuous position in the household.

As time went by, I was beginning to get anxious as Celeste approached the age of a full-time school schedule. I was aware that Madame was also in the process of securing information about the additional classes her daughter would soon be enrolled in to learn the manners and decorum expected of young ladies in their social class.

Music lessons that had been introduced at an incredibly young age would, of course, continue. These included piano and violin. For these classes, various teachers drifted in and out of the house, as did tutors in Latin and Greek.

Was there still to be a need of an au pair in the household? I dreaded a day when I would be told that it was time to seek employment elsewhere, now that Celeste would no longer need a daytime companion and caretaker. My fears kept me from broaching the subject, but I found that my anxiety was increasing as Fall approached and the new school term became imminent.

I learned that I was not the only one who was contemplating the changes that were about to occur because of the passing of time.

Monsieur Marshand opened a conversation pertaining to the matters at hand one evening at supper in the dining room. Celeste was now old enough to eat with the family and no longer had her evening meals in the nursery.

The conversation was light and airy as we enjoyed Cook's famous bouillabaisse. Madame Marshand mentioned that she and Celeste would be going to the shops in the city the following afternoon. The outing was scheduled for the purpose of obtaining Celeste's school uniforms and the shoes designated as part of the outfit by the nuns.

Celeste would be attending the private school near the Cathedral. The mother and daughter shopping excursion was a first for Celeste and I was already aware of how much she was looking forward to spending the entire day with her mother. They would be joining a fellow classmate and her mother for lunch at the Regency Hotel.

Monsieur Marshand cleared his throat and began a small speech as dinner was concluding.

I found his words to be quite unexpected.

"My dear," He began as he looked directly a me. "Perhaps you've been wondering if we were going to set you out on the street now that

Celeste will be attending school most of each day."

I believed then that his attempt at a smile was for the purpose of injecting a sense of humor into his words. It did nothing to ease my nervous state. I think my heart stopped for a moment, while I waited for him to resume.

"Madame Marshand and I have been discussing your future for quite some time now, and I would like to offer a proposition for your consideration."

Monsieur Marshand went on to say that he had taken on a rather involved court case over the past month and it had already begun to be very time-consuming. Since he did a good portion of the composition of his court papers here in his study, he was accruing paperwork at a rapid rate and his workspace was beginning to look like a disheveled library.

It was then that his offer to me took shape. He said he needed a secretary to help him organize his research and notes. He added that it would be most beneficial to him if that person could update his calendar on a regular basis so that upcoming client meetings and court appearances were not missed.

"An intelligent young woman like yourself, would be able to help get me organized. I'm sure you would learn what I needed from you in a very short period of time. And, of course, the nice thing is you would still be part of our household."

Madame Marshand spoke then, saying that I would have my evenings free, from the secretarial duties, and perhaps I would be able to assist Celeste with her school assignments.

She added that it would also be a great help to her if I would continue to see to the child's bedtime routine, as well.

I was invited to think over the proposed ideas and to advise them of my decision at breakfast. But I didn't think that would be necessary. I accepted the offer immediately, relieved that I no longer had to be concerned about my future.

"Oh, I forgot to mention." Monsieur Marshand continued. "I will also be mentoring Jules who has decided to pursue a legal education like his brother. You may have some secretarial duties to perform for him as well. I hope that is not too much to ask."

I assured him that I would find a way to handle the tasks at hand and thanked him and Madame Marshand for their faith in me.

I almost danced my way to my room that night. Change was upon me, but I was certain that I could rise to the challenges at hand.

Madame and Monsieur Marshand both accompanied Celeste on her first day at the academy. I stood in the doorway and watched as the three of them departed that morning. I admit to having a tear in the corner of my eye as I observed the child all dressed for school, carrying her small satchel of notebooks and pencils. Her hair was done in the customary bun, which made her look older than her ten years. I don't know if it was the fact that our daily routine would now be so different or simply the observation that another phase of my life was beginning, but I felt a sense of melancholy take hold of me that I could not shake.

Monsieur Marshand informed me that it would be a few days before he would be ready for me to assume my secretarial duties. He and Madame Marshand agreed that I could have the rest of the week off during the day, until Celeste needed my help after school.

Dix-huit

Summer Stories

So much free time was an odd occurrence and at first, I hardly knew what to do with this gift. When Bernard, Cook and Clair, the morning maid, were the only ones in the house, I paused to reflect on my choices.

After some deliberation, I decided that a nice, brisk walk was in order. It would be good to be out of the house in the fresh air with virtually no distractions, and no responsibilities.

The sky was a bright azure blue with several wispy white clouds off in the distance. A slight breeze wafted through the air, bringing with it the lovely scent of wisteria as I stepped from the front porch. I brought my small volume of poetry by Lord Byron, whose verse I felt matched the dour mood I could not yet put aside.

As I set out on the streets of Paris, I found I was not the only one taking exercise at this early morning hour.

I found myself being even more depressed as I observed various au pair with their small charges, stopping to tie a child's shoe, or holding a small hand as they crossed the street together. There was, of course, no way to go back in time, but how I craved such an opportunity that morning. I found myself standing outside of Madame Fournier's bakery across from the Eiffel Park and I basked in the solace of the wonderful scents emanating from her shop.

As on any other Paris morning, the locals were there to purchase their croissants and baguettes. Businessmen stood in another line at the counter where Madame Fournier's son, Philippe, grown now into a handsome young man, poured the dark black cups of espresso caffe.

I sat at a small table in the back corner of the shop, as I waited for the crowds to die down before I caught Madame Fournier's attention. She smiled in acknowledgment. A few minutes later Philippe was serving me a fresh warm croissant and a cup of the delicious brew he had just prepared.

He patted my hand, and then wordlessly returned to the counter to serve the customers that were still arriving, although in a less steady stream.

I sat there with Lord Byron enjoying this welcome repast for almost an hour before Madame Fournier joined me at the table. She was always happy when I paid her a visit, and she was excited to learn of the new assignment I was to be given in the Marshand household.

"I think of you all the time, my dear." She said. "It has always been my hope that you would have a happy life, considering the perils that you underwent as a child."

"It was never Mama's fault." I said.

"I know, my dear. Your poor mother was too fragile for this world, I think. She was a good person, though, of that I am sure."

"Perhaps she was too good." I said.

Noticing my dark mood, Madame Fournier began discussing some local gossip she thought I might like to hear pertaining to the neighborhood people with who I was familiar.

She told me about the girl who lived next door who was moving to America. She mentioned the scandalous husband of husband of Madame Lacharite, who apparently was seeing a girl young enough to be his daughter. As she spoke, I found it was not what she had to say that held me enthralled, but rather the connection her presence provided to the few warm parts of my childhood.

Lately, I had become overwhelmed as I sensed that time was speeding by me. Madame Fournier was still the vibrant, busy woman my mother loved to gossip with. In truth, she was my touchstone. She helped me to hold on to the past that was rushing by and the memories that were slipping from my grasp.

Madame Fournier leaned forward in the chair as she asked what it was like to live in the Marshand household. She expressed a keen interest in everyday lives of the family, especially Madame Marshand. Instinctively, I was aware that she wanted me to help her peek through the window that would permit her to observe a lifestyle very foreign to her own.

The lives of the affluent were a world apart from her everyday existence. I felt as though I were describing to her what life might be like on the moon.

I studied Madame Fournier's labor worn hands as we sat there and made a mental comparison to the graceful fingers of Madame

Marshand as she poured tea with such grace into her fragile porcelain cups.

I strung a series of recent events together to feed Madame Fournier's curiosity and give her some wonderful stories to share. I began by telling her that a particularly good friend of Madame Marshand had recently invited her to an afternoon tea, which unbeknownst to Madame was to be a celebration of her recent birthday.

Surprised and delighted, Madame enjoyed a lovely afternoon with friends, returning home feeling well liked and appreciated by her peers. She brought with her a gift that was to charm the entire household.

When the butler, Bernard, met her carriage outside the door, she pointed to a lovely carved bird cage that needed to be brought into the house. Bernard was further instructed to install the cage in the corner of the drawing room near the window and to fill a small container with water for the bright yellow canary perched on one of the bars inside the ornate cage.

Celeste was so excited when she saw the little bird. Madame stood aside for a few minutes as her daughter admired the creature, who began pleading for the cage to be brought to her room. A request which Madame Marshand gently denied.

"The bird and the cage were a birthday gift from my friend Camille, dear." She told her. "I believe I shall enjoy its company as I sit here and read in the afternoons. And besides, you have your dear pet, Ami. The bird shall be my pet."

I was somewhat amazed that Madame Marshand denied her daughter's request. I think it was the first time Celeste's appeals were not met with a positive reaction.

As her rapt attention focused on my story, I observed that Madame Fournier was hanging onto every word as she enjoyed her coffee and the rare break in her routine.

"There was to be another birthday surprise for Madame, that was totally unexpected." I said as I continued the saga much to Madame Fournier's delight.

I told her that Madame Marshand was in the sunny drawing room enjoying what had become her regular afternoon activity during the summer months. In this lovely setting with fresh flowers on almost every surface, Madame spent her time reading and doing needlepoint. These pastimes always seemed to refresh her spirit, providing a sense of relaxation before she supervised the evening meal.

Monsieur Marshand, knocked lightly on the door, opening it slightly to observe his wife as she hummed to herself, engaged in an intricate cross stitch pattern that was stretched on a floor easel. Pushing the door open quietly, he cleared his throat to announce his presence.

Madame was surprised to see her husband, calling on her like this, during the middle of the day. He could usually be found in the study, sifting through stacks of papers while dictating case notes to me.

I had helped to secure the gift that he was now presenting, and both Celeste and I were invited to witness the gift giving, with the condition that we stood back and observed quietly.

Holding a beautifully wrapped square parcel, Monsieur said, "Happy birthday, my dear."

Then he laid the gift on the side table near Madame. At first, I believe she was overwhelmed as it took several minutes for her to react or reply.

I believe that Celeste was just about to burst into the room to give her mother a hand with the unwrapping, but a glance from her father warned her that it would not be a good idea.

Finally, Madame arose, approaching the package with some trepidation. I wondered if kindness of any type was something that Madame did not receive often from her husband. She seemed to be struggling to create the proper response. When she unveiled the contents of the box, Madame sent her husband an inquisitive glance.

He approached her and removed the item in question. Neither Madame, nor I, nor Celeste, had any idea what it was. Placing it on the nearby table, Monsieur explained that it was a delicate musical instrument called a "serinette." It was designed to teach birds how to sing a tune.

Monsieur opened the lid, turned a crank and to the surprise of us all, the box emitted a high-pitched sound, much like a bird tweeting, in a tuneful serenade. Although the response was not melodic, the caged canary responded by singing a song of its own when the music ended, and we all laughed.

Madame was thrilled with the gift as was made obvious by the fact that she gave Monsieur a small kiss on his cheek, a gesture quite uncustomary for her to make while there were others present.

Madame Fournier was immediately intrigued, with the details of my story.

She asked me if Madame Marshand made use of the serinette every day. I told her that on most afternoons it could be heard through the closed doors of the drawing room, and that I was certain Madame Marshand was enjoying the gift immensely. Only recently, Madame told us that her little canary, who she had named "Chanteuse," had learned several tunes and was singing beautifully.

I was happy to entertain my dear friend with these kinds of details of the lifestyle in the home where I lived. These were innocent stories of high society that did not contain the dark contents of most of the city's street gossip. If Madame Fournier felt the need to share the details with her neighbors, there would be no harm done.

My stories fueled the satisfaction of the local shopkeepers, regarding how the other half lived, without soiling anyone's reputations. And, besides that, they pleased my friend, so much.

Her son looked over at the two of us a few times as he served the dwindling number of customers arriving now that it was mid-morning. I swear he winked at me more than once and I felt myself blush slightly thinking that he somehow found me attractive.

Hadn't we been children playing on the street together only a few short years ago? How did we become young adults interested now in each other for entirely different reasons?

Dix-neuf

My Introduction

MADAME Fournier returned to the kitchen to resume baking for the afternoon and evening patrons, so we bid each other adieu.

I was not ready to return home with this lovely afternoon still at my disposal. Instead, I occupied a bench at the Eiffel Park and began to read more poetry as I soaked in the rays of the sun.

Without Celeste, I need not be concerned about the restrictions imposed on visiting the Eiffel Park, and it was nice to be here so close to the apartment where I spent my youth and where my mother died. When I rose to stretch my legs, I began to walk toward the Tower. I was enjoying seeing the ever-present tourists stopping for photographs with the iconic structure.

Soon, I was underneath the Tower's four pillars looking up through the filigreed metal, a view of the Tower that always left me in awe, for it seemed to reach to the sky when observed at this angle.

I felt, a slight breeze as the corner of a black cape whooshed by me and I was sure that someone, or something had reached out to touch me. Then, it was as if the other occupants of the park were moving in slow motion except for the specter who appeared before me. This time he did not evaporate into thin air as he had during my earlier sightings. And then we were alone somehow, and we whispered to each other.

"I never caused the unrest at the Tower."

"I didn't think it was you."

"I saved the dog that day."

"I felt that you had. Thank you."

"The Masked One had her in his grip. But I stole her back for you."

"I am most grateful."

"I couldn't always save the young girls. He delights in their demise when they fall from the Tower."

"But you have saved some?"

"More than you could know. I swore them to secrecy after saving them. I told them that any notoriety of what was happening at the Tower, would only encourage the Masked One to kill even more, for the attention that it garnered. People have seen me here on the lawn. He, the Masked One, has always stayed hidden, so they believe I am the killer. They call me the Eiffel Spirit. But I need for you to know that I have never caused any destruction or death."

"Who is the Masked One?"

That question went unanswered. He was gone.

The cool breeze brought me back to reality and once again I heard voices around me and saw the movement of the people at the park.

I would never forget this encounter with the Spirit. I felt that he made this appearance in order to assure me of his protection. I was safe and loved and I would never be the same.

Vingt

Judgment

A new routine was soon established. I rose as early as I always had and after dressing and putting my hair up, I went upstairs to attend to Celeste and get her ready for school.

The two of us then stopped at the kitchen, where Cook had a small bowl of oatmeal waiting for her. Ordinarily, she would then hand the child a bag she had prepared for the mid-morning break in classes. The bag would contain a cut apple and a few slices of cheese, or perhaps a sausage cut into small bites and a pear cut in half. Celeste informed us all that the nuns insisted on this break, telling the children that it helped to keep their brains sharp as they learned their lessons for the rest of the morning.

A hot lunch was prepared by the Sisters who worked in the kitchen. Students were encouraged to eat silently and to wait until afterward to make noise on the playground.

Madame Marshand waited by the front door each morning with Celeste's cape and her schoolbooks. She accepted a kiss on her cheek from her daughter and then closed the door behind us as Celeste and I set out.

I walked Celeste to school and waited to see her enter the gated enclosure guaranteeing that she was always in someone's care.

I returned to the residence, shed my coat and gloves, ate a baguette and some fruit with my coffee and then proceeded to join Monsieur Marshand in his study to resume my secretarial duties.

When I began this assignment, Monsieur Marshand described what was expected of me. After that, being a man of few words, he worked silently while I tended to the organization and filing of the papers that he had worked on the previous day.

Eventually, I learned to take dictation, which pleased him very much. I was often asked to pick up law books at the library and return the volumes when my employer was done with them.

Jules arrived the first of October.

I had put aside my feelings for him during the time that he had been gone, but as soon as I saw him again, I felt a tingling sensation that reminded me of the crush I had on him from those days gone by.

If it was possible, he had become even better looking. As before, his smile and warm attitude toward me occasionally caused me to stammer. I blushed with embarrassment as I was certain that he thought me to be an idiot who was unable to complete a full sentence without sounding like a child.

Another desk was set up in the study for his use, although it was quite a bit smaller than the one used by Monsieur Marshand.

Jules was not yet an official member of the legal system, awaiting an examination scheduled for the Spring. It was apparent that Monsieur Marshand was serving as his mentor prior to the test, spending several hours each day discussing various court decisions with the younger man.

The next few months were a flurry of paperwork and court appearances. Monsieur Marshand commented more than once that he was so relieved that I had become his assistant.

The case he was currently working on had escalated to an overwhelming amount of court papers being processed daily. At dinner, he often praised Jules and I as the team of workers sent to him by a higher power to help with the inordinate number of documents that needed to be reviewed, responded to and filed in a manner consistent with his demanding requirements.

It was on a day of court appearances when I was left to tidy up the study and put the papers in order that I made a discovery I wish to this day had been avoided.

To straighten out the top drawer of Monsieur Marshand's desk, I came to the realization that it had been a long time since the drawer had been stocked in an orderly fashion with the requirements of this busy attorney. Sharpened pencils and an assortment of pen nibs were badly in need of replenishing. I smiled as I tended to the upkeep of the drawer, imagining my boss' face as he reached in there during the rest of the week to find what he needed at hand and neatly cared for.

There was a piece of paper and a broken pencil stuck in a slot at the back of the drawer which prevented it from opening all the way. Again, I smiled as I pictured Monsieur Marshand, trying to grab hold of the paper with his fingers, much thicker than my own, and him finally giving up on the attempt. I thought to myself how thrilled he was going to be when the drawer slid open with ease henceforth.

After some gentle maneuvering, I was able to wiggle the pencil free and then to gingerly remove the stuck paper. I then sat down with a thump in the office chair, astonished at what I was seeing.

I had unearthed a photograph of a young woman with long blond ringlets cascading over her bare shoulders. Her face was heavily made up with what I considered to be enough rouge that it could have been shared with several other pairs of cheeks in order to present a pleasing appearance.

The woman in the picture was smiling in a way I considered to be coquettish. Her low-cut blouse revealed more cleavage than I had previously beheld. A locket on a thin gold chain hung between her breasts.

But what perhaps was more disturbing was the inscription at the bottom of the picture. "To my darling Pierre. The locket and your picture that it contains remain always close to my heart." And it was signed, "Your Jeanette."

How was this possible? I asked myself. Was Monsieur Marshand having an affair with this person? Who was this wanton woman? Did she know he was married?

At that very moment I heard footsteps approaching the study.

"It is lunchtime, my dear." Madame Marshand announced. "You have been working too hard in this stuffy office. Come join me on the patio. Cook has prepared a wonderful meal for us both."

I stuffed the picture in my apron pocket and softly closed the top drawer of the desk.

"Right away, Madame." I said. I prayed that she would not take notice of my pale complexion or trembling hands as I joined her for lunch.

For several days I pondered whether I should act upon my discovery, or simply let it lie, in hopes that nothing would come of it.

I could no longer look Monsieur Marshand directly in the eyes and was continually averting his glance while working beside him in the study. Thankfully, it did not seem that Jules noticed any change my behavior. In part, this was due to his energies being consumed by composing court briefs and arguments. I give no credit to my acting skills because I would not have been able to refrain from blushing had he paid much attention to me.

Occasionally, he would request that I join him in the garden so that he could orate one of the arguments he had composed so that it could be heard aloud. He would ask if I thought they sounded cohesive and always requested that I be honest with my critique.

As time went on, I began to feel more secure making comments that I believed would be useful to him. I blushed on the afternoon he told me that he did not know what he would do without my help. I turned abruptly to head for the kitchen so that he would not see my color rise, using the excuse that Cook might need a hand setting our luncheon on the table.

My schoolgirl crush on Jules was becoming something more as I spent more time with him as his secretary. My work was meticulous and efficient more to please him than for any other reason. I took pleasure in sending him out the door with Monsieur Marshand, armed with anything either of them might require in the courtroom.

"Would you like to come hear me argue before the magistrate?" Monsieur asked me one morning.

"Are you certain that would be allowed, Monsieur?" I asked.

"Of course, you would be attending as my secretary. You will take notes of the proceedings. It happens all the time."

I did not hesitate to dash to my room for my cape and a notebook. I was back at his side within minutes.

"Well, therein lies my answer." He said.

I was in awe sitting in the gallery observing the other cases being heard that morning prior to Monsieur Marshand rising to present his own arguments. He would be introducing a new motion and making the Jury and the Magistrate aware of precedents that supported his statements.

Jules, still a month or so away from taking exams, sat in the first row of the visitors and witnesses directly behind Monsieur Marshand. He was consumed with observing the jury and making his own notes about their reactions to what was being said.

Quite often, Jules leafed through the paperwork in his briefcase. If he felt his brother should glance at a note he was writing, regarding a pertinent case, he would merely tap on the banister in front of him. At this cue, Monsieur Marshand would nonchalantly walk by, glancing briefly toward the banister and Jules' handwritten comments that offered the relatable information.

I was thrilled to watch Monsieur dramatically present his arguments and watch him interrogate expert witnesses with a knowledge of wills and estates. It was an honor to sit in the courtroom as his secretary.

After a slight break, the lawyer for the plaintiffs presented his own motions to the bench and spoke directly to the Jury about the portions of estate law that pertained to his clients and their demands.

There were many people in the gallery since the case had been the subject of several newspaper articles and had become a topic of conversation among the people of Paris.

A rich aristocrat had died leaving the mass of his fortune to his adopted son. The remainder of his family were in the process of contesting the will, producing what they believed to be proof that they were meant to receive more compensation than the will provided for them. There were inferences that codicils to the will had been coerced. Dramatic reference was made to testimony from family members who swore that verbal promises had been made to them.

The adopted son sat next to Jules, apart from the other family members in a clear demonstration of the growing animosity they felt for the adopted man, who they considered an unworthy upstart.

The Jury appeared to be unmoved by the theatrics of either attorney as their voices reverberated throughout the courtroom presenting arguments and interviewing experts.

The whispers in the gallery, where I sat were all about money and greed. A young mother sat behind me, nursing her small baby. Continually, she whispered to her friend that the old man had more than enough money to share if these rich folks were not so stingy. The contempt of the working class pervaded the space all around me.

Unfortunately, this made it difficult for me to hear the arguments, as uncomfortable as it was there in the crowded gallery. But I could not take my eyes off the handsome man writing feverishly in the first row, occasionally brushing the hair back that kept falling in his eyes. I wanted to tell everyone that not only was I acquainted with that man, but that I would be returning home with him when our day in the courtroom was over.

"I'll be needing your help." Jules said as we exited the courthouse.

"Of course."

"This book has been updated of late." He told me. "I need the library's latest issue by this evening. Can you stop by there before returning home to pick it up for me?"

"Most certainly." I replied, more than happy to run this errand. "I'll return home with the book shortly."

Monsieur Marshand and his brother were deep in conversation about the case as they walked off toward home. I turned toward the park. I would take a shortcut to the library and be home within the hour. I knew my haste would please Jules, and I wanted nothing more.

Whenever I approached the Eiffel Park, I was filled with so many memories of the mystical experiences it held for me. I seemed to be drawn toward the Tower, somewhat afraid I might encounter the Spirit and at the same time wishing for nothing more.

Vingt et un

Who Are You?

I felt his gaze grow stronger the closer my steps took me to the base of the structure. I told myself there was no time for this type of distraction. I was supposed to rush home with the book that Jules needed, but I could not help myself.

When I looked up, I saw him standing on the first landing of the Tower watching me. I was now mere steps from one of the supporting feet of the Eiffel and suddenly he was right in front of me, as if he had wings that propelled him downward.

"Ah, you are here again. I have been waiting for you."

"I cannot stay."

"Of course."

"You must tell me who you are and why you stay here. I must know if I am to be afraid."

"You must never fear me. I am only here to protect you."

"From what?"

The Masked One. It is he who would harm you and I swore this could never happen."

"Have you always been my protector?"

"Yes, my dear, and I always will."

And then, like before, he was gone, and I was as mystified as ever. I was left standing there aware that the sun would soon be going down. How long had this encounter lasted? It had seemed like only a moment or two when I was conversing with the Spirit and yet it seemed to be later in the day than it should have been.

I ran the rest of the way to the library, arriving just before the doors were going to close. Thankfully, since I knew which book, I wanted, the librarian let me retrieve it. While she processed it with her stamp, she shook her head and mumbled about being on time and not causing others to go home late.

I ran all the way home with the book and was met by Jules at the door.

"I wondered if you'd gotten lost." He said as he grabbed the book from my hand.

He headed for the study and closed the door, without thanking me for running the errand. I knew he was displeased with the length of time I had taken.

Vingt-deux

Jeanette

*I*T seemed to me that the trial would never end.

Jules and Monsieur Marshand were confined to the study more and more as the days drew near for the presentation of closing arguments.

More than once, Cook was requested to serve their meals on trays and the only glances I received from Jules were through the crack in the door when Cook entered. I was even banned from going into the office to organize the paperwork or provide sharpened pencils.

Finally, the day came when they left the house at the crack of dawn, both dressed to perfection in expertly tailored suits and newly purchased dignified neck pieces. A man had been hired to accompany them with a small, wheeled cart carrying several books and worn files stuffed with notes.

The occasion was made rarer by Madame Marshand standing at the door and planting a small kiss on her husband's cheek before he left for court. It was the first time I had seen any type of affection between the two, in quite a while.

I stopped on the stairs, so as not to make a noise. I did not want to distract from this touching moment. Monsieur Marshand took his gloved hand and gently stroked Madame's cheek. And then, the moment of affection was over, and he was out the door with the hired man and Jules on his heels.

Since it was the last day of the trial, and since I had the afternoon free, I decided to meet them at the courthouse mid-afternoon, when I calculated their part in the events would have been concluded. I have since wished I had gone shopping instead, for at the courthouse I would witness a scene I wished I had not.

Jules and the man who was hired to help that day raced down the courthouse steps. The hired man almost fell as one of the wheels of his cart got stuck on a loose brick. They appeared to be scurrying in the direction of the library together and I was still too far back on the sidewalk to call out to him.

I almost turned back then but decided instead to wait there and accompany Monsieur Marshand back home when he emerged from the courthouse. However, a moment later as he was exiting, adjusting his scarf at the top of the stairs, she approached him, and he encircled her in his arms. It was the woman in the photograph, I knew her at once.

I was breathless as I stood there in awe, witnessing the scene.

How could Monsieur Marshand be so daring as to embrace this woman, this harlot, in a public place? Didn't he fear that he might be seen, and that word might get back to Madame Marshand?

I turned and ran back to the house, slowing only a block away so that I could calm my breathing.

I no more wished for the knowledge of this seedy affair than I would wish for the sky to fall. This family, in whose debt I would always be, was not the tight knit group that I had so long imagined.

Did not Monsieur Marshand realize what he was risking by such behavior? How could he shake the very foundation of so many other lives with such recklessness?

I must compose myself, I thought. It dawned on me that the picture I had hidden away no longer represented an innocent flirtation. There was more to the relationship between my employer and this wanton woman, this "Jeanette."

Was Jules aware of her existence? Had he too betrayed his sister-in-law and risked the future of the niece he proclaimed to love so much? I prayed he was ignorant of the circumstances. I prayed, too, that I would be able to handle the information myself.

I took a deep breath and entered the house. As cheerfully as possible, I asked Bernard if Celeste was home from school as yet? When he answered "yes," I leaped up the stairs and concentrated on playing a card game with her until supper was announced.

I detest keeping secrets. This time it was torture.

At the supper table I barely looked up from my plate. I did not want my emotions to be visible. I was concerned for Madame Marshand, for whom my heart ached because of her husband's thoughtless betrayal. I could barely face him without feeling as though I would give myself away with an accusatory stare.

I was thankful that Celeste was bubbling over with stories to tell, and that Jules was so enthralled with the child's re-creation of her day at school, he did not seem to notice my unusual silence.

The next day, I made up a story that my former landlord and friend was not feeling well.

As the family assembled for breakfast, I scurried off to Madame Fournier's bakery.

Although I missed sharing the meal with the family, it was my way of avoiding the uneasiness I had felt the evening before. Instead, I grabbed a warm croissant and slipped it in the pocket of my cloak before the family had even registered my lie about my sick friend. I ran quickly toward the Tower park.

My feet slowed as I neared the iconic structure, and it was then that I realized that my cheeks were wet with tears. The entire situation had left me so dismayed. How could I continue to work for the Marshand family knowing what I knew? I felt betrayed myself, although not as much as I knew Madame Marshand would be if she found out. I felt sorry for her plight and dreaded that she might discover the infidelity.

I sat on a park bench for what seemed like an eternity. The sun was just beginning its climb barely reaching the mid-point of the Tower, filling the sky with an orange glow.

Then, I saw him lying on the ground. I held my breath as I slowly crept toward the Eiffel Spirit. I was sure he was dead.

I wanted to touch him to find out if he was breathing but could hardly bring myself to come within two feet of his emaciated form.

"Monsieur," I whispered. "Can you hear me?"

Nothing.

I approached him carefully. Kneeling beside him, I reached out tentatively, barely brushing my fingers against his pale hand.

Suddenly there was an intake of breath and his eyes opened. His gaze pierced my soul.

"Are you alright Monsieur?"

No answer.

I waited.

Finally, he rose, with much effort. I watched in mixed awe and terror, offering my hand to help.

"Do not touch me."

"No sir, I will not. What happened?"

"It was him. He is trying to destroy me."

"Who is this being you are so afraid of, and why does he want to destroy you?"

"He is the Masked One. He loathes me for my interference in his heinous endeavors."

"Did he do harm again?"

"Yes, but it has yet to be discovered by anyone but you. I am too weak to exert much energy now. But I still need to offer protection from his demonic pursuits."

"Can you escape somehow from his evil clutches."

"I will find a way."

I closed my eyes a moment, wiping my face of tears. When I opened them, he was gone?

I quickly ran to the boulangerie. Philippe was in the shop that afternoon and he was incredibly pleased to see me. Within minutes, he brought an espresso over to the table where I sat and began to regale me with stories of what he had been up to. He asked questions about my life as well, since his mother was busy with customers and had only been able to wave a cursory bonjour when I first arrived.

Philippe served me a pastry, smiling shyly as he gently laid the plate down. To my surprise, he joined me at the table despite the line of customers standing at the counter who glowered at his lack of service. I do not think he even noticed that my mind was elsewhere that morning, or that I barely responded to anything he said.

Madame Fournier did take a moment to come over and give me a small hug, soon waving her son in the direction of the waiting clientele.

I was suddenly aware that Madame Fournier had begun to show her age. Her movements were slightly slower, and I believe I detected some pain in her step.

It was Philippe's final year at university, so it made sense that his mother was aging. I guess I was not ready to face the fact that time had been taking a toll on this lady who had been so supportive to me when I had no one else in the world.

Soon, Philippe would pursue his own career and I worried about what his mother would do without his assistance in the shop.

I started to feel guilty sitting there with my coffee like I was a rich customer with nowhere else to be. I dismissed my thoughts of worry for my friend, my concerns for the emaciated Eiffel

Spirit and my distress over the unfaithfulness of Monsieur Marshand.

I gathered my cloak around me and prepared to walk back home. Philippe held the door for me and leaned toward me to whisper in my ear. He said he hoped I might have a free evening that he could escort me to dinner before returning to school.

I must have looked quite shocked at his invitation because for a moment my stunned look left him speechless. I cleared my throat and said that I would love to join him for dinner. The words were out of my mouth before I could take them back, and before I knew it, Philippe was planting a kiss on my cheek and asking if he could come by to get me on the following Friday around seven in the evening.

I believe I nodded. At least I think that I must have because he was suddenly kissing my cheek again and saying he would see me soon. I was on the path outside the shop and the door had closed behind me. As I walked back home, I thought about the handsome young man who was so happy to spend an evening with me.

I had been carrying a torch for Jules for so long, I wondered if I could even be interested in the romantic overtures of someone else. But Philippe was not just someone else. I had known him most of my life and felt a connection to him as a childhood friend. I now wondered whether he could be anything more than that.

Vingt -trois

Philippe

I put aside any conjecture about the seeds of romance growing like the wildflowers in the Eiffel Park. I turned my focus toward the joys of going out for an evening with an attractive and charming young man. After all, this was a chance to dress up and to expand my extremely limited social life partaking in an activity that didn't involve Celeste or anyone else in the Marshand household.

I must have had a schoolgirl grin on my face when I arrived back home because Cook gave me an inquisitive stare as I passed by the kitchen. After returning my scarf and cape to my room, I changed for dinner and then went upstairs to see what Celeste might need.

At the dining table, I barely offered any comments, lost as I was in my daydreams about Philippe. I may have had a crush on Jules for years now, but I had to admit to myself that it felt good to have a young man interested in me, who had just kissed me on the cheek more than once.

Jules had yet to invite me for an evening out and I must admit that I hoped he would feel a spark of jealousy when Philippe arrived to escort me to dinner.

I wondered if Celeste or anyone else in the family could sense my uplifted spirits as we dined that evening, and I could not wait to be alone in my room, resting on my pillow devoting my thoughts entirely to Philippe. It was odd to think of him in this new romantic light. He was always somewhere in the back of my mind as a childhood playmate, nothing more. It struck me as curious that he had been thinking of me as more than that.

I'm not sure if it's possible to fall asleep with a smile on one's face, but if it is, this was the night that I did.

I mentioned the evening out to Madame Marshand because I wanted her to be aware of what I was doing. After all, I was still in residence in her home, and I believed that gave her the right to know what I was doing even during the evening when my workday was over.

She appeared happy that I was planning an evening out and commented to me that she was glad I was seeing a young man on a social basis. She asked a few questions as I tidied up Celeste's closet and organized her schoolbooks for the morning. I believe that she was relieved that I had known Philippe for most of my life, and that he was the son of my mother's friend of whom I had spoken often.

Her only concern was voiced when she asked what I planned to wear for the dinner out. I had not really given my wardrobe much thought and her question left me momentarily baffled. My clothes were practical and appropriate to wear as an au pair or a secretary, but they were not well suited to a social occasion. I found that I was speechless for a moment before saying I really was not sure what I would wear.

Madame Marshand smiled and assured me that this would not be a problem. She asked me to allow her to be of service to me for a change.

"My dear." She said. "You have been such a dedicated employee to our family for these past several years, rarely asking for time off or any special favors. It is my turn to do something special for you. Besides, I believe you and I are close to each other in size so we will just look in my armoire, for something suitable for you."

Although quite surprised at her kind offer, I was more than happy to accompany her to her suite to view what she might offer.

I tried on several outfits that were stylish and appealing, but none registered with me as becoming until she produced a dark green velvet dress with a high bodice and slightly puffed sleeves. As soon as I put it on, I felt like a member of the elite. The shade of green was exactly the color of my eyes and complimented the auburn highlights in my hair. Madame gasped when I stepped from behind the changing screen. She announced that this was most definitely the dress for the occasion.

When the evening arrived, I took extra care dressing and arranging my hair. Taking one last look in the mirror, I was pleased. It had been a long time since I'd felt pretty, and I found the feeling quite enjoyable.

There was just one more thing to do before going to the parlor to await the knock on the door. I opened the small box on my dresser and reached for the cameo that had been Jules' gift to me and placed it around my neck. It was as if the dress had been made to accentuate the lovely necklace because it was the perfect complement to the borrowed outfit.

With my wrap over my arm, I headed toward the parlor just as Monsieur Marshand and Jules were headed toward the dining room. They were engaged in conversation about a particular judge who would be hearing an upcoming case.

Their conversation came to an abrupt halt as they both looked me over and seemed to be collectively holding their breath. I bid them both a good evening as I made my way to the parlor. My heart was beating a little faster as I wondered what Jules might be thinking.

I wanted to stand outside the dining room door as they gathered for dinner to hear what inquiries might be put forth regarding my plans for the evening. Instead, I refrained and sat lady-like on the edge of the sofa waiting for my escort. Assessing the occasion, as I sat there quietly, I smiled to myself and felt as though I had crossed the threshold into womanhood that evening.

I no longer thought of myself as the lost teenager who came to this house desperate for employment, living in utter uncertainty about her future. Right then, I knew that whatever my destiny might be, I was able to take the reins in my own hands and make things happen. If simply putting on a fashionable evening dress could transform how I saw myself, then what might I accomplish if I took some big steps to transform my life?

The future seemed to be filled with possibilities waiting for me to take the reins. Up to this point, my prospects were narrowly centered on the Marshand family and what opportunities they may present to me.

Philippe had taken me down a different road simply by adding another dimension to where my life might be headed.

As if I had just emerged from a cocoon, it was dawning on me that there were other people in the world outside of this family. Other young people who were enjoying themselves.

I had allowed myself to occupy a cloistered environment living up to the demands of the Marshands, afraid that I could find success only under their protection.

I asked myself if I had the faith and conviction to leap forward into the rest of my life trusting that I would make the right decisions. Lost in these thoughts and convincing myself that indeed I could become a self-assured woman, I failed to hear the knock on the door.

The butler entered the parlor to announce that a young gentleman was waiting for me in the foyer.

"Thank you, Bernard." I said.

Philippe was wearing a suit and scarf and I was momentarily taken aback by how handsome he looked. This was not the little boy I had played in the park with. This was a far cry from the young man who served coffee in his mother's bakery. This was a handsome man who turned toward me with a smile, who reached out for my hand and kissed it gently before taking my wrap and expertly putting it over my shoulders.

"You are stunning this evening, Natalie." He whispered in my ear.

Then, he took my hand and led me through the door and down the porch steps.

I was surprised to see the hired carriage waiting for us at the curb. I thought we would be walking to our destination. Philippe held open the door and gently assisted me as I took my place on the leather seat. After seating himself next to me, he lightly tapped the roof of the cabin to let the driver know we were ready to take off.

Reservations had been made at a bistro close to the Eiffel Park. It was a popular night spot noted not only for its cuisine but for the view of the Tower at night.

I told him that we most certainly could have walked to the restaurant, but he said that he wanted to go to the extra expense, comically adding that after all he was trying to impress me. I laughed and it felt good. We were at ease with each other the entire evening and had a delightful meal.

He inquired about my life as an au pair and I assured him that I seemed to be a perfect fit for the job. I briefly spoke of the family and how they had always made me feel like I belonged. I became quite animated as I expressed the joy that I felt caring for Celeste and how much she now meant to me.

At one point I paused in the conversation as I thought about the uncomfortable development of what I had recently discovered regarding the suspected infidelity. I wondered briefly if I might disclose to him the secret of the photograph that I found. I wanted to tell him about the scene on the steps of the Courthouse. I played with the idea of getting another opinion about my suppositions.

But quickly I let the thought pass by and picked up the conversation with an inquiry about news of the boulangerie.

"My mother works too hard." He said. "I worry about her sometimes. She is up so early to begin baking each day and does not retire for the night until every table is wiped clean and every inch of the kitchen sparkles."

"Madame Fournier has always put in those kinds of hours, as I recall." I said. "I have admired her all my life as a woman with incredible stamina and determination. Of course, I must add that besides all of that, she makes the finest pastry in all of Paris."

"That goes without saying." Philippe smiled as he agreed. "I may be concerned that she overworks herself, but there is no question about her talent in the kitchen. I could not be prouder of her. It is my hope that the day will come when I will be in a position to be more helpful to her so she can finally have some time to be kind to herself."

He raised his glass in a toast. "To my mother, a woman who is dear to us both."

Philippe also had a few stories to share about his college experiences. Now that he was graduated, he missed seeing his friends from school. He particularly missed life in the dormitory, where apparently there were pranks played and camaraderie was encouraged.

Philippe almost spilled his wine laughing about the time his friend Rene entered the dorm room looking incredibly sad. He explained that he had just seen the test scores posted in the main hall for the term's passing and failing students. He said he was too broken up to tell Philippe how badly they both had done on the finals and that he would just have to go see for himself.

Philippe said that he ran down the flight of stairs in the dorm building, He ran all the way to the main study hall and pushed his way through the crowd of students to get close to the list of grades. When he was just about there, a few of his friends turned toward him and broke into applause. His name was at the top of the list of honors students indicating that he had passed with the highest grade possible. Philippe said that he returned to his dorm room and began throwing pillows and books at Rene, who feigned injury as he fell onto his cot in fits of laughter.

As Philippe recalled, Rene held his hand up and while still laughing asked his friend not to beat him up too much. He produced a bottle of champagne and told Philippe that it would be better to spend the evening celebrating than throwing things at each other.

Before they popped the bottle open, the dorm room was inundated by a few more of their classmates who burst in with similar celebratory intentions.

Philippe said that the party continued at local bistro until the early morning hours.

His delight in telling the story was infectious and I found myself laughing with him as I pictured the scene.

Our evening passed by quickly and I was sorry when it was over.

When I arrived home, the house was incredibly quiet. I thought for sure everyone was asleep or at least in their own quarters. However, when I went through the kitchen on the way to my room, I saw a figure in one of the chairs by the kitchen table.

I was surprised when I discovered that it was Jules, who inquired if I had a good evening. I replied that it was most enjoyable and asked what he was doing there in the kitchen at this hour.

He hesitated. Later I wondered if he slurred his reply. I am fairly sure I caught him off guard by questioning what he was up to. He mumbled something about not being able to sleep and that he was getting a glass of milk to help with this problem. He did not look me in the eyes when he spoke. I detected the strong odor of whiskey on his breath. I had never thought of Jules as much of a drinker, but he had clearly had more than one drink before I got home. As I stood before him, I noticed he could not take his eyes off the cameo necklace, his gift of long ago.

I believe he expected me to console him, whether for allegedly betraying him by going out with Philippe or because he was unable to sleep. Perhaps he thought I might at least offer a couple of minutes of companionship, but instead I proceeded toward my room. I mumbled under my breath that it had been a long day, and that I would see him tomorrow. I said I hoped he was able to sleep now, and then I closed the door to my room.

Maybe he was a little miffed with my conduct or maybe he just wanted me to pay attention to him, but I was too busy recalling the details of the evening, which I had thoroughly enjoyed.

I fell asleep hoping to dream about the enjoyable meal and the even more enjoyable company. Philippe had proven to be charming, well-educated, and more than pleasant to be with. I hoped it would not be long before we would see each other again.

That night, I believe I outgrew my girlish crush on Jules. The fascination was being overshadowed by another man who looked at me as more than a governess and enjoyed spending time just being with me.

I was still young and felt no pressure to decide which of these men I liked more. Time was on my side and even if the perceived jealousy that Jules had displayed was imagined, I found I was amused by the fact that it might exist.

Either of these men, at least from my current perspective, had plenty of time to make themselves more important to me. I could not wait to see if they would and if so, how they would go about it.

Vingt-quatre

Finality

*I*T was obvious that there would be no more musing about romance and dreams of the future as the events of the following morning developed.

I awoke to the distressing sounds of stamping feet and slamming doors. Soon after the noise became overwhelming, Cook knocked on my door and abruptly entered my room without waiting for me to respond.

Her face was noticeably pale, and it was obvious she had dressed in haste. Normally, quite fastidious, she appeared somewhat disheveled. She announced that I must rise and dress quickly and that I was to appear in the dining room. Breathlessly, she muttered something about a family emergency and then she was gone.

I shot out of bed and was dressed within minutes. I hoped that Jules had not received a similar summons, since I wanted to avoid seeing him.

In the few minutes before I was seated at the table, several potential scenes took place in my mind. I imagined Celeste being taken to the hospital. I imagined that a fatal accident had occurred in the pre-dawn hours to Monsieur Marshand, perhaps as he left for an exceedingly early appointment.

Jules was seated at the table sipping coffee when I arrived, so I dismissed the fact that he might have been the victim of some type of traumatic event. Neither of us said a word as we sat motionless waiting for the terrible news that it seemed we both feared. Shortly, Cook silently served us coffee and put a plate of croissants in the center of the table.

Madame Marshand entered the room and without looking either of us in the face took a seat across from Jules. Her usually composed demeanor was nowhere to be seen. Her eyes were red and swollen and it looked to me as though she had not slept all night.

Not being able to stand the suspense any longer I blurted out the main question of my initial concern, asking outright if anything had happened to Celeste.

Slowly, Madame turned toward me. She offered me small smile as she replied.

"I'm sorry that I caused you to worry about my daughter." She said. "But you can put your mind at ease in Celeste's regard, for she is well and unharmed." She hesitated before adding, "Although she will certainly be impacted by the events of this day, she is physically fine, and nothing has happened to her."

She succeeded in putting my mind at ease, but now I found myself holding my breath while waiting for an explanation of what was happening in the household.

Cook appeared again to serve coffee to her mistress, again in complete silence. No other food was served, and the room was quiet and still. It seemed like each second dragged on like the tortoise in one of Celeste's books who was in a race with a hare.

Finally, Madame spoke again. Her voice was flat as if she purposefully was holding back her emotions, not wanting any of us to see what she was going through.

She explained that Monsieur Marshand had not gone to bed the night before until the early morning hours. He had been indulging in an unusual amount of libation and was quite tipsy when he did pull back the bed covers. She disclosed that he just fell into the mattress, still completely dressed.

It amazed me to hear her speak of a scene that occurred in her private rooms. I glanced toward Jules, wondering if he thought it was odd as well. He had not looked up since the conversation began, instead staring down at the dining table. It looked as though he were in a trance as Madame continued her story.

Madame told us that she was disturbed by her husband's inebriated condition and somewhat repulsed by the odor of liquor he brought with him to bed.

She said that she pulled back her own covers in order to get up from the bed and leave the room. She said that she had resigned herself to sleep on the sofa in Celeste's room rather than endure the indignity any longer.

But just as she was about to rise, Monsieur Marshand reached out for her arm. He asked her not to move. She said her pulse quickened and she was momentarily afraid of what was going to happen next.

She said that Monsieur Marshand issued an order that she was forbidden to leave the room until he spoke to her about an urgent matter. He said that he had a confession to make and although it would change their lives completely, it had to be done. Apparently, he disclosed that he had terrible secret that he could no longer keep to himself.

My heart was in my throat at this point. Had Madame been told about Jeannette and his affair? My imagination got out of hand. Had she perhaps reacted to the knowledge by killing him? She was not a frail woman. I could picture her picking up a candle holder or heavy book and hitting him over the head.

She went on to say that she breathlessly awaited the revealing of her husband's dire secret but that it was never disclosed. Instead, Monsieur took the hand which he had used to restrain her and pressed in on his own chest.

"I will never forget the look of pain and surprise on his face. Madame said. "Next, he merely fell forward, gasped loudly and then stopped breathing." I felt as if I had just witnessed a one act play take place in the Marshand dining room. I prayed that the described events could not possibly be true.

As she openly shed tears, Madame continued.

"I have no idea what this secret of his was." Madame Marshand continued. "And I suppose I never will know, for now my husband, Celeste's much-loved father, is dead. I am a widow and I do not know what the future has in store for me."

At this, Madame rose from the table and left the dining room.

Jules, I, and the butler remained frozen as if in a tableau for several moments. Then, without a word to anyone, Jules rose and proceeded to go to the study closing the door behind him.

The butler disappeared soon after and I was left at the table with my cup of cold coffee and a million unanswered questions.

The events of the next couple of days occurred as if in a dream. People came and went to the house, all dressed in sedate dark clothes. Several catered meals were delivered, and many tears were shed. Cook still baked and prepared food, so there was an overabundance of things to eat. A buffet was set up for all the mourners who came to offer their condolences. Cook managed to keep the food fresh and replenished, so it always looked as if no one had touched anything.

My main obligation was to care for Celeste's well-being.

After the coroner left the house on that fateful day with her husband's body, Madame sat down with her daughter and held her hand. Calmly, as they sat together on Celeste's bed, Madame explained to the child that her father had passed away in his sleep and that he was at peace during his last few minutes on earth.

I stood in the doorway of Celeste's room silently observing the scene as it unfolded.

Madame was careful to conceal the truth of what really happened during those ugly, last few minutes of her husband's life. She held her daughter close and for several moments neither of them spoke a word. Madame then summoned me to take over as she left the room.

A soft, gentle, rain was falling the day of the funeral.

The house was disturbingly quiet as we prepared to leave in the waiting carriage.

I dressed Celeste in a plain black frock with her hair tied back in a black grosgrain ribbon. I believe the saddest thing about the entire day was seeing this beautiful child dressed in mourning clothes.

The Butler assisted Madame Marshand, Celeste, and myself into the carriage where we waited for Jules.

Several minutes passed before he joined us. It was obvious to me that he had been crying. I wondered if he had used the time while we waited to steady himself to hide his devastated emotional state.

I was surprised that he reached for my hand when the carriage pulled away. I doubt if Madame even noticed the gesture, and if she did, she most likely did not care.

Several of Monsieur Marshand's legal colleagues stood over to the side at the burial site. Their heads were bowed as the preacher offered words of comfort to the family.

I felt as if everything was happening in slow motion. It appears we were suspended in another worldly dimension, apart from the events of the rest of the population.

As I momentarily surveyed the mourners while lost in my own thoughts, I was surprised by the presence of one young woman who stood slightly apart from the rest. A breeze briefly lifted the veil she was wearing to cover her face. I recognized her immediately.

It was the woman in the picture from Monsieur's desk drawer. The same woman I had seen him with on the steps of the courthouse. I was astounded that she had shown up at Monsieur Marshand's funeral and that she was standing only a few feet away from his wife.

I quickly glanced at Jules to see if he was aware of her presence. He caught my eye and saw my slight nod, toward her.

I was holding my breath. I did not want Madame to see the woman, even though she most likely would not know who she was. She was standing in close proximity to the Monsieur's colleagues and for that reason I hoped Madame would think she might be one of their wives. As my thoughts were spinning about the woman and her reasons for being there, Celeste reached out for my hand and held it tightly in her own as tears streamed down her cheeks. My concern for her well-being dwarfed my worry about the woman whom I believed was her father's mistress.

I put my arm around Celeste and led her away from the mourners. I thought she might need a moment to grieve by herself. I hugged her gently as she cried and waited patiently for her to pull gently away from me.

Soon we were all headed back to the carriage, thankful that the rain had stopped as we made our way through the cemetery. I was more grateful that Madame had paid no attention to the woman in the veil.

I glanced back toward the burial site and saw Jules with the woman. They stood next to a nearby tree. His hand was wrapped around her wrist and he looked at her with a menacing expression. I could not hear what they were saying but they appeared to be arguing. Quickly, he released his grip and left her standing there alone. Madame was looking straight ahead walking as if in a trance, for which I was greatly relieved.

As if that moment was not already infused with sufficient anxiety, I was aware of being watched by a penetrating stare. Although I saw no one distinctly, I caught a glimpse of a dark cloak floating through the nearby trees several feet from the grave. I gripped Celeste's hand tighter and led her toward the carriage.

The black wreath on the front door greeted the mourners as they entered the Marshand home. Madame was in an obvious state of shock. She seemed to glide from one place to another never really landing anywhere for long. I noticed more than once that she would turn away right in the middle of a conversation as a friend was offering their condolences. She did not seem to be relating to the reality of the situation. It was as though she was an actress playing the part of a recently widowed woman, and completely unaware of her lines or the correct stage direction.

I was relieved to be able to go upstairs to settle Celeste down for a nap and forego milling about with a house full of strangers.

Later in the day, when everyone had gone, a pervading air of melancholy lingered behind. Cook left a cold buffet out for the family to partake of rather than prepare a meal for us to share in the dining room. Little of it was touched.

Vingt-cinq

Mourning

*I*T was my hope that Madame would begin to show some signs of recovery from her loss, as the next few weeks went by.

I became even more protective than usual of Celeste who was existing in a fragile emotional state since the day of her father's burial.

I was also concerned that in addition to trying to deal with the loss of her father, she was contending with a lack of support from her mother as she grieved.

Madame was so lost herself that she was unable to give comfort to her child. Celeste was more withdrawn as each day passed.

I wished I knew if this situation was temporary. Was it possible that Madame Marshand was to be this detached entity forever? If so, I believed that Celeste would rely on me more and that I would have to become her mother's emotional surrogate.

More than once I witnessed the child reaching out to her mother, only to be brushed away, nonchalantly. Her face took on a confused and hurt look. I tried to fill the gap by pulling her toward me in a caring embrace when I had the opportunity. I could not find the words to offer her comfort since I did not know the future impact of Madame Marshand's mourning, but I knew the current detachment was leaving an indelible mark on the child's psyche.

I was reminded of my own mother and her deterioration during her last year, and I prayed that Madame Marshand would not find escape in a bottle and thereby ignore the emotional needs of her daughter as my mother had.

I watched as Celeste began to withdraw. Slowly she was transforming from the carefree, happy child I had cared for all those years. She was becoming a serious, introspective young woman who now at twelve years of age had pulled a veil over her emotions that was not going to permit anyone to know what she was feeling inside.

I was determined to help her in any way I could, as I now felt she was a kindred spirit to myself at that age. I wanted to assure her that I could be trusted with any disclosure of her inner turmoil if she were to open to me. It was important that she realize I was there to be a steady ship in the current storm.

I looked out the window of my room and saw Jules sitting alone on one of the garden benches. Celeste was busy with schoolwork and I saw this as an opportunity to spend a few minutes with her uncle.

I hoped he might evaluate the household situation and help me to put it into some type of perspective that I could understand. But I was cautious about how to begin the conversation since he had his own emotions to deal with about his brother's death.

"Jules." I said after getting his attention. "I have not had an opportunity these last few days to speak directly to you and tell you how sorry I am for the loss of your brother."

"Ah, don't be concerned." He said, brushing his hair back from his forehead in that endearing gesture I had come to love. "As far as I am concerned, you are just as much a member of this household as am I, and I know you have been dealing with your own grief concerning Monsieur Marshand's passing."

I had been so worried about Madame Marshand and Celeste's ability to cope with their loved one's death that I had not given myself a chance to deal with my own feelings. Suddenly I felt a flood of tears well up in my eyes as I gave in to my own sadness.

It was not that Monsieur had ever reached out to me with many kind gestures or smiles, but during the time we worked together we achieved a healthy respect for each other's work ethic. And, after all, it was he who gave me a second career in the household when Celeste began going to school each day.

Jules reached out for me and held me close as I cried. It had been so long since I had let any tears flow, perhaps it had even been since the death of my own mother. Now, I could not seem to stop the tears and the uncontrollable sobbing for several minutes.

I cried to compensate my own feelings and more importantly because of how sorry I felt for Celeste.

Jules reached in his pocket for a handkerchief which he gave me for the tears and for my nose which to my embarrassment was running profusely.

I felt that I must say something about the change I had seen in his niece. I asked if perhaps he might reach out to her and offer her some consolation. I told him of my concern that she was closing herself off emotionally since her father's death and even went so far as to say that Madame Marshand was so involved with her own mourning that I felt she had not taken an opportunity to console and comfort her daughter. I held my breath after making this disclosure, wondering if I had overstepped my boundaries being so frank about his sister-in-law's detached state.

We sat on the bench together for quite a while. I know because the light in the garden changed to the late afternoon glow that would soon leave the daylight behind.

"Jules, I saw you with her at the funeral." I said.

"What are you talking about, Natalie?"

"I know who she is. I saw them together once."

"My God." He said. "Does Monique know?"

"I don't believe so. I certainly would never say anything to Madame about that woman. What did you say to her that day at the funeral?"

"She threatened to tell everything if she doesn't receive some money. She said she would go to the press. She has no qualms about ruining my brother's reputation by announcing their illicit affair to the entire city of Paris."

"What did you say, then?"

"I told her if I ever saw her anywhere near my sister-in-law, she would be sorry. But, all the while, I knew she would approach Monique as well as the newspaper if I didn't offer her a monetary compensation."

I must have looked incredulous over this disclosure as I stared at Jules in disbelief.

"Natalie, you mustn't worry. I'll take care of the situation and I swear to you neither Monique nor Celeste will be hurt in any way."

"What kind of person would resort to blackmail during a time of such distress?"

"The kind who would have an affair with a married man. This woman is lacking in morals and judgment. Not only did she wantonly fling herself at my brother, but she also apparently cares nothing for his family's preservation of his memory."

This type of behavior was more than shocking to me. I realized that if this kind of treachery was an example of the way adults think and treat each other, perhaps I did not want to be part of this grown-up world.

Finally, Jules rose and took my hand. I stood and faced him, both of us speechless as we looked into each other's eyes. Then, as naturally as the morning dew on the bright green grass, he bent his head down and kissed me deeply and with a passion I had never encountered.

Again, we searched each other's eyes. Neither of us said a word. I felt as though I was drowning in the sea of his blue eyes and that there was no escape.

Slowly, I turned and went into the house. I closed the door to my room gently and leaned back against it. I was transported from the spot as I felt a glow throughout my body. Although the words had not been spoken, I felt loved and cared for and it was all that I needed.

The next morning, I was hurt and confused when at the breakfast table, Cook informed me that Monsieur Jules had left earlier with a suitcase in hand. She said a carriage had arrived around 5 am for him.

She said that she was beginning the breakfast preparations when she heard the hall door open to the drawing room. When she left the kitchen to investigate, she was surprised to find the Butler assisting Monsieur Jules with his coat and scarf. She stood in the hallway for a few minutes to figure out what was happening.

The Butler answered the knock at the front door. A carriage driver stood on the top step with is hat in his hand, as he waited for his passenger. Within minutes, Jules wrapped his scarf tighter and headed out the door.

The Butler followed, delivering Monsieur's case to the carriage. He returned and closed the front door behind him. Cook said that he glanced briefly in her direction before proceeding down the hall to his own room.

How could Jules have left after what passed between us yesterday in the garden? Had the incident been a dream? Was the kiss something Jules had conjured up to make fun of me, the young au pair with no romantic experience? None of this made any sense.

"Was there no note for me?" I asked Cook.

"Not that I know of. There were no notes for anyone from Monsieur Jules, Mademoiselle. Are you ready for coffee now?" she asked.

I do not recall answering her. I do not recall much else that happened that morning. I was overcome with confusion. The glow of the kiss was forgotten. I now questioned the feeling of being loved that I was so sure of mere hours ago.

Was I nothing to this man? How could he kiss me with so much passion and tenderness and then disappear as if it were nothing, without even saying au revoir? Perhaps I was just so naive and vulnerable that my own emotional needs were exposed to those around me, setting me up to be hurt. I told myself that I was taking this too hard and should not give it so much importance.

It was a kiss after all, not a proposal of marriage. Jules had not professed his love, nor had he made any promises.

I vowed to myself not to think of that kiss again. I would not let this man, or any other man, become so important to me that they could control my happiness and disturb my poise and self-possession. Wherever he had gone, I resolved, good riddance to him. I could not be in love with someone who tossed my feelings in the air and toyed with my heart as Jules had. I simply would not think of him anymore.

Despite my resolve, I knew this was not going to be easy. As I walked in the garden with Celeste that afternoon, I paused as I reached the bench where I had sat with Jules. For an instant I closed my eyes and swore I could feel his lips on mine again. I hoped that when I opened them, I would be looking into his eyes as deeply as I had the day before.

Celeste watched me as I stood still. She looked perplexed as I evolved from my reverie. Even though it had not lasted exceptionally long, it was as if I was coming awake after a deep sleep.

"What is it?" She asked in a concerned tone.

"Oh, nothing. For a moment I thought I was coming down with a migraine." I lied.

"Are you all right now?"

"Quite all right. Shall we sit and read some poetry now?"

Celeste opened the small book she was holding and began reading Elizabeth Browning's verses out loud. She was so adept at her poetic cadence. I enjoyed her musical tones and found myself relaxing as she read.

In the midst of the romantic verse, I felt a tear escape and trickle slowly down my cheek like the last rain drop on the window when a rainstorm draws to a close.

Love, I thought. Certainly, this was an emotion I would rather not feel anymore. It brought hours of anticipation, a moment of joy, and days of heartbreak in its wake. I could live happily without love and would no longer dream that it might be waiting for me around the next corner.

When we went inside for supper, Celeste looked as though she enjoyed the time in the garden. I believe that it had been soothing for both of us.

Her father's death had left a gaping hole that she was trying hard to fill. He had been like a pillar to his daughter and she cherished his memory. I did not have the heart to tell her that even though time would dull the pain, I knew from my own loss that the void would remain with her like a hole in the pocket of one's favorite coat. A person might put their finger in the worn-out hole over and over again as a reminder that it was still there and that even if it were mended, the torn spot would not be forgotten.

Vingt-six

Captured

I asked for a day off in the middle of the week.

I walked briskly to Madame Fournier's bakery, picking up my pace as I neared the Eiffel Park. I could not face an encounter with the Spirit. My emotions were raw and unable to handle such a confrontation. I needed the consolation of the closest person I had to a mother. I was relieved that the bakery was not crowded.

A young girl, I did not know, was serving the customers.

As I stood back to observe the scene it was apparent that her friendly and pleasant demeanor was appreciated by the clientele.

Madame Fournier brought a fresh tray of pastries from the kitchen and busied herself arranging the delicacies in the glass case. Looking up, she saw me standing close to the door. With a big smile on her face, she beckoned me over to the counter.

"Cherie, I am so happy to see you." She said. "You are like a ray of sunshine on this cloudy morning."

"Madame, it is you who are the ray of light; a light I needed to see today."

"Natalie, I'd like to introduce, Chloe. She has been helping me every morning during our busy hours and already I am totally dependent on her assistance."

The girl blushed at the compliment. She smiled shyly and nodded her head toward me.

"I have heard so much about you, Mademoiselle. Madame tells me stories every morning of the time you lived upstairs with your mother."

"You must be bored to death by those stories. Chloe. I'm afraid our lives were not overly exciting."

Madame Fournier poured the two of us an espresso and signaled for me to join her at the small table nearest the kitchen.

"My dear, you look so tired." She said as she smoothed my hair back from my forehead. "I don't think you have been taking very good care of yourself."

"It has been a difficult few weeks." I said.

"Ah yes, I read about Monsieur Marshand's death in the paper. I wanted to send my condolences but thought it better just to wait until you visited again. How is the family?"

"Madame has been noticeably quiet. Her brother-in-law, who was in the legal practice with her husband left rather abruptly after the funeral.

My poor Celeste is still experiencing the shock of the loss. The whole thing happened so unexpectedly, and I believe that was the most difficult part."

"And it has obviously been a strain on you as well."

"I suppose it has. Emotions can be draining. So, how are you? And how is Philippe? I want to hear some good news. Have you any?"

"My son is well, although he has not visited for a while. I expect to see him at the end of the week. He has finished his classes and has applied for a position with several architectural firms here in Paris. It would do my heart good if he settled down here."

"And what of the new girl that you've hired."

"The bakery has been more prosperous than ever this past year. The girl is nice to the customers and good at serving them at the tables as well as at the counter. I believe she wants to learn to help with the baking too, which would be most appreciated. Philippe inquired in his latest letter if I had been in touch with you. I think he wants to secure a good position and establish himself in his field. After that, if I may be so bold, I believe he would like to court you further if you are amenable."

"I believe I've given up on men." I told her flatly. "It seems that love only causes confusion and pain, and I don't believe that I should solicit those feelings."

Madame Fournier smiled and reached across the table to take my hand.

"Don't give up on love completely." She said. "Perhaps it has just not shown you its kindest face. You are still young, and love can still entice your heart. Wait my dear, and someday you may find there is kindness and gentleness that can accompany what a young man may offer you wrapped inside of the passion and desire he displays at first glance."

"Now you are beginning to sound like a poet, my dear Madame Fournier. But you have made me smile and given me some hope. I thank you for this, and for all the love and support you have shown me all my life. Just knowing that you are here on the other side of the Tower gives me strength and a feeling of belonging to someone. You are my childhood family and will always be like a mother to me."

Abruptly, Madame Fournier rose, saying she and I needed a pastry to go with our coffee.

I had a feeling she was escaping from a conversation that touched her heart. I believe that she was uncomfortable being praised for her past support. Moreover, I saw tears well up when I told her how much she meant to me.

The wind had picked up quite a bit and a few raindrops landed on the bakery window as we continued our visit. Although I was thoroughly enjoying the conversation and the delectable repast, I thought it wise to start walking home.

The force of the gale made it difficult to walk against its direction. I pulled my cloak tighter and tried to accelerate my advance. But it seemed that the effort I used to go forward was rewarded with a stronger wind that blew me backward with each step. The storm had become an entity unto itself. One that was filled with rage.

And then, I saw him.

The Masked One was on the landing of the Tower's first level. His cape was pulled out from his shoulders and he resembled a giant bird of prey about to swoop down in my direction. A quick inventory of the lawn and the linden trees revealed that there was no one else in the Eiffel Park.

To my horror, he began to drift toward me. Was he floating or flying? I could not tell at first. He was so nimble in his rapid climb down the side of the Tower that the moment became surreal. I wanted to scream for help, but I had no voice. I wanted to run but found that I was frozen to the spot and could not move in any direction.

I did not see a weapon, but I was possessed by fear and felt more powerless than I ever had. I would die today; I knew it.

The Spirit had warned me before that the Masked One wanted me, but until now I did not comprehend the extent of his evil desire.

As he got closer, I saw that the Masked One was enjoying this. His smile was such as I had never seen before. It was filled with malevolence. His face, with the skin drawn back, displayed sharp cheek bones. His eyebrows were arched, adding to the diabolical smile which was a threat to my very soul. And yet, there was something so familiar about him. Even with the red mask, I knew those eyes from somewhere. But his identity was out of the reach of my memory.

In an instant the moment ended.

The wind died down.

The Spirit had his arms around me. He carried me to the edge of the Park and then put me down on my feet. My legs were weak, but I was somehow able to stand.

"Run." He whispered. "He will not let go of you the next time. You must get away now, at once."

I ran, although my muscles were as weak as newly formed bread dough.

I ran, although my breath was coming fast, and my heart was working like a worn out gear on an old bicycle. I ran until I reached home and then I dissolved on my bed, not waking until three days later.

He was there in my dreams, taking the form of a red-eyed hawk swooping overhead. No matter how much I darted behind trees and rocks he would be there waiting. I was in a state of restless sleep and delirium. Fear rippled through me during these terrible nightmares leaving me covered in a cold sweat.

In my fevered state the bird of prey became a tangible presence overwhelming me with dread.

Madame Marshand was sitting on the edge of the bed when I awoke. She held a soothing washcloth to my forehead. Her face was consumed with concern.

"Thank the Lord." She whispered, as I slowly opened my eyes.

"You have had a terrible fever, Natalie." She said. "Thank God you woke up, we haven't been able to revive you for several days. The doctor was here. He said that you had probably come down with a fever as a result of being caught in that very ominous storm, without enough warm clothing to protect you."

"I will ask Cook to bring you some hot soup, at once."

I pulled myself up and leaned back against the wall. Suddenly, I recalled the scene in the park. I did not remember how I got back home, but I could still picture the sinister look on the face of the Masked One as he glided toward me.

I knew I had come awfully close to death.

Madame Marshand brought Celeste to see me later that day.

"I didn't want her to disturb you." She spoke quietly. "But she wanted to see for herself that you were all right."

Celeste bent down to hug me, and although she didn't say anything, her sighs told me how worried she had been for my wellbeing. When she pulled back to look down upon me, she smiled and then went to stand by her mother, without making a sound. They left the room, quietly closing the door behind them. I fell into a deep sleep, finally feeling at peace.

Thankfully, this sleep was not interrupted with dreams of the Masked One or the form he had taken as a sinister, red-eyed hawk. Instead, I was somehow comforted by the remembrance of the Spirit's arms around me as he rescued me from the malefactor.

Vingt-sept

Going Forward

A mere two weeks later, there was a note from Phillipe telling me that he had returned to Paris and that he had finished school. He wrote that his mother mentioned that she and I had seen each other recently.

He further noted that he would enjoy the pleasure of my company if I would care to go out with him again, perhaps for an afternoon coffee or a bite to eat on an upcoming evening. He said that he had missed me and had been thinking about me while at school.

He asked if I would send him a reply, so that he might decide for us to get together. I smiled, reflecting on the formal way in which he approached the subject of seeing me again.

He is so different from Jules, I thought. Jules is so much more worldly and self-assured. I always felt as though he believed I should be the one flattered to be seen in his company.

Surely, it would not hurt to spend an afternoon or evening with Philippe. Our one and only evening out had been a pleasant experience. Then, I contemplated my resolve to have nothing to do with men anymore and never to subject myself to becoming emotionally involved and vulnerable to hurt.

I would wait a day or two to respond to the note. I had to decide if I was willing to participate in an event that may or may not force me to analyze my feelings for Philippe. Or worse, to subject myself to any disclosure on his part about his feelings for me. I would just have to give the matter some thought.

In the meantime, I approached Celeste with an idea that I thought might pick up her spirits. "Why don't we redecorate your bedroom?" I asked her. "It might be fun to change your curtains and perhaps get new wallpaper. Maybe we could select some new colors that you haven't used before to decorate your space."

It made me feel good when she perked up at my idea. I told Madame about my suggestion the next time she showed up at the dinner table. She glanced at me and then over at her daughter. Nodding soundlessly in my direction, I believe she understood by the inflection in my voice that I was proposing the project to help raise her daughter's spirits.

Madame did not join us every night at dinner anymore, so I was glad we didn't have to wait long to get her permission. Celeste and I immediately prepared for our shopping expedition.

We spent a wonderful day in town investigating several tasteful shops displaying the latest in popular design schemes. One pattern appealed to Celeste so at the end of the day, we returned to that shop to order the wallpaper and matching drapes.

Celeste was in fine spirits during lunch. She reminded me of the carefree child I had helped to nurture. We dined at one of the new sidewalk bistros that had opened in the district.

Celeste recounted stories of her current classmates, which she had not done in quite a while. I laughed and almost choked on my wine and cheese when she described the handsome boy who had recently fallen down the stairs of the school while he stared after a girl, he had a crush on. She described the red face of the poor boy when he got back on his feet, with the knees now torn in his uniform pants. Unfortunately for him, the incident had been witnessed by several students who were now aware of his unrequited love and would soon be whispering about it all over the schoolyard.

We did not arrive home until the late afternoon, laden with packages containing a couple of art prints Celeste had selected for the walls of her room, and a new lamp for the bedside table.

"How long do you think the order for the paper and drapes will take, Mademoiselle?" She asked. "Not long, my dear. The fabric is made right here in Paris and the matching paper comes from a factory not too far away. I believe you should have both delivered within the month."

Giggling and talking nonstop as Bernard held the door for us, we then headed for the stairs to take everything up to her room. We declined his offer of assistance, Celeste saying she wanted to unwrap everything immediately and spread the parcels on her bed, barely noticing that someone was standing in the doorway on the landing to the bed chambers.

"Good evening lovely ladies." A voice said.

It was Jules who approached Celeste displaying a big smile, as if we had just seen him that morning. With no words of explanation for his lengthy disappearance, he inquired as to where we had spent the day.

I was speechless. I was astounded and angry all at once. I resolved that there was no way I was going to speak to him or let him think we had not noticed that he had been away and had left without saying a word.

For a moment I almost gave in. He stood there holding the door open to Celeste's room, exuding a boyish charm and looking down at the floor with an assumed air of humility. Casually, he brushed the stray wisp of hair from his forehead, as was his habit. I had to hold myself back in order to maintain my resolve.

I took the packages that I was holding into Celeste's room without even acknowledging his presence and made up my mind I would not come out until Celeste was asleep in bed and the house was quiet for the night.

I did not come downstairs at all that night. Not wanting Celeste to see how angry I was with Jules, I fussed over the purchases we made and exaggerated my excitement about the changes we were going to make to her bedroom.

Celeste was thrilled with the colorful art prints and the swatches of the fabrics that we brought home. Her exuberance helped me to offset my anger against Jules.

I told Celeste to clean up for supper but that I was not hungry this evening and would rather just rest here on the chair in her room for the time being. I perused the furniture catalog that we brought home as the sun began to set.

Celeste felt bad that I had not gone downstairs since we returned home, and I wasn't going to share with her that it was because I did not want to encounter her uncle.

When she joined me, she brought a small plate of cold meat and cheese and a cup of wine for my supper. For a moment, it seemed our relationship was reversing, and she was taking care of me.

Rain began beating hard against her bedroom window as we both sat on the bed and leaned back into the soft pillows. I found myself drifting off to the rhythm of the falling drops, thinking about how pleased I was that my efforts had the positive effects of lifting Celeste's outlook.

She was still talking about the treasures she had seen in the shoppes as I fell asleep.

I wished as I dozed off, that there was a way I could affect Madame Marshand's mood as well, but her grief was not about to be dissuaded by a new set of drapes or a comforter. I had a feeling that only time would heal the young widow's heart.

Vingt-huit

Sabbatical

*A*MI awoke me the next morning licking my face and then racing back and forth to the bedroom door with her tail wagging, announcing that she needed to go outside.

Since Celeste was still deeply asleep, I rose from the bed and proceeded to go downstairs with Ami. The rain had stopped during the night leaving sizable puddles in the back of the house. I opened the garden door for the dog and decided that I needed to wait by the door in order to let her back in.

She would need to be wiped dry when she came in, so she did not track mud into the house. I gathered some rags from under the sink as I began regretting my impulse to answer the dog's plea to go outside. The ordeal was going to take longer than I had initially hoped.

I watched out the window for the dog to return to the back door and was startled when I felt a hand on my shoulder.

"You ignored me when you got home yesterday." I did not answer him.

"You're angry with me?" Still, I said nothing.

"It was wrong of me to leave Paris without telling you. Please listen to me. I had to get away then, I had to sort through my feelings. I didn't know what was happening between us, and I needed to get some perspective to think it over."

Though I did not turn my gaze his way, I could tell by the tone of his voice that his blood pressure was rising.

Ami scratched on the door. I picked up the soaking dog, wrapped her in the dry rags and began to dry her paws. I still said nothing to Jules.

"You're not going to let me apologize, are you?"

I put the dog down on the floor and filled her water dish before I retired to my room. Jules was still standing by the back door. I acted as though he did not exist.

Madame made an announcement that morning when we gathered for breakfast that was a surprise to us all. Celeste had just completed the school year and was free for the summer. Madame Marshand told us that she and her daughter would be spending the summer months in Spain at her sister's villa. She said she needed to get away from Paris, more specifically from the house.

She explained that she needed some new scenery and further that it would be beneficial to be with her sister's family. She mentioned that it would be good for Celeste to spend time with her cousins, as well. She and Celeste would be leaving the following Monday and would be gone for two months.

It surprised me that I was not invited on the trip to Spain, but I reasoned that since Celeste was no longer a small child, I was not needed in the capacity of an au pair during their time away. I wondered briefly what I was supposed to do exactly during the time they were gone. I supposed I would be able to fill the time somehow.

As an afterthought to the announcement, Madame mentioned that it would be a great help to her if I would stay in the house and take care of overseeing the daily operations and overall security of the place in her absence. Of course, I could not decline.

"What about Ami?" Celeste asked. "Of course, Ami will go with us, darling." Madame Marshand said, rising from the table and smoothing her skirt.

I was pleased that Madame had found some type of distraction that might help her cope with her grief, but as I looked at her that morning, I saw that she still had a faraway look to her expression. It was as if her body was there in the room with us, but her mind and her spirit were far away. I wondered if she would ever become again the vital woman I once knew.

I helped Cook to clear the table, waiting for a comment or two from the normally opinionated servant. She merely gave me a look from the corner of her eye that said she could not understand how I had become such an important member of this household as to be left in charge.

Celeste ran up the stairs behind her mother. She seemed quite excited at the prospect of the trip to Spain and as her voice trailed off, I could hear tidbits of the questions she was firing off, like the firecrackers on Bastille Day. Would all her cousins be there during the visit? What kinds of activities might they be involved in? Would there be any parties to attend?

I wondered if Madame had planned the sabbatical more for Celeste's sake than her own, but it did not matter because I believed it would be a great help to them both. And then I was struck by the reality of my own commitment to Madame Marshand to watch over the house in their absence. While I did not regret having agreed to this arrangement I suddenly wondered where Jules planned to be during the summer months. Surely, I, as a single young woman, would not be expected to stay in the house alone with a single man although Cook, and Bernard would still be in residence.

I would have to bring this matter up with Madame Marshand. As a devotee to decorum, I was sure she had considered that it would be totally inappropriate for Jules to be living there with me, while she was away. Perhaps, after reconsideration, she might invite me to accompany them to Spain and put Jules in charge of the house instead. Or, perhaps Jules had advised her of plans he had made to be away for the summer as well.

As I tidied up my room that afternoon, I contemplated the various scenarios that might solve the dilemma I was stressing over. Whatever the outcome, I only knew it would not be acceptable to spend the summer in the Marshand home with Jules living there as well.

Besides, I did not trust myself where Jules was concerned. Without being able to escape an uncomfortable moment by using Celeste's care as an excuse, I wasn't sure that he would not overwhelm me with that smile.

The house became a beehive of activity as preparations were made for the trip. Trunks were packed. Last minute shopping was done. Bernard and I were both sent to the shoppes for last minute items Madame required.

Bernard was sent to find appropriate pillows for Madame's comfort on the train and warm lap blankets for she and Celeste. It was my job to approach the milliner for ribbons and feathers so that Madame's hats matched her current wardrobe. While on that errand, I promised Celeste to explore a shoppe where she had recently seen some decorative hair pins that she liked.

Finally, the morning arrived when all the parcels and trunks were stacked by the front door. Bernard was appointed to order a hired carriage with an extra porter who oversaw handling the parcels.

Celeste clung to me for a while before we were summoned to join Madame downstairs.

"I shall miss you." She whispered.

"And I, you." I said.

I wanted to be philosophical and tell her that she would have a grand time with her cousins. That there would be fabulous experiences and even new foods to try in Spain. But I was dealing with my own struggles knowing I would miss her these next couple of months. Truth be told, I needed cheering up myself. I could barely find it within me to bolster her frame of mind when my own needed some positive support.

Celeste busied herself with a last-minute check in the mirror as I went downstairs to seek out Madame.

A very brief opportunity arose while Madame awaited her daughter in the parlor. Bernard was getting frustrated as he gave orders to the waiting coachman. It was easy to detect that he trusted no one when it came to caring for his mistress. I believe he would have gone all the way to Spain with them if it were allowed just to be sure their needs were met.

I used the moment to express my concern.

"Certainly, you have considered my position, Madame, being here in your home with a single man and no chaperone." By forming the words in this way, I hoped she would realize that I was giving her the benefit of the doubt, even though I perceived that as her mind was wandering a lot lately, she had overlooked this socially unacceptable situation.

"Of course, I have considered this, Mademoiselle Natalie. I would be derelict in my duties to let this matter go unattended. You need have no worries about my brother-in-law's presence while I am away. He will be staying in our apartment in the center of the city while we are gone. It is near the courthouse, which will be a great benefit to him during these next few months."

I pretended not to notice when Madame signaled to Bernard as he returned inside. She took the butler aside a moment, spoke to him quickly, and then procured a set of keys from the drawer in the parlor sideboard. I said nothing, but it seemed as though the plan to have Jules stay in the city apartment had just now been conceived.

I stood at the doorway as the carriage departed, waving and smiling until my face hurt, but as soon as the door closed, I found myself in tears, alone and already hearing the echo of silence reverberate against the walls.

I decided that I would commit myself to the enterprise of updating Celeste's room during her absence. The new drapes and wallpaper would certainly arrive in the next few weeks. I would be busy looking for the best craftsmen available to hang the paper and put up the new window coverings.

I made it my mission to delight Celeste upon her return. Perhaps I could help to instill some excitement into her for her own future, planting the idea of the new memories that could be made in this house.

As her governess, and surrogate big sister, it was important to me that the child be allowed to enjoy what was left of her innocent years without constantly living under the shadow of her father's death and her mother's emotional abandonment.

I was also determined to spend my time reading several of the books I had stacked up on my nightstand. I read their reviews in the Le Temps newspaper, which was on our porch each morning.

And I made up my mind I would also get some exercise more often, walking in the neighborhood as I used to do when I cared for Celeste as my young charge. It would be fun to do some window shopping on my own and perhaps buy something nice to cheer up my own room. I found myself looking forward to the time I would be in the house while Madame and Celeste were on holiday.

Changes had been happening lately to the family that I had come to care for, and I supposed I needed to accustom myself as much as anyone else who lived there to the new ways.

Perhaps even I needed a respite from the same old daily activities as a kind of vacation of my own to make my own life more interesting. I could not have known then as I entertained these pleasant thoughts the impact of these next two months and how they would change my life forever.

Vingt-neuf

The Truth

$\mathcal{A}$LTHOUGH, I had plans for how to spend my time, the first couple of days in the quiet house, I merely moped around, looking out the window as I sat on the bed or the rocking chair in Celeste's room. I was concerned about Madame and Celeste's train trip. I hoped that Madame had the ability to come out of herself long enough to devote some attention to her daughter.

Celeste was so in need of reassurance. She needed to be made aware that the trip would be a good diversion for both. I prayed that her mother would assure her that their lives were going to be secure and that their future was not dangling by a string.

On the Thursday of the week they left, I could hardly deal with my own depression. I hurriedly dressed, barely combing my hair. This was a very odd thing for me to neglect but I needed some air, and I needed to be out among the people of Paris. I convinced myself I would be in a better state of mind if I were out in the crowds, listening to their chatter and observing them live their daily lives.

Out of habit, I found myself heading for the Eiffel Park, and Madame Fournier's boulangerie on the opposite street. It was as if a magnet was pulling me in the direction of the place, I spent my childhood. This particular morning, I seemed to have no control over my own feet. I was being swept toward to the Tower as if my destiny itself were a living thing.

I became aware as I approached the Park that I had an appointment on this day, at this hour, that had been a long time coming. I felt a cloud lift from the atmosphere. A light appeared that it seemed only I could see, leading me like a beacon toward the bench where I used to read poetry. He sat on the bench among the linden trees, alone and huddled in a tattered shawl.

When he saw me, his eyes seemed to penetrate my very being and I was incapable of not moving toward him. I joined him on the bench and sat there in silence looking straight ahead and hoping I was not making the biggest mistake of my life.

"You are old enough now to know the secret." He said.

"Secret?"

"Yes, I could not tell you before, you were just a child. You would not have understood. Perhaps you still might not."

"I will try." I whispered.

"It began long ago." He said.

I glanced over at him briefly and was overwhelmed by how fragile he appeared. His green eyes were luminescent, and his long white hair seemed to float about his head like the feathers of an exotic bird.

"The Masked One was not always an evil force." He continued.

I waited for him to go on with his story, holding my breath in anticipation.

"His downfall was caused by someone you loved dearly."

At this moment, I gasped and began to rise from the bench to avoid hearing any more of what he had to say. Gently, he stretched his thin arm and his long pale fingers across my chest, encouraging me to stay where I was.

"I must tell you this story now, before it is too late." He said "Please indulge me for a few more minutes."

I glanced furtively around the area where we sat. There was no sign of imminent danger and for some strange reason, the entire area was devoid of people. I repositioned myself on the bench.

"Madame Fournier can reassure you of the truth I am about to depart to you, for she knew us all back then."

Now my head began to reel. Was I somehow unconscious? Was this some kind a dream state, perhaps he was a hypnotist. I read in the paper that they performed for people's amusement at the Folies-Bergère. They supposedly had the ability to make people think things were real that were not.

How could there be secret that Madame had kept for so many years as she was taking the place of the only family I had? The Spirit said I may not understand, and I was already in a state of disbelief.

"You are the one that's called the Eiffel Spirit, are you not? You are the one that the City of Paris is afraid of. Why should anything you say be considered the truth. People say you are a murderer."

"Before you reach any conclusions, please hear me out. When you have heard the whole story, you will re-evaluate things you believed that you knew."

Once more, I paused. But already I vowed to myself that I would run away if I felt the least bit threatened.

"You see, my dear, when your mother was a young woman, she was the most beautiful girl in Paris. Many young men wanted her to notice them. She was literally the toast of the town, and a certain young man was determined that she would be his.

This person, stole, gambled, and even killed so that he could amass a fortune and look the part of a person of wealth so that he might be accepted in the proper social circles in order to lure the beautiful debutante into finding him to be an attractive suitor. He even bestowed a title upon himself as Viscount of a province that no one was familiar with. His lifestyle and manners never caused suspicion on his false identity."

"My mother inspired such behavior?"

"It was never her intention. She was young, and pure as the driven snow. I am sure she had never been made aware of the existence of such a disreputable character. I would venture a guess that most young women never encounter anyone like him."

"Did it work, was he able to court her?"

"It might have, except for the fact that she was already in love."

"Really, with whom?"

"With the man who would become your father and who at that time was merely a clerk at the haberdashery where your mother's family shopped.

"She and the young man had innocently flirted with each other for years and he had finally gotten the nerve to ask her to have coffee with him only months before the Masked One, known then as Joaquin, made himself known to her."

"So, she pretty much ignored this Joaquin?"

"Although that was her intention, her mother encouraged her to see him.It was her desire that her daughter wed a rich man, rather than a store clerk, so she promoted a relationship with the fake Viscount.

Claire consented to go out with him and for the first couple of encounters he managed to conduct himself as a gentleman, but this man would stop at nothing to have what he wanted even if he had to use force. He contained his manly desires if he was able, but he was determined that he would have what he wanted at any price. He knew that the innocent, young girl would be his for life if he had his way with her, just once. And his dark soul plotted to plant his seed within her."

I took in a big breath of air and clasped my hand to the bench to steady myself.

"The night of his determined plan however, the young clerk was at the same restaurant where Joaquin took your mother. The clerk was there as the guest of his wealthy aunt who was visiting from out of town.

He watched the two of them eating their meal, aware that there was an electricity in the air that was somewhat unnatural. When they left the restaurant, the clerk made his excuses and followed them out into the street.

Young Joaquin did not hail a carriage but instead walked arm in arm with Clair, leading her to an ally a short distance away. The clerk bounded quickly in the same direction arriving just as the pretend Viscount was lifting the skirt of the petrified young woman forcing his mouth over hers at the same time to stifle her screams.

Without a thought for his own safety the clerk took hold of the rascal by the shoulders turning him around with one quick motion and then bringing his right fist in contact with the man's jaw, using so much force the man collapsed to the ground covered in the blood that gushed from his nose and the back of his head where he fell.

Seconds later the young clerk took your mother's arm and led her back toward the street hailing a carriage and gently helping her inside. He rode home with her in the hired cab and waited outside her house until she was safely in the door before heading home himself."

"My God." I said. "He saved my mother from complete dishonor; how did she thank him."

She was housebound for several months after the night of the attack. Her family was enraged and saw to it that the man responsible was brought up on criminal charges which led to his disgrace and to the discovery of all his past crimes. His title was proved fraudulent and what money he had left was paid in restitution to those he stole from. Besides having to serve prison time, he was ruined in Paris society. The masquerade was over.

The girl's family was so grateful to the young clerk that they offered him money as a reward for saving their daughter's virtue and possibly her life."

"Did he take the money?"

"No, he asked only that he might be able to see the young woman from time to time, and perhaps take her out for an evening at an affordable establishment in his neighborhood. They and she were more than happy to agree."

"So, did she marry the young store clerk?"

"Before I answer, I will finish the story. Eventually, the pretender was released from prison, determined to enact his own justice on the person who had stood in the way of his plan. He was obsessed with revenge since he had been prevented from deflowering your mother. In his twisted mind, the young clerk had ruined his life of status and luxury. The way he saw it, the clerk and his bride were the ones at fault.

By then, there was a child born to the couple and they lived in the small apartment above Madame Fournier's bakery. He worked as a delivery person in the garment district and though they were not rich, they were incredibly happy.

Joaquin was determined to enact revenge on his sworn enemy but did not want to hurt the woman he had been infatuated with. He determined that he would go after the child."

He turned then and focused those crystal-clear eyes on me.

The truth struck me like a bolt of lightning.

"I am the child." I said.

"Yes, you are. He realized that your mother would die of a broken heart if you were killed so he substituted other young girls for you. He coerced them and then pushed them from the Tower.

"They died in place of me?"

"Yes. And when your father realized what was happening, he was determined to stop the killings, so he left you and your mother behind letting you both believe that he was dead. He became the Eiffel Spirit determined to eliminate the coward who hides behind the red mask. He has tried for years to annihilate the Masked One. But he has only been successful in saving some of his victims."

"It is you." I said. I felt as though I had just walked through a thick fog, one that had kept me from clearly seeing all of my life.

"You are the Spirit." I said.

"Yes, I am the Eiffel Spirit, but it is not I who you should fear."

Perhaps, I should have handled things differently all those years ago, but I had to offer protection to the only daughter I would ever have."

I closed my eyes as the tears fell freely. I felt as though I had been living a half-life until this moment. Things I was sure were true, were not. Things that I believed in had no foundation. I was aware now why the Eiffel Spirit had come to my aid more than once.

I knew why he watched me the way he did and seemed to care for me all those years. I knew why one glance from him made me feel like I was loved.

And even more so, I knew why my mother became the woman she became. Why she drank as she did, why she lived her life trying to escape her devastating past. I wanted to put my arms around her and tell her I was sorry for any judgments I had made as a foolish child. Suddenly, I understood why she could no longer face another day.

When I opened my eyes, the Eiffel Spirit was nowhere to be seen.

Trente

Revelation

I drifted as if on a cloud as I walked across the street. Still in a beguiled state, I sat at one of the outside tables of the boulangerie. It felt like years passed before Madame Fournier joined me.

She held an old brown envelope in her hand, from which she produced some photographs and a news clipping. We sat there silently for a while.

"Today was the day." She said. "He told you everything, didn't he?" I merely nodded. Words simply would not come.

First, she showed me a picture of my mother and father on their wedding day. My father was right. She was the most beautiful creature I had ever seen. Her smile was like sunlight, her hair the finest shade of gold and her deep blue eyes, which looked right at the camera were full of the joy and happiness of a woman in love.

He was tall and thin, but also good looking, in an ordinary kind of way. His happiness also shone through in the photo. She told me that everyone who met Claire and Henri were aware of how much they cared for each other.

Madame Fournier announced that she had been my mother's attendant on her wedding day. The women had been friends since their school days. She had another picture that touched me even more. It was one of my father's holding me as a baby. He was smiling into the camera as he cradled me close. He looked so proud, as if he was the first man in history to hold the daughter that he loved.

And then, she showed me the news clipping about the sentencing of Joaquin Picard listing the heinous crimes he had committed. The picture of the man startled me, for those were the eyes that had penetrated my being when the Masked One came toward me that day at the Eiffel Park. Although this picture was from decades ago, his face was already a study in evil intentions.

I had seen the news clipping once before, as a young girl. My mother was holding it, mesmerized as if in a trance. I approached and asked who the man in the picture was. Hastily she tried to hide it behind her back. But I had already seen enough of that intense look as he stared from the newspaper page. His strange countenance left an indelible impression.

"I was told my father died in a factory fire that took place when I was quite young."

"There was a fire. Henri used the tragedy as a means of disappearing. Though the fire was investigated, there were very few remains to sift through. Those who had reported to work on that shift were declared dead without much deliberation."

"This is more than I can take." I said as all the pieces fit together. "My entire life has been a lie."

"I'm sorry that you now have to deal with what happened all of those years ago."

"It is not just the past, Madame. The crimes at the Eiffel Park are a continuing part of the twisted story. Joaquin became the Masked One still seeking revenge. My father was transformed into the Eiffel Spirit attempting to prevent death and destruction, out of the goodness of his heart. The problem is that the public has never realized that there are two entities involved in the malicious acts at the Tower.

Those who have seen the Spirit have been scared by his demeanor. Being so frail and thin, he appears like a transparent creature that puts fear into people. As he maintains this countenance, he fulfills another aspect of the Masked One's vengeance. He laughs all the while as his evil deeds are blamed upon his arch enemy.

"The Spirit, my father, risked his life first to save my mother, from Joaquin's evil grips and now, it is up to me to save him."

I scooped up the photos and the article and headed back to the Marshand home. This afternoon was not one to be wasted on tea and croissants. I simply could not engage in idle chatter after this new revelation.

Tears practically blinded me as my pace increased. I wanted to get home and land on my bed. I wanted to pull the covers over my head and stay there for days. I did not want to cross the park after the sun went down. Now, I would live in dire fear of the man with the red mask.

I had to come up with some type of plan to save the Eiffel Spirit. I was determined to help the man who had fought his entire life to save the innocents and was denounced and feared as a villain.

What could I do? I was overwhelmed as I played the facts over and over in my head. I had been walking on quicksand for years without being aware of the stark nature of the truth. Could I go to law enforcement with my story? Would they believe me, despite the evidence that made The Spirit look like the guilty one? Madame Fournier would certainly be a credible witness on his behalf, would she not?

I feared that the authorities would think I was putting the pieces together from stories of a long ago past that sounded more like a legend than the truth.

They wanted hard facts and evidence when it came to solving crimes, and I had neither. I imagined a police investigator listening to my story and concluding that I was a lower-class girl who had been deprived of a normal childhood. I would probably sound like someone with a rapid ability to concoct a story about the Eiffel Spirit by adding my own drama to punctuate the few facts.

Trente et un

Crushed

*J*ULES had been in trial all week. I knew, because he had to come back to the Marshand house occasionally to use the study and the resources his brother had left behind.

Thankfully, he had been staying in the city apartment, so I had not seen very much of him, which was just as well.

I had way too much on my mind to sort through my feelings for Jules or for Philippe, or even to devote any attention to the decorating I planned to do in Celeste's room, But I did finally turn myself over to the latter occupation, as it kept my hands busy while my mind worked out a solution to my father's dilemma.

My father.

Contemplating that reality was too much to absorb. A man I thought had been long dead was only a few steps away from us and was devoted to protecting us from harm.

My father, a man who had saved the lives of countless young women whom the Masked One tried to destroy. My mind was fuzzy just trying to make sense of all of this. I had spent my entire life under the delusion that I was not loved, when in fact I was loved and cherished by the purest of men with the purest of intentions.

Jules beckoned me to join him in the garden when I spied him through the kitchen window.

With all that was swimming around in my head, I suddenly relished the diversion. I decided it could not hurt to find out what he had on his mind.

He held out a small bouquet and smiled sweetly as I approached.

"You are as lovely as ever." He said.

I lowered my head, demurely taking the bouquet and then standing silently waiting for him to go on. Somehow, he seemed so much older to me at this moment than he had before he disappeared on whatever secret mission he had undertaken. I found this maturity attractive.

Maybe I was throwing caution to the wind, but I was curious to discover if Jules was going to offer up an explanation for his mysterious behavior. I supposed that he deserved a chance to be forthcoming.

"Please sit down for a minute, Natalie."

I wanted to speak to you about my interaction with a certain woman at my brother's funeral. I was certain you noticed when I was speaking with her."

I focused my gaze on the bouquet.

"When I left town, it was to make sure that the woman in question would not be interacting with the Marshand family in the future. I am now the male head of this household, and it was up to me to solve the situation." Jules had wasted no time getting to the point. I was spellbound as he continued.

"I escorted her to a town far from Paris and set her up in an apartment. I established a modest trust fund, which will become void if she ever utters a word to Monique. You need not worry that my sister-in-law nor my niece will hear a word about what transpired between her and my brother."

"She will be well provided for if she keeps her secret to herself. Besides, women of her kind always find a way to make a living. It is my hope that she finds another man to use to her advantage and that we will not hear from her again."

"You did all of that to protect Madame?"

"Yes, my brother may have been a scoundrel, but that certainly was not his wife's fault and, like you, I would never want any of his shame to spill over into her or Celeste's lives. I believe it would be devastating."

At that moment I was full of gratitude to this man, whom I had not thought of as sensitive to the feelings of others.

"I've thought of you so much lately, Natalie. I am much fonder of you than you know, dear. Much more than even I realized until now."

"Jules, I don't think this is the right time for us to have this discussion."

"Why, it is what I feel and what needs to be said."

"But we are unsupervised right now. We should not approach the subject of feelings when there is no chaperone nearby. I have to think about decorum."

"How old fashioned you are my dear. This is a new age. Young people are behaving differently here in Paris. We are not the generation of your parents or mine and we are making our own rules."

"I don't know who this 'we' is that you are talking about, Jules, but I guess I am a bit old fashioned. I need to protect my reputation and it is important to me."

"This is not the conversation I wanted to have with you." He said.

I knew he was perturbed, and I wanted to get away from him, so I turned toward the kitchen door.

He grabbed me then by the shoulder and abruptly turned me to face him as he took me in his arms. He kissed me with a force I could not believe, hurting my mouth as he thrust his tongue inside of my lips. He let go of me briefly to gaze into my eyes. I could tell that he was surprised to find fear in them.

Again, he pulled me close and again he forced his mouth on mine.

I shuddered as a cold chill spread through me. My knees were beginning to buckle, and I was sure that I would soon be on the garden floor unable to move or breathe.

At that moment, Cook opened the kitchen door and proceeded to dump the sink water on the plants that were near to the house.

I took the opportunity to push Jules away from me and hurry toward the door, dropping the crushed bouquet on the ground. I went directly to my room and did not leave it for the rest of the night. My thoughts were swirling, and I questioned everything I thought I knew about Jules and his intentions.

As I pondered the experience in the garden, feeling dumbfounded and confused, another encounter was happening elsewhere in the City of Lights that would have a devastating effect.

Trente-deux

Confrontation

*T*HE events of this evening had been planned since the beginning of time.

As they stood on the precipice of the Tower's landing, they both knew it was inevitable. This confrontation was destined since the prison doors slammed shut on Joaquin Picard twenty years before. It had smoldered like the embers of a fire about to set blaze to a dry forest.

Although freed from the iron prison doors, he remained encased in his own world embarking on a rampage fueled by hate and vengeance. The rage was at its height and the devil would be paid his due.

"You had to tell her the secret, you mangy dog, you had to violate my existence one more time. You had to expose me to Claire's daughter so that she would fear me as her mother did."

"She already feared you. That was your own doing. In fact, she and all of the young women of Paris have feared you for ages. I did nothing to make that happen."

"It was you that they feared, you fool. You and your pale vestige. The young girls who see you scream with fright. But even so, you took it upon yourself to tell her. You had to appear to be the hero. The hero who saved her mother and now her from my evil clutches."

"You are pure evil, you are the Masked One, hiding your identity behind that red mask. You have always served the Master of Evil every day of your life."

"And you are so pure." In his rage he spat out the words. "You, who abandoned the only woman I ever loved. You who left her in despair so that she eventually took her own life out of the desperation you caused. And what of the daughter you supposedly love, how much heartache did you cause her? Certainly, you did not ease those years of suffering when you told her that you left her and her mother behind to save others from my vengeance. You have caused her more pain than I ever could."

"That was never my intention. I always acted in her best interests. I had an obligation to protect her."

"Does that diminish what was done? You killed her mother as surely as if you stabbed her in the heart and the scars you left on the heart of your little girl will never heal. I think it is time for what is left of your pathetic existence to come to an end. Even I have become tired of seeking retribution for the life you stole from me that night in the alley. I will now put an end to the Eiffel Spirit.

And I will have the ultimate satisfaction of knowing that when they find your body, they will believe they have found the specter responsible for countless evil deeds. I will win in the end and I will see your daughter grieve for the hero you convinced her you are."

With that, the Masked One gave a push that sent the body of the Spirit tumbling to the ground among the linden trees. The echo of his evil laugh could be heard throughout the Park and for several blocks in each direction.

Madame Fournier was clearing the table in front of the bakery. She felt her skin crawl as the haunting sound permeated the air. She yelled for Philippe to hurry and to follow her to the Park.

Instinctively, she felt that somehow Henri was in danger. It was as if an inner voice, perhaps based on their years of closeness, struck her like a bolt of lightening. This time the diabolical noise seemed to signal a very personal cry for help. She knew at once that it was him when she saw him on the ground. Bending over his body, she checked for a pulse.

All the while, she glanced furtively around the Park. People were approaching and she knew something must be done fast. Philippe stood at his mother's side, unable to figure out why she was showing so much concern for this feeble, old man who had obviously met his death.

"He's breathing." She whispered. "Philippe lift him up, carefully and follow me. Quickly."

Sirens could be heard approaching. She knew they must hurry to spare being discovered.

She led her son, as he carried the injured man back to the bakery and up the stairs to the apartment that had once been Natalie's.

"Lie him on the bed, with utmost care." She said. Now, quickly go to the Marshand home and bring Natalie here at once."

Philippe stared at her as if she had issued the most preposterous order that it was possible to proclaim.

"Do it now. She said, her words becoming a loud command. "And do not come back without her."

As happened every so often, a local reporter appeared on the scene prior to the arrival of the police.

As the crowd drew near, the accounts of what had occurred were diverse and filled with conjecture. Some said they saw a body on the ground, others that they were sure they saw the Eiffel Spirit trying to overtake another victim under the linden trees.

Looking for a sensational tale for his readers, the reporter came upon a woman who was sure she had seen a dead body carried away in what appeared to be a hurried fashion. She testified to the fact that she saw the coroner's wagon parked nearby, most likely there to claim the corpse.

Without waiting for further police inquiries, or confirmation from the coroner, the story was written to arouse suspicion and entertain the thrill seekers.

Newspapers flew off the stands bearing the headline: "Is this the end of the Eiffel Spirit?"

Trente-trois

Devotion

*A*FTER running all the way to the Marshand residence, Philippe waited in the foyer. The butler knocked heavily on the door to my room.

"You must come at once." He said. "The boy insists that you accompany him now."

I was shocked to see Philippe waiting for me with his hat in his hand.

"My mother sent me. She said that I must bring you back as soon as I could. There is an old man she is taking care of. I think he may be dying." I grabbed my shawl off the hook in the hallway and hurried out the door, without giving an explanation to Bernard.

We ran all the way back to the bakery. Both of us arrived, breathing heavily from the exercise. Philippe bolted up the stairs. I was at his heals.

The door opened to a scene I would not soon forget.

He looked so small on the cot by the window. Madame was sitting by his side gently stroking his hand. His eyes were closed. Hesitantly, I approached the bed, hoping above to hope that he was still alive.

Madame Fournier rose so that I could take her place on the cot. His hand was cold, but I could see his chest rising with each measured breath. Quietly, the door was closed behind

Philippe and his mother as they exited the room, and I was left alone with this man. This man who had lived the most unnatural of lives.

I did not know if he could hear me, but I spoke to him as I continued to hold his hand.

It was evening now, and the lights of the city were being lit. I observed the changing light within the room that once was my mother's as I wondered if this was the same cot on which she took her last breath.

"I am so happy that I finally know the truth." I whispered, as I drew closer to his ear.

"It amazes me that I spent so many years so close to you and never knew who you were. I wish that I had known.

My whole sense of reality has changed since I learned about the past. I regret not having the chance to know you and to love you, and finally to say thank you for all you have done to keep my mother and I safe from the One who would do us harm."

I leaned across his fragile frame hoping that I could warm him up and somehow restore his strength. I vowed to stay as close to him as I could wishing with all my heart to impart my own resilience onto him. If only there was a way, I could absorb a portion of his pain. I wanted to heal not only his present wounds but the suffering of so many years he spent desperate and alone.

In the morning, Madame Fournier found me sleeping next to the haunting figure that I was beginning to love.

"I've brought you some strong coffee and a croissant. I must take care of you now, so that you can take care of him."

He was as pale as ever, and I do not believe his hands felt any warmer than they had the night before, but he was still breathing and for that I was relieved. I rose and sat in the tattered chair next to the cot and slowly sipped the hot brew. Madame Fournier stood by the cot for a long time without saying a word.

"I made a promise to your mother." She finally said. "She made me vow that I would not tell you the story of how your father had saved her when she was a young woman. She was quite ashamed of the encounter in her past with Joaquin Picard. She wanted so badly to hide her story from you and not let you think she had almost succumbed to the evil desires of that wicked man." As she spoke, I could see that she was playing scenes from the past over in her mind.

"How did you know then about my father, if she did not know herself?"

"I found out from him, Natalie. He allowed me to know about his presence in the Park, and his identity as the Eiffel Spirit, swearing me to secrecy."

"Henri is a good man. I can still picture him, here in this apartment with your mother when you were a baby. There really were a few years of happiness back then. Recalling those memories was the only way I could cope with your mother's death."

"They lived a simple life here in this small space and yet the love they shared and the way they cared for each other transformed this meager apartment into a home as lofty as any mansion. I wish you could have seen the way they looked at each other. I have not before or since seen a couple so in love. And, when you were born, the love that they had for you was an extension of their devotion."

"So many times, I have reflected on what your life would have been if there had been no Joaquin Picard. The three of you would have had years of happiness. I have cried into my pillow more than once when these thoughts have crossed my mind. If I entertain them for exceedingly long, they bring with them a heightened sense of despair at the unwarranted injustice."

"After your mother died, Henri came to see me. It was only a brief encounter but one I will never forget. He explained that Joaquin was determined to seek revenge on the innocent young women of Paris in retribution for your mother's rejection. He had become obsessed with the destruction of the innocent and more and more determined to impart his own warped sense of justice on random surrogates. Henri believed he could counter the evil that Joaquin was determined to carry out. He told me he believed that he had to try, in spite of the price his wife and daughter were forced to pay for his diligence."

"I was to be the only one who knew the truth. It was important that you believe he was dead. He made me swear I would never disclose his identity to you. He wanted only to protect you from the Masked One and to preserve as many innocent lives as he could."

"And all of those years that you knew," I replied. "Did you not see that as some type of betrayal. I loved you and trusted you. You were the only friend I had."

"I did not believe that I was doing anything wrong." Madame Fournier said. "I had to respect Henri's wishes and keep my promise. I had to keep the vow I made in your mother's memory. I hoped during that entire time that you never would need to know the truth."

"But now that I do, my world is upside down. I hardly know where to go from here."

"You needn't go anywhere. Stay here if you must. Care for him as long as he needs you. I will do all that I can to help you to heal from this terrible pain and to give him the comfort he has earned through his loyal service to the blameless victims sought out by the Masked One."

"When Madame Marshand arrives back home, I must tell her that I can no longer be in her employment. As long as my father is here, I must be here to care for him. I must do all that I can to help him to heal."

"Of course. You are not alone, Natalie. Philippe and I will be at your service, and it will be an honor for me to sustain you both while he is suffering so gravely."

"Thank you. I am appreciative of the support, for while I am still in shock over this recent discovery, I was concerned about being able to care for my father and myself since I would no longer be employed."

"In spite of the anger I have shown you since the recent discovery, you have turned out to be a true and lasting friend and the only person I can count on."

We hugged for quite a while in silence as we both absorbed the emotions of the current moment. For myself, I was consumed by exhaustion. My entire existence felt surreal as if I had been living without my feet ever touching the ground.

The next morning, I returned to the Marshand's home only long enough to pack a small bag of my things. I explained to Cook and Bernard that I needed to be gone for a while although I gave them no detail. I merely explained that there was a family emergency that needed tending to. I left Cook with instructions for the men who were hanging the wallpaper in Celeste's room and showed her how the new drapes should be hung.

Then, I wrote a letter to Madame Marshand which Bernard assured me he would post. Naturally, I did not reveal all the particulars to her but merely implied that I was needed to care for someone that was dear to me. I allowed her to interpret that to mean that Madame Fournier was suffering in some way and needed my help. I signed the note and included the address of the bakery under my name. I had spoken of Madame Fournier on a few occasions over the years, mentioning that she was the closest thing to family I had.

Jules was walking down the sidewalk as my carriage pulled up in front of the house. He tried to waylay me, asking where I was going and why.

"Natalie, you must forgive me for being so forward and treating you as I did in the garden. Surely, you can't be leaving because of that embarrassing encounter?"

"This is neither the time nor the place for us to have this discussion Jules." I said. "Please just let me go, I am not in the mood for explanations right now." He still held my arm, and I was becoming concerned that the moment might turn ugly.

Bernard approached the carriage at that point. He addressed Jules directly and rather firmly telling him to let go of my arm and that I needed to board the carriage at once.

I believe that Jules was stunned by the actions of the servant and stepped back merely because he was having trouble processing the extraordinary event. Bernard stood firm, displaying an unrelenting grimace which said more than any words he might utter. None of that mattered to me because, although I was grateful for the butler's intervention, my mind was already miles away, picturing the scene I had left in the small apartment where my father lay dying.

During the next several days a routine was established. I rose early every morning and tended to my father immediately. Although he had regained consciousness, he did not communicate with us to any degree. We could hardly get him to eat anything, and this was a cause of great concern. Either Madame Fournier or I spent a great deal of time spooning soup into his mouth, as that seemed to be the only nourishment, we could persuade him to take. I opened the curtains each day so he could feel the sunshine spilling over the cot where he lay. I read him stories from the newspaper and when it looked as though he was drifting off to sleep, I would curl up next to him and sing softly to muffle the noises in the street.

Each afternoon, Madame Fournier came to keep him company so that I could bathe and then take a brief walk on the sidewalk outside of her shop. It was all that I needed so I did not go stir crazy in the small room to which my life was now confined.

I received a reply letter from Madame Marshand two weeks after leaving her house. She expressed her concern for me and hoped that the situation was improving. She also offered any help she might be able to give me and asked that I let her know if there was anything I needed. Enclosed with her letter was a small drawing that Celeste had done. It was a picture of a heart and within the heart was my name, carefully scripted. I knew at once it was her way of saying that she loved me. I felt a tear roll down my cheek as I held her picture close. Such a short time ago my life had been so different.

I had been used to the routine at Madame Marshand's home and despite the events following her husband's death, I had felt secure in the knowledge that I had a home there as long as I wanted one. I could never have known the turn my life would take, and that a secret buried for so long would enfold me in such an uncertain future.

Every evening, I closed the curtains and rearranged my father's bedclothes to make him more comfortable. It was difficult to know if he was in pain as his demeanor remained stoic as he was still mostly unresponsive.

Weeks went by and it seemed as though we would go on in this manner forever. Nothing changed, and without any signs of a positive progression I felt myself becoming more and more depressed.

In the evenings, I swept up in the bakery and helped clean up the kitchen. I prepared the pans that Madame Fournier would need when she began baking early the next morning, a task that started each day while the city was still asleep. In these small ways, I could express my gratitude for her generosity.

Philippe spent several hours each day searching for employment with various architectural firms. He set out impeccably dressed with his portfolio tucked under his arm, looking very professional. I hoped that he would find what he was looking for after working so hard at the University. And I knew how much he would be able to help his mother if his employment proved to be lucrative.

What I did not know at the time was that Philippe's main reason to be situated with a reputable firm was his love for me. We had been so close as children, during a time in my life when my mother's health was my main concern. He had always been a kind friend and a dear playmate, but I failed to see that when he looked at me he had feelings of which I was totally unaware.

The day he received the job offering he desired, he appeared at the bakery with a bottle of champagne and the biggest grin I had ever seen. He coaxed his mother into closing the bakery early. He declared that the three of us should celebrate his good news as he gleefully popped the cork pouring the delightful bubbles into three glasses and raising a toast to better times.

My father's condition had stabilized during the previous week and although he was still bedridden, he was breathing better and taking a small degree of sustenance. I began to believe that there might be better times ahead. He was not speaking very much, but when I looked into his eyes, they spoke volumes. There was so much pain hidden there, I felt nothing but compassion. I imagined how he had suffered. Living all those years as a vagrant must have been full of desperate moments. How was he able to find food when he was hungry? I wondered. How many nights had he spent freezing during the cold Paris winters? And, perhaps worse than these basic human needs, had he lived with the ongoing fear wondering which form the Masked One's depravity would take next?

Along with the hurt that I detected in the Spirit's demeanor, there were also fleeting looks of appreciation for what was being done for him now. Finally, he was no longer alone. He was beginning to look less like a ghost, but certainly not yet like a man.

I joined Madame Fournier each evening in her small apartment behind the bakery. I did not want to disturb my father's rest and it was comforting to spend this time with my dear friend.

She was deep in thought on a particular night, as I joined her after pouring us each a small glass of wine. The strain of her long workday was evident in the crevices on her face. She did not see me watch her gently massaging her hands and fingers as she eased the stiffness in her joints. I imagined that plying the dough of a thousand loaves of bread had left an indelible mark.

"I think I need more than tea this evening." I said. "Lately, I have been contemplating the future with very little sense of assurance that it holds anything good."

"We are just in a state of suspension right now, my dear. We may not know where we are headed with certainty right now. But I'm sure things will work out and they will be all right."

"Do you wonder if the Masked One, I mean, Joaquin, will strike again at the Tower?"

"Of course, I do. I am certain he will not be able to avoid inflicting peril for very long. Doing harm is in his blood and I await with dread whatever plans he is harboring."

"The only good that can come from his future deeds is that my father won't be there to blame. Perhaps Joaquin will leave himself wide open to the punishment he deserves if the Spirit isn't there to set things right and intervene." I said.

"And the other side of the coin is that your father won't be there to save the innocent victims."

Philippe found an apartment close to the architectural firm where he worked. He told me that he had to put in more hours than the older associates.

"I need to prove myself right now, Natalie. But it will not always be like this. I will be paying my dues until I am an accepted part of the firm. I am confident that my work will speak for itself eventually, if I am patient. And if I need to sweat harder than anyone else for a certain period, I am prepared to rise to that occasion. When I finally have these first couple of years behind me, I'll be able to entertain plans for my future. Perhaps having a wife and family."

He looked at me intensely as he said those words. They hung in the air taking on their own weight and a resounding importance. I wondered if he might be thinking of me somewhere in his dream of a future. He had not said so, and I did not want to presume. Did his plans include someone else, I wondered, or perhaps there was no one specific at all?

"Philippe, I'm sorry." I stammered. "What is it you want me to say?"

"I don't believe you've heard a word I've been saying."

"Oh, but I have." I reassured him. "I'm sure your hard work will pay off and as one of your oldest friends, I can only wish you the best."

He leaned forward in his chair as if ready to say something especially important, but after a long pause he said nothing at all. I watched as his body relaxed from the tense attitude of a man driven to make a strong argument into a deflated shell not willing to make the effort.

For my part, I could not offer much interest or support for Philippe's hopes and dreams as my father's health was foremost in my mind. It was as if I was a captive of the present time, unable to think of any kind of future while I helped to heal the man my mother loved.

The evenings settled into a quiet routine. Most of the time I fell asleep on the small sofa in the apartment as I watched my father rest on the cot. The window curtains fluttered in the breeze and the lights from the Tower illuminated the room, so that it was never completely dark.

I wondered if it was just a matter of time before the Masked One began to undertake another spree of destruction. I pictured the entire city of Paris holding its collective breath, anticipating a resurgence of crime and grief. And then one terrible night it happened. The sound of an ear-piercing scream drifted through the narrow window followed by the most unearthly evil laugh echoing through the night and filling me with terror.

I ran down the stairs and found Madame Fournier staring through the window of the bakery.

"Do you think it is him again?"

"It must be."

"I think that we should go investigate what we heard."

"It would not be safe, my dear. We will find out in the morning. We cannot expose ourselves to harm, just to satisfy our curiosity. As long as Henri is safe, we need not worry. Now you go back upstairs, I will come to get you when I know what happened."

"I know that the Masked One is responsible." I said. "He has been waiting to resume his diabolical acts, and it seems that he has finished waiting."

The nightmare had begun. Quietly I ascended the stairs to the apartment, hoping in my heart that my father had not been awakened by the eerie noises in the middle of the night. I thought that I must close the window in case any more disturbing sounds were forthcoming.

I did not need to be concerned about the noise. He was gone.

Trente-quatre

A Matter of Trust

GOSSIP pervaded the bakery in the morning bringing with it a tense excitement that could be seen on the faces of all who gathered there. Stories were told about what had happened in the Park during the night, embellished by the imaginations of those who had no concrete facts. Others stood awestruck listening and reacting with fearful glances that darted all around them, landing on no one person or item in the vicinity.

I helped Madame Fournier behind the counter to speed up the process of taking orders and to thin out the number of people murmuring in the small shop. I was able to whisper to her briefly about my father's disappearance. She looked at me in sheer surprise.

"Do we know anything of what really happened in the Eiffel Park last night?" I asked.

"Unfortunately, the only fact I could discern from the constabulary earlier was that a woman had been attacked and was taken to the hospital. But that is all."

Later in the morning I walked to the park, but there was no sign of the man I had been helping to heal. I did not know then that I would not see him again for quite a while. Once again, he had assumed the persona of the Eiffel

Spirit and became hidden to keep his nemesis at bay.

Instead of diminishing, the story of the latest victim of terror became even more fantastic as the newspapers disclosed that the woman had suffered a memory loss during the trauma she endured. She could not recall who she was or if she had relatives or friends who might be contacted on her behalf.

In an effort to discover the woman's identity, the authorities launched a campaign to help resolve the mystery. They issued a series of posters depicting her picture with the caption: "Do you know who I am?"

The telephone number of the police station was listed and anyone with information was encouraged to contact the number or to speak with any one of the local gendarmes.

The mystery became the most significant issue of that day and the next several days. Madame Fournier's boulangerie was a gathering place each morning for more tittering and tongue wagging as Parisians submerged themselves in an avalanche of hearsay.

When one of the local constabularies asked Madame Fournier to display a poster in the bakery window, I had a chance to take a close look.

I sucked in my breath as I looked at the picture and then I ran from the bakery at lightning speed, clutching the poster in my hand. There are times in life when sheer coincidence is the only explanation for a chain of events but accepting this as a possibility can sometimes be more than our psyches can handle.

I look back now on that morning at the bakery. My mind had been so preoccupied worrying about the whereabouts of my father and the condition of his health. I was sure he should not be living on his own again. His fragile condition made him susceptible to a variety of hazards from the natural elements.

Further, I believed that the Masked One had been honing his evil intentions to harm him while he came up with ideas to terrorize the city's population at large. But, as I ran down the streets of the city, I wondered if it was possible that I had somehow incited the current situation. When I went out to find my own life, had I somehow started a chain of events that caused the evil events of the Tower to penetrate the Marshand household.

I never could have known that there were underlying events coming to a head that would unite past and present. I felt I was poised at the edge of an eruption that had the power to cause devastation to the people who had become the center of what was once my somewhat ordinary existence. And now, one act of desperation, one development, and one photograph threatened to unravel the lives of several people who were undeserving of the consequences.

Hardly able to catch my breath, my thoughts were spinning out of control.

I conjured up a picture of a younger me, eager to please my employer by organizing his office. Why did I have to be so diligent? Why was I more eager than I should have been?

Why did I have to unearth a hidden photo that should have stayed in the back of a drawer?

Now, as my heart beat wildly in my chest, I wished I had not been so good at my work.

I turned my glance toward heaven and asked God why I was placed on this path. In my current emotional state, I blamed Him for allowing me to intercede in a situation that I should have had to the sense to stay out of. If only I had left well enough alone. But, with all of the images of the past that were appearing in my head, I knew for a fact that it was impossible to alter the past, no matter how much I wished that I could.

"Your Jeanette." She had written on the photo. Jeanette, the temptress. Jeanette the homewrecker. Jeanette, the harlot.

Unable to speak a word when Bernard opened the big oak door, I simply fell into his arms. I believe I might have gone into a dead faint if he had not supported me and led me to the nearest chair in the drawing room. Cook appeared briefly and was commanded to bring me some water.

The minutes ticked by on the large grandfather clock before I could finally ask if Jules was in residence. Bernard told me to sit still and went at once to summon him.

Although she had left the room, I knew that Cook would find a way to eavesdrop. She simply could not miss a detail that concerned the Marshand household.

Jules entered the room smiling, appearing surprised and happy to see me but the smile quickly faded when I handed him the poster with her picture on it.

He slumped down on the sofa and just stared at me.

"Where are Madame and Celeste this morning?"

"They are gone to the country manor this week for some socializing and relaxation before school resumes."

"Have you been aware of the terrible events at the Tower?" I asked.

"I've been submerged in a case at court." He said.

"The picture. It's her, isn't it?"

"There can be no doubt. It says here that she can't remember anything and doesn't know who she is."

"Yes. And the authorities are asking for help. Sooner or later someone will come forth, Jules. We cannot allow the woman to receive any notoriety. God forbid she regains her memory and someone associates her with Monsieur Marshand. This is a secret I was sure would never come to the surface. We must protect Madame and Celeste."

"She came to see me last week."

"What are you saying? This woman came to see you before being attacked?"

"Apparently. I swear I didn't know about what happened to her after we spoke."

"What did you speak to her about?"

"She wanted more money to keep her silence."

"My God, Jules. Did you give it to her?"

"I told her she would have to wait for me to get the funds together. I asked her to meet me at the Law Library in the middle of the week. But she did not show up."

"So, you were going to pay her off again?"

"Of course, I didn't want her to contact Monique and I was determined to protect my dead brother's name."

"And what now? Now that these new circumstances have arisen. How can we be sure this goes no further?"

"You must leave that to me, Natalie. I will have someone posted at the hospital who can report her condition to me every day. If she suddenly is aware of her identity, I will go there at once and arrange to pay whatever she demands. I will be sure this time to put an end to the blackmail and threats."

"It is hard for me to trust you, Jules. You assured me once before that the matter was taken care of."

"You have no choice, Natalie. I promise I will take care of this woman. You can put your mind at ease."

"I'll be leaving then."

"Wait, please." He said, softening his tone, he reached out and touched my hand as it lay on the arm of the overstuffed chair.

"It has been some time since we have spoken. I realize I was quite a cad the way I approached you in the past, but I would like to begin again. I would like to call on you and perhaps take you out for a meal, or perhaps an afternoon tea."

Gazing into those deep blue eyes that once had left me mesmerized, I was swayed by his gentle tone. Memories of the afternoon in the garden came flooding back and I experienced a sense of dread knowing what this man was capable of.

"I'm asking for another chance, Natalie. I know what proper decorum is and I would like the chance to show you that I can be a gentleman." And there was that familiar gesture, as he brushed his hair back from his forehead. Again, he endeared himself to me as he did this, assuming for a moment a certain boyish charm that I found attractive and alluring.

"Perhaps an afternoon in the public eye for tea would be all right. But I would like to be sure that this matter is dealt with first." I said, pointing to the photograph on the poster. "And I believe I shall take this with me, as I'd rather not leave it here in this house."

"If and when there are further developments, I will find a way to let you know, my dear." He said. "Maybe you will learn to trust me, when I have solved this dilemma."

My pace was much slower as I walked back toward the bakery. I directed my footsteps as far from the Tower as I could when I neared the park. But still I glanced over the area for a sign of my father. It was to no avail.

Physically, I was exhausted, weighed down by my worry for his well-being and concern for what might happen to the Marshands if that woman were to disclose her secrets from the past. I knew as I climbed the stairs to the small apartment that I was overburdened. I dropped onto the bed and fell immediately into a fitful sleep full of haunting nightmares that were punctuated by the echoes of the Masked One's evil cackle.

Trente-cinq

Before the Storm

*T*HE next few nights were eerily calm. I am sure there were many who were able to put aside any thoughts of danger and perhaps even forget the tense atmosphere so apparent mere weeks earlier. I was unable to embrace this state of mind. I was full of foreboding, believing that evil was hanging in the air just out of reach and ready to strike. The customers in the boulangerie had resumed speaking of petty things. The mood returned to the carefree manner of neighbors meeting for coffee. Office workers stood at the glass display cases selecting pastries for us to wrap up.

Occasionally, I observed a questioning gaze from one of the patrons. I wondered if they recognized me from my outings with Celeste. I averted my eyes at those times avoiding any kind of interaction that might cause further speculation regarding where they might have seen me before. The structure of Paris society would certainly frown on the idea that a common sales clerk was assigned to the care of a child of the social elite.

One morning as I handed a customer a freshly baked loaf of bread, she displayed a curious expression and it appeared she was about to say something. At that exact instance, a metal baking pan slid off the kitchen counter and reverberated on the bakery floor. In the midst of the startling noise, all heads turned, and a few surprise giggles were heard. When I turned back to the counter, the customer was no longer there. The discarded loaf of bread was left abandoned.

It was then that he entered the door. I sensed his presence before I realized it was him, occupying the doorway. He stood back, avoiding the line of patrons. As he held his hat in his hand, he assumed the attitude of a patiently waiting patron willing to stand there all day.

It was a good time for him to appear, since the morning rush had eased up. I told Madame Fournier that I would need to step out for a few minutes as I hung my apron on the nearby hook. I told him he would be able to find me at the bakery, but that was all he knew about my private life. He was unaware that I lived upstairs, and he was most definitely not informed about my relationship with the dreaded Eiffel Spirit.

"Natalie, I hope this is a good time, can you spare me a minute?"

I led him to one of the patio tables and waited for him to speak. The humility of his demeanor struck me at once. I had never seen Jules behave with such subservience.

"I told you I would keep you informed and that's why I'm here. I have had the woman under surveillance and although she is about to leave the hospital, she is still suffering from amnesia. I have also discovered that the authorities have received no leads from the public."

"So, nothing has really changed?" I said.

"No, but I thought that if I gave you the latest information, it might help to ease your mind."

"Thank you, Jules. May I ask how Celeste and Madame Marshand are?"

"Of course. They are both well. Celeste has begun her new term and you will be happy to hear that my sister-in-law is more like her old self again. She smiles, and even sings along with her little canary occasionally. It is a great relief to see her emerging somewhat from her grief-stricken state.

More importantly, I want you to know that I am happy to be of service to you my dear Natalie. It has been my pleasure to reassure you and see you sigh with relief. I must be off now to court but not before I ask again if I may take you to an early supper soon. I would be most honored to spend an evening trying to impress you with the best of manners."

I smiled at his remark and told him I would not mind an evening away from my own daily routine.

"Wonderful, I will contact you shortly to set up a time and place and will anticipate the event with great joy."

I watched as he walked down the street toward the courthouse.

Jules had always impressed me as a confident, well-bred man. His carefree stride reflected the ease and confidence of his entire countenance as he walked on the sidewalk. Even as he disappeared from my sight, I pictured him smiling at passersby, tilting his hat to the ladies and causing more than one to feel a thrill.

Despite my reservations, I found that I was smiling more in the days that followed, looking forward to seeing him again. The youthful feeling of anticipation caused my heart to beat a little faster. I wonder how many young women become so lost in thoughts of fancy that it becomes hard to embrace the realities of their surroundings.

Trente-Six

Upheaval

*T*HE middle of the week brought fresh terror to the neighborhood. The night was shattered by an earsplitting scream, followed by a ghostly silence. I did not have the strength to go downstairs and possibly meet Madame Fournier on the landing. I pulled the coverlet over my head and lay there in the dark awaiting the morning. I was much too afraid to go back to sleep.

When the dawn broke, I was pulled apart by conflicting emotions. My curiosity about another suspected incident at the Tower was mixed with my fear of discovering the possible impact on my father, myself and whoever the innocent victim might be.

I bolstered my courage and silently assumed my stance behind the counter at the bakery, eager to learn what the patrons might disclose in their rapid-fire dialog.

More than once I heard the word "dead." The words "murder and blood covered" were bandied about. But perhaps the most devastating gossip being put forth concerned the hole in the ground that the body made as it contacted the earth below the Eiffel Tower.

There was no specific description of the victim, except for one person who said that this time the body seemed to have been hurled from the highest level of the tower and with so many broken bones in every part of the skeleton, including the face, a positive identification would take some time.

My skin crawled as I overheard the semi-whispered tones. Horror and curiosity were the perfect combination to feed the gossip and rekindle the dread of the entire population of Paris. The Masked One had accelerated his heinous acts. Fear and dread were growing with each story that was told.

Madame Fournier made an announcement that the boulangerie would be closing earlier than usual and that business would be conducted on a limited daily schedule for the foreseeable future. Her own trepidation was reflected in her face and it was a contagious condition that morning.

I read the newspaper with my coffee to see if there might be more details, but it seemed that the essence of what had happened was the same as I had discerned through the gossip in the bakery. There could be no identification of the victim due to the condition of the woman's remains. I read that sentence twice, and both times it sent a chill down my spine.

Each evening, I drew the curtain closed and shut the window tight in my bed chamber. I needed more than ever to know the fate of my father and would have run outside despite my fears if I thought I could help him. But there was no information forthcoming about where he was and my despair grew with the realization, he had not been able to stop the Masked One's destruction this time.

As I wiped off the table on the sidewalk outside the bakery, I gasped as I saw Bernard approaching me.

"What a surprise to see you here." I said. The man looked so out of place there on the sidewalk, dressed in the full livery of a town butler.

"It is good to see you, Mademoiselle Natalie. I have brought you a message from Monsieur Jules. I hope you are well."

"Yes, of course. Thank you, Bernard. I hope you are well also, and that Madame and Celeste are in good health."

"I can tell you that they are, Mademoiselle. Here is the note from Monsieur Jules, I hope you will come visit soon, I believe Mademoiselle Celeste would be happy if you would."

"Please tell her that I will and please tell her that I miss her company."

"I will be glad to. Monsieur asked that I await your response to his note if that is convenient for you."

I sat down to read the note from Jules.

"My dearest Natalie, I wanted to let you know right away that the cause of our concern has been addressed. There is no further need to be worried about a possible incident occurring that might embarrass anyone we care for.

"And now to celebrate, I hope that you might join me for an evening out this coming Friday, at one of my favorite bistros here in town. If you agree, I will pick you up at 7:00. Please let Bernard know if this is acceptable to you. I hold my breath as I await your reply. J."

I decided, maybe too quickly, that I might find the evening enjoyable. It would be nice to replace the thoughts I had been obsessing over with a meal and some light conversation.

I told Bernard to let Monsieur Jules know that I would be available on Friday.

I hoped I was not making a mistake.

I breathed a sigh of relief as I watched Madame Fournier filling the display cases with pastries the following morning. The usual clientele began arriving and the look of dread and fear seemed to be abating slightly.

Madame and I were able to share a cup of coffee when the morning rush died down.

"Every night I fear he will strike again." She said.

"I am scared too." I told her. "Some nights I find myself straining to hear a sound from the Tower and petrified that I might."

"I'm sure that having no word about your father has been difficult."

"I am tempted to search the Park for him but terrorized by the idea of an encounter with the Masked One."

"You would be foolish not to be afraid. Perhaps I should get in touch with my son and ask his help to search for Henri."

"I would be concerned for Philippe's safety if he were to interfere. I have convinced myself that I must trust that my father will resurface when the time is right and that he is occupied trying to protect the innocents for the time being."

"I would agree, especially in light of the recent death of the poor girl who made an imprint in the ground under the Tower.

Apparently, your father was not strong enough to fend off his evil opponent that night."

"Even so, Madame, I must hope that he will be able to protect others and I cannot lose faith in his determination. I believe that he has saved many from similar fates."

Her words haunted me that night as I pulled the covers back. Was my father lacking in strength, or had the Masked One finally eliminated him and made his dark deeds easier to carry out?

Friday, after the shop closed, I dressed for the upcoming evening I was to spend with Jules. It did not take long to prepare for our excursion, since I only had two dresses to choose from. I hoped that we were not going somewhere elegant because I would look out of place. If Jules did not change his plans when he saw me, then I would not be concerned about what I was wearing. I opened the small box on the dresser containing the elegant cameo and fastened the ribbon around my neck.

The carriage was right on time. Jules alighted and took my hand to help me board.

"You are as lovely as ever, my dear." He said.

"Thank you. I am looking forward to the evening."

To my great relief the bistro was not too upscale, and I was dressed appropriately. Jules was obviously a regular patron, treated by the waitstaff as if he were coming home. The wine steward appeared at our table with a selection before anything was ordered. Jules sipped the small taste that was offered and nodded his approval.

He then offered a toast to the night, as we shared the delightful beverage.

I told him he could order for both of us, since he was familiar with the menu, and I believe he was pleased that I did.

His mood was lighter than usual, and he began by regaling me with stories of his latest courtroom appearances.

"I believe my brother would be quite proud of me. I have had successful verdicts in four out of five cases of late, and although none of the decisions will go down in history, they are assuring me of a winning reputation."

"What types of cases have you been taking?" I asked.

"Recently, I handled a petty theft and before that a man who had embezzled funds from his employer."

"Sounds challenging at the least."

"I was able to be of assistance to the boy who had been responsible for the petty theft. He was able to offer restitution for his crime and did not have to serve time."

"And the other case?"

"I have to say that even though I defended the man, I abhor the underhanded larceny involved when funds are misappropriated in this manner. The man was given a job and entrusted with responsibility which he then repaid with a slap in the face."

"I understand what you're saying. Was justice done?"

"Yes, to the fullest degree. I am not too unhappy to admit that this was the case I lost. The man will be locked up for quite a while."

After a few moments of silence, Jules went on.

"This is no discussion to be having during our pleasant night out. I'm sorry for being such a bore. Tell me how you are doing. Do you enjoy working in the bakery with your friend?"

"Yes. I really do like spending time there. I feel I owe so much to Madame Fournier, for being there for me when I was young. We get along well, and I can offer her a lot of help since the bakery requires many hours of hard work."

It had been some time since I had enjoyed a meal so good with rich sauces and savory spices. I had forgotten how well I had eaten as a member of the Marshand household.

It wasn't until the meal was almost over when Jules leaned toward me in a conspiratorial posture.

"You received my note, but I wanted once again to reassure you that we would not be hearing from Mademoiselle Jeanette again."

"Yes, I read the note, but there were no details."

"There is no need for you to know the details. Just be assured that she will never pose a threat to my sister-in-law in the future."

"You were pretty sure of this once before, Jules, after you escorted her away from Paris."

"Natalie, you are not to worry about the woman again." He said, assuming a rather fierce demeanor suddenly. "She will bother no one ever again."

"And, what exactly does that mean?"

"You heard about the woman who died at the Tower earlier in the week?"

"Do you mean the woman who fell from the top tier and left a hole in the ground?"

"Yes, that was the one." His answer was sharp and direct as he looked me straight in the eyes.

"Was that her? Did she go back there again after she left the hospital?"

"Natalie, you ask so many questions. Please just don't worry.

Believe me when I say there will be no more threats from her. And there is no reason for you to know more than that. Now, I will take you home, unless you would like me to take you back to the bakery?"

"Yes, the bakery will be fine, I can help to prepare the kitchen for the morning baking. There is always more than enough to do." Inwardly, I was filled with gratitude knowing that Jules was unaware that my living quarters were only one flight up from the ground floor of that shop.

No words were spoken during the carriage ride. I was filled with an ominous dread about the fate that had fallen Monsieur Marshand's lover. I wanted to ask more questions but was convinced they would go unanswered.

Jules had become defensive and cold and seemed anxious to put an abrupt end to the evening. I wondered what I really knew about the man. Was he capable of violence to eliminate a tentative threat? Why did he bring up the incident at the Tower when we had been discussing the fate of Mademoiselle Jeanette? Would I ever discover the truth behind this veiled implication?

I felt quite a sense of dread as these questions plagued me.

I closed the shop door behind me and watched the carriage disappear around the corner. Another mystery had fallen into my lap and I was unprepared to deal with it.

The newspaper reports concerning the recent death at the Tower were now relegated to the fifth page. The event was fading from recent memory and no updates were reported. The papers said that the authorities were not pursuing any leads as to the victim's identity. No witnesses had come forth to say what had happened that fateful night.

Resorting to what had been said during similar episodes in the past, it was reported that the Eiffel Spirit was once more wreaking havoc upon the city. Apparently previous reports of the Spirit's demise had been overturned.

My heart stopped when I read the accusations against him. If only the truth were known by the populace regarding my father and the reasons, he had stood watch at the Tower. If only the innocent people he lived to protect could be aware that he was a benevolent spirit and not the entity their imaginations associated with fear.

I wanted to scream from the rooftops that it was the Masked One, Joaquin Picard, they should fear. Not my father. It was the Spirit whom idol gossip had shrouded in all manner of evil, when it was he who was the one concerned for their safety.

After briefly scanning the paper, I took my place behind the bakery counter on that bright winter morning. Madame Fournier was in an exceptionally good mood. She smiled at each customer as she waited on them and told each one to enjoy the beautiful day. I let my thoughts wander as her clientele politely smiled back. I let my gaze follow them as they opened the door and merged into the pedestrian traffic on the sidewalk.

Madame Fournier was right. It was a beautiful Parisian day. The weather was neither hot nor cold and the sky was punctuated with bright white clouds which seemed to be made of spun sugar.

I waited as the morning passed, until I could have a word with her to discover the cause of her bliss, although I found myself enjoying her mood so much that finding a reason was not necessary. There were so few moments lately that were profoundly joyful, and I found myself clutching this one close to me, reluctant to let it dissolve.

Trente-Sept

Good News

"PHILIPPE will be coming for a visit beginning Saturday." She said as she handed the last customer a fresh loaf of crusty bread.

"How lovely." I said.

"He sent a note saying he has so much to tell us both about his job and what has been happening since we last saw him. I am looking forward to seeing him again. It feels like he has been gone such a long time. Although, to a mother, I believe it always seems that way."

"Well, that is particularly good news, Madame. I look forward to his visit as well. I think I've really missed him, too."

"He would like to take us both to dinner on Saturday evening."

"I will enjoy that very much." I said, thinking about my recent evening out with Jules. I believed that spending time with Philippe and Madame Fournier would be much more enjoyable. These were the two people in the world I felt most comfortable with and whom I believed sincerely cared for me.

We closed the shop on Saturday and then prepared for our evening out. Madame had been in the most cheerful of moods all day, humming about in the kitchen as she worked and hardly containing an almost giddy countenance as she waited on the customers. I wondered if Philippe was aware of how much his visit meant to his mother, and how much she had missed him.

Madame knocked on my bedroom door to let me know when he arrived. Although I had been looking forward to the evening, I had not realized how much I was anticipating seeing Philippe again. Even though it had only been a few months, I could have sworn that Philippe had aged by a couple of years. He stood there near the bakery counter, helping his mother on with her wrap as I entered. He turned and smiled, and I was suddenly drawn to this man who exuded a mature charm and a warmth that I wanted to become more familiar with.

He kissed my cheek and said how happy he was that I was available this evening to join he and his mother for dinner. He held the door as we left the bakery and then assisted us into the waiting carriage, all the while saying how nice we both looked and how fortunate he was to be escorting the loveliest women in Paris.

I heard all of this as though I were underwater and I'm sure I must have appeared to be in a daze, but the moment seemed surreal. It was as if I had this experience before and knew what was going to happen and what was going to be said. All that I seemed able to do consciously was to smile. So that is what I did.

Finally, as we enjoyed a wonderful meal, accompanied by a genuinely nice bottle of champagne, I regained touch with reality and was able to participate in the conversation at the table.

Philippe delighted in telling us about the firm where he worked and how rewarding it was to be recognized for his talents in the architectural field. He was in the process of designing some new shopping areas on the city's outskirts that were to be modern with all of the latest techniques being developed. He drew a picture on his dinner napkin to explain the concepts he was working on and it was exciting to share in his delight as he explained that so many of the ideas were unique to his firm, and more specifically to him.

"We are going to use a lot of glass in the design of this structure." He said.

"The concept is not entirely new, but we are adding some interesting things, such as tinted glass to accentuate some of the building angles. I believe the public will be impressed by the appearance of the building exteriors. We are also incorporating some interior surprises as well, such as live plants and trees interspersed among the sites of the proposed store fronts."

His mother beamed with pride as Philippe told us that the firm was thrilled when they were awarded the bid on the shopping area, giving credit for several of the innovative ideas to their new, young associate. Raising his glass, he told us that for him it meant an increase in pay and position after many long hours at the drawing board.

"I simply had to share this good news with you in person, Mere, since I knew it would make you so happy to hear of my success. And, of course, I could not think of celebrating without including you, Natalie, my dear friend."

Motioning to the waiter, Philippe signaled for the dessert cart to be brought over. The display of mouthwatering delicacies was inviting and difficult to choose from. Philippe commented that he was curious to see which selection his mother, the best baker in Paris, would pick for herself.

I looked up as Madame Fournier pondered her choices to see that someone standing next to our table. It took me a moment to realize that this was the little girl I used to care for, now grown into a lovely young woman.

"Celeste? My, Celeste, is it really you?"

"Yes, Mademoiselle. I saw you across the room and I had to come say bonjour."

She bent to offer me a small hug. I introduced her to Madame Fournier, and Philippe.

"You must come by and see me, Mademoiselle Natalie. I have a few days free this week and would love for you to come to tea."

"I would enjoy that very much, Celeste. Shall we say mid-week, I can come by on Wednesday, if that is good for you."

"I will look forward to it. So nice to meet you both." She said, and then she left to rejoin her friends for dinner.

"I'm happy to finally meet Celeste." Madame Fournier said. "After all of the years that I have heard you speak about her. She is a lovely young lady."

Suddenly, I was filled with an awareness of how fleeting time can be?

Sitting at the table that evening, observing the dignified young woman that Celeste had become was overwhelming to my senses. How could this confident person be the little girl that I used to tuck into bed at nap time?

The three of us lingered over our coffee and dessert in a manner that said we wanted the evening to last. For the first time in weeks, I gave myself over to laughter and enjoyed the pleasant company of the two people I considered my family.

I was able to put aside for a brief while the concern that I constantly felt for my father's well-being as I wondered if I would ever see him again.

Philippe mentioned on the carriage ride home that he would be free for the next day or so and wanted to spend the time visiting with his mother.

"I have been so preoccupied with work and with making my own way, that I feel I've neglected you." He told her. "And that was never my intention. You always have a special place in my heart even though I don't tell you often enough."

Madame Fournier was noticeably moved by her son's words.

I offered to run the bakery for her in the morning, so that she and Philippe could spend the day together touring the city or just having a day out. It would be the first time she spent the day away from the shop in many years and would be a well-deserved holiday.

I had to reassure her several times that everything would be taken care of in her absence. I listened more than once to her instructions for handling the register and filling the display cabinets. And I laughed as I reminded her that I had worked in the bakery long enough to know my way around.

Finally, she left on her son's arm, happier than I had seen her in a long time. Philippe was like an elixir of energy and joy that pervaded her spirit and made her look quite young and spry as they set out together.

It turned out to be a perfect day to be alone in the bakery. It was somewhat overcast, bordering on gloomy, which seemed to forestall the usual rush of customers. Although sales might be less than what Madame Fournier might have hoped for, I was relieved that the day was quiet and slow moving. More than once I looked up suddenly feeling as though I was being watched through the store window.

I saw him, just as the first spots of drizzle were falling on the sidewalk. The store was empty and there was a hazy cloudiness that seemed to drift inside from the dismal Parisian day as I held the door open for him. I locked it after he entered.

"I have waited to see you when you were alone."

"I have been so worried."

"That is why I had to see you. To let you know that you needn't be concerned."

"Can you finally stay with me and let me take care of you?"

"Not while Joaquin is still a viable enemy."

"You were not able to protect the girl who recently died at the foot of the Tower."

"I don't believe it was he who caused her death. Another force was responsible. I am always watchful of Joaquin and stand ready to come to the aid of his victims."

"Another force? You mean the Masked One is not responsible for the death of the girl who fell from the top of the Tower."

"Yes, daughter. I had him in my sights as her body flew by us both."

"And, what of you, my darling father? How much longer can you offer protection against him and still preserve your own life?"

"As long as I must be there, I will be there. For now, however, I must be going. My love for you is the only reason I have lived this long."

He pulled the hood over his head, unlocked the door and was gone.

Those brief moments felt unreal. I wanted him to stay with me. I wanted to take care of him and to give him the opportunity for some restful hours during what was left of his remaining years. I wished I could spend some time just getting to know him. But this was not to be, not while the Masked One continued to be obsessed with terror and destruction.

I told Madame Fournier about the encounter as we shared dinner in her small kitchen with Philippe.

She made a delightful onion soup after returning from their afternoon excursion.

Philippe opened a bottle of burgundy that he bought when they were out. I set the table and procured a crusty French loaf from the bakery shelves.

"I am sorry that I missed seeing your father. But I am relieved that he is well." She said. "Maybe you will be able to sleep better now that you have been reassured."

"I am happy that you had that short visit, Natalie." Said Philippe. "I can only imagine how often you think of him, wondering the whole time if he is dead or alive."

The rest of the evening passed in relative quietness, with just the sound of the rain beating on the windows. The three of us were lost in our own thoughts as we enjoyed our meal and the comfortable silence of each other's company.

My father's words resonated with me as I lay in bed that night, sending a chill through me.

"Another force was responsible."

What force?

I was becoming obsessed with suspicions that the dead woman might have been Jeannette, the harlot who had seduced my former employer. I imagined that Jules was somehow involved in her destruction. And now, my father cast doubt on the Masked One's responsibility for her demise. I had to let this go, I was being consumed by this crime and its implications. Pulling the comforter over my head, I spent the rest of the night in fitful slumber.

Philippe rose early and was already having coffee at one of the cafe tables when I entered the bakery.

"Please join me a moment, Natalie." He said as he rose to pour me a cup.

"You are off to an early start this morning." I said.

"I was hoping I might have a moment with you before the shop opens."

"Of course. I must tell you, Philippe, how much your mother is enjoying this visit with you. It has been a while since I have seen her so happy."

"I am happy to be here too and glad I planned these few days away. I was hoping that I might speak to you on a more personal matter."

Philippe paused a moment before going on.

"Natalie, I've always cared for you. I think you must have known this as the years have gone by. But, what you may not have known was that you were always my inspiration for doing well in school and eventually becoming successful professionally."

I found I was looking deep into Philippe's light blue eyes as he spoke. He leaned forward and his tone of voice was so intense, I felt myself holding my breath.

"It has all been leading up to this moment. I wanted so much to offer you a life of comfort and contentment, Natalie. I think about you all of the time. You are my motivation and reason to succeed. Now I am asking if you will share my life with me and let me be the one to care for you always."

I was at a loss for words. Philippe was waiting for me to say something, but I could not speak. Time stood still as his hand rested on mine. I wanted to ease his anxiety by saying yes immediately. But so many thoughts were playing in my head that I seemed to have no control over a response of any kind. Patiently he continued waiting and I could see that he, too, was holding his breath afraid of being rejected.

I was in a state of suspended animation, questioning my own emotions.

Philippe was frozen to the spot in anticipation. The muscles in his face and neck were tight as he waited for me to speak. From somewhere inside I simply blurted out, "I am not sure I can make this decision right now, Philippe. I don't feel as though my life is completely my own to live as I wish."

I attempted to gently free my hand from his grasp, but he held it tighter.

"I love you, Natalie. I am willing to wait for a response if there is hope that you will eventually be mine. Can I at least carry that hope within me?"

"It would not be right for you to put your life on hold for me." I said, as one small tear escaped the corner of my eye.

"I care for you, Philippe. You are very special to me, but at this moment my life is still consumed with my father's fate and the destiny he believes that he must fulfill. I am not free to give myself completely to anyone, while he is in danger every day. I must be nearby if he needs me, and I can't let go of the worry that I always feel for him."

"Of course, I understand your concern for him, and I know you must be available if something happens to him, but you are willing to put your life on hold because of your love for him. I am willing to do the same for you, if it is simply a matter of waiting for the time, we can be together. I love you that much."

"I'm not sure I can make a promise about a future which is still shrouded in the darkness of the unknown. I would never want to inflict disappointment or pain on you and I'm not sure it is fair to have you live your life in a state of suspension as the future unfolds."

"So, I am to leave here with no answer at all? You won't even give me the slightest hope that one day you will be my wife?"

"If I were free right now, I would not allow you to leave with your future in such doubt. But I am not free, and things must stay as they are now, with no inclination toward any type of decision. I am sorry, Philippe, but this is how it must be."

I rose then and went upstairs to my apartment without turning around to look at him. I needed to be alone. I needed to cry.

When I looked out the window later in the day, I saw a carriage parked outside of the bakery. I watched as Philippe kissed his mother on the cheek and then boarded the carriage with his valise in his hand. I backed away from the window seconds before he looked up in my direction.

Madame Fournier commented at supper that he had been called back to his office to make an important decision regarding the design of the shopping area. She said that he was sorry he was unable to say goodbye to me, but that he asked her to say he would hopefully be back soon for another visit. I could tell that she was disappointed that he left so abruptly, but I was quite sure she was not aware of the conversation he and I had earlier that morning.

We made up our baking schedule and settled into our regular routine. I must confess it was a relief that she was in the dark about the proposal. I was not ready to discuss my feelings for Philippe and the reasons for my indecision. But, more than that, I did not want to face the impact all of this would have on our relationship.

Trente-Huit

Tea and Memories

I welcomed the break on Wednesday afternoon when it was time to accept Celeste's invitation to afternoon tea. Bernard extended a warm greeting when he opened the door. He took my wrap before setting off to announce my arrival. I did not have to wait long before I heard the rush of steps descending the staircase and turned to a warm embrace from Celeste.

"You must come and sit down at once." She announced as she took my hand and led me to the drawing room. There was a very inviting tea service set up with perfectly delicious looking sandwiches and sweets.

"I am so glad you came and that we will have the time together to catch up."

"I was happy to be invited, and I have been looking forward to coming since we met at the restaurant. It has been such a long time since we've had a chance to talk, and I want to know everything that has been going on with you. I assume your mother is not at home."

"She said she would have loved to join us if it were not for a previous engagement.

You will be pleased to hear that mother is more like her old self again. She still has moments where I believe that she dwells on father's untimely death and drifts off into a sad reverie. But, for the most part she has assumed a social life of her own and found interests and pursuits that help her pass the time pleasurably."

"I am relieved to hear that. I can tell you now that I was concerned about Madame Marshand for a considerable length of time after your father's passing. Would it be fair to say that she has become an active part of the social life of the ladies of Paris once again?"

Celeste poured the tea and handed me a cup and saucer as I perched on the edge of the plush settee.

"Oh, that would be more than fair to say, Mademoiselle Natalie. She has even become somewhat of a fashion plate among the women she spends time with. Today, for example, is lady's day at Longchamp and mother set the pace for what one might wear to the races. Just this week she purchased the most elegant, fringed dress and a pair of daring ankle strapped boots. I wish I could have seen the expression on the other ladies faces when she emerged from the carriage."

It was easy to imagine Madame wearing the latest Paris fashions, with her long legs and slender physique. It did my heart good to hear Celeste talk about her with a certain amount of pride in her mother's taste.

"It sounds as though she was looking forward to having a wonderful time with her friends, and I am thrilled that she is again taking pleasure in dressing well and enjoying herself."

"Speaking of enjoyment, you must try the little cakes set out there on the tray. Cook made them especially for you and she will be so happy to hear that you liked them."

"I'm very sure that I will."

"Oh, yes, Mademoiselle. Mother's friends are remarkably busy planning social activities that keep them quite busy and entertained. Just last week one of them had a card reader at their home for the afternoon. Mother came home quite giddy as she told me about the future of travel and romance that was predicted for her by the fortune teller. Later this week there are plans to go to the opera and I believe there is a concert or two scheduled for the near future."

"And what about you, Natalie? Are you enjoying a social life of your own?"

"I have some friends from school with whom I like spending some of my free time. The evening I saw you at the restaurant I was with several of them. We had just spent the afternoon at the museum and ended the day with a lovely supper. And, I still enjoy sitting down with a good book, thanks to you for instilling the love of reading in me at a young age. I find the time speeds by when I get caught up in a story that I enjoy."

"That is a pleasure I can certainly relate to; I find a good book one of the most pleasurable parts of life."

"I was hoping that Uncle Jules would be here when you came to tea, but he had to go out of town on a legal case he has recently taken. He did tell me that you and he had recently gone out for an evening and that he had enjoyed seeing you."

"Yes, we did have supper recently."

"I have to tell you, Mademoiselle that I have always hoped you and Uncle Jules would become a couple. I know it's not my business to discuss this, but I have entertained the thought, and even secretly wished you might become a member of my family by marrying my uncle."

"Celeste, that is the farthest thing from my mind. I consider your uncle to be friend, but no more than that can be deduced from our relationship, and certainly not marriage."

"You can't blame me for hoping, it would just be so wonderful to call you my Aunt, and to have you in my life again on a permanent basis."

"I plan to always be in your life, dearest Celeste. You mean so much to me, and you should know that. I always want to know how you are, what you are doing and what kinds of plans your future holds. You will never be rid of me."

She smiled and replied that she would always feel the same.

While she poured us another cup of tea, I had the opportunity to sample the tiny baked sweets that had been prepared for the afternoon.

"You never saw my room after it was completely decorated." Celeste said.

"I would love for you to come see it, since you did help me select the fabric patterns and the wallpaper?"

So many memories were contained in that room. Even though it no longer looked like a child's bedroom, I could still recall the hours of reading bedtime stories, brushing her hair and tucking her in after a warm bath.

The room now belonged to a young lady. It contained a vanity and mirror, a small settee on which were stacked a couple of her current reading materials and a nightstand which contained a small lamp and what looked as though it might be a diary.

"The room is perfect for you, Celeste. I can tell that it is a place of retreat and relaxation befitting a smart and beautiful girl like you."

"I do enjoy my privacy." She said. "When I am not out socializing, or playing the piano downstairs, I love spending time in here and I am happy to have this space of my own.

I must show you the most delightful gift that Uncle Jules gave me recently."

She opened a small jewelry box which sat on the dresser and withdrew a necklace with a fine silver chain.

"Actually, I should wear it more often." She said, as she opened her hand to display a silver locket.

"It has my father's picture inside. Isn't that just the most thoughtful gift? Sometimes, Uncle Jules can be so kind and so good to me."

I felt the blood drain from my face as I recalled the last time, I had seen the necklace as it adorned the neck of another young woman.

"The locket and your picture remain always close to my heart." The words stung like a knife.

I sat on the edge of Celeste's bed and listened to her speak lovingly of her uncle. Since her father's death, Jules had become more important to her than ever before. She spoke of him with a devotion that I found difficult to contend with as I entertained doubts of what he may have recently been up to.

There was no doubt that the locket he presented to Celeste was the same one being worn in the signed photo of Monsieur Marshand's lover. There was only one way it could have come into Jules' possession.

I wanted to spend more time with the charming young woman who played such an important role in my own life, but I was finding it difficult to not let my mind wander. I rose under the pretext of extending a personal thanks to Cook for the afternoon repast and then gracefully took my leave.

I went about my routine for the next several days without really thinking about what I was doing. The only thing on my mind was the locket. I needed to know how Jules came to own it. I knew it was going to be a very necessary part of a puzzle that had to be solved. At the same time, I was reluctant to find out what the puzzle may reveal, and what implications there would be to those I held dear.

Of course, I was also entertaining thoughts of my last conversation with Philippe. I had been surprised by his marriage proposal. I grew up with him. I cared for him deeply and cherished our friendship. I just was not sure I could love him the way a wife should, and I never thought he considered me as someone he loved enough to marry.

I felt as though time was standing still for me. I was trapped by events that were out of my control and decisions I felt unable to make. If only my father was free from his self-imposed role as protector of the innocent. At least then, I would have more freedom to pursue my own future.

If only I knew the details of Jules' involvement, if any, regarding the demise of Jeannette.

If only I were free of worries and concerns and could concentrate on my feelings for Philippe and whether, we had a future together.

Something had to give, and I was at a loss to know how to initiate what changes needed to be made. And it was at this time of my own self-doubts and recriminations that the city itself came to an abrupt halt all around me.

Trente-Nuef

All Consuming

THE local constabulary was being harassed every day as a result of the recent events at the Eiffel Tower. After the devastating death of the unidentified woman, the Masked One was enjoying a rampage of violence.

The police were put to shame by the citizenry, who decided it was time to visibly protest what they believed was a lack of protection by those hired to do that job on their behalf. The newspapers exploded with stories of the Paris citizenry rising en masse at the Tower Park with placards. Signs were printed with slogans stating, "We Must Protect Ourselves;" "Where Are Those Paid to Protect?" and "It is Time to Stand Firm."

Every morning crowds assembled. There were women with small children in tow; au pairs arrived pushing prams with signs and banners attached to the front of the baby carriages; and businessmen made brief appearances an hour or so before showing up at their offices.

Housewives seemed to spill from their front doors in an endless stream to join the throngs advancing on the Eiffel Park with their home-made signs. As they congregated on the lawn, they assumed an almost festive air, gossiping among themselves until some speaker or another commanded everyone's attention at the front of the crowd.

These random citizens spoke loudly demanding safety for the women of Paris. They stirred people up and were encouraged by the cheers of support they received from those gathered on the Park lawn.

Madame Fournier and I watched through the window of the bakery each morning. The larger than usual number of people on the streets meant there was always a line outside of the shop, for which we were grateful. But, on occasion when the crowd became more boisterous as the speakers incited a reaction, there was cause for concern because of our close proximity to the activity.

One afternoon as the crowd seemed to be reaching a fevered pitch, Madame Fournier locked the front door during what would usually be our busiest hours.

"I simply cannot take any chances. These peaceful citizens might just throw all caution to the wind and take out their frustrations on whatever or whoever is near them. They can't do any physical harm to the authorities who they are frustrated with, so no one knows when or where that pent up anger will boil to the surface."

We sat in the back room of the bakery that afternoon, listening to the muffled sounds of the crowds outside. Sharing a pot of tea, we relished the pause in what had become a daily barrage of energy both within and surrounding the small shop.

Earlier that morning, while we waited on our clientele, we were subjected to a steady stream of gossip about their conjectured rumors. The entire City of Paris seemed to only have one thing on its mind and people seemed to enjoy entertaining each other with stories about the mysterious Eiffel Spirit.

All conversation centered around their fears of what was going to happen next at the Eiffel Park.

"That girl's death will never be solved." I heard more than one person say.

"How am I to bring my children here. I am much too fearful that something terrible could happen to them."

"How can I ever consider this park a safe place for a picnic? I am sad that this is no longer an option for me and the children."

"I am concerned to even walk through the park on my way to go shopping."

"I have nightmares of what could happen here next."

Such was the substance of the whispered conversations as our patrons purchased croissants and baguettes. It became obvious that one person's fears fed those of others as surely as the bread they were buying fed their stomachs.

Quarante

The Locket

*E*ACH morning I woke up thinking that the protests would no longer be such an important part of the Parisian atmosphere. But, even as the weeks went by there was still a steady stream of mothers and children, au pairs and prams, and the occasional office worker.

Madame Fournier and I lived with the fear of what might happen as a result of the frustration and rage that was displayed right outside of our windows. And, as if our own imaginations were not enough to fuel our unease, we were subjected to the constant chatter of customers who, by now were concocting all kinds of stories based on a combination of supposition, hearsay, and legend.

My own nervousness was further fed by my concern for my father's welfare.

I worried that it might be discovered where he was hidden in the Park. I pictured scenes of him being subjected to persecution from the crowd. Other times, I imagined that the constabulary would see him hiding and arrest him as a murderer to put an end to the idea that they were negligent in finding the perpetrator of the recent crimes.

I prayed daily for the protests to end without my father's involvement in any way.

Early one afternoon, the tide changed. The officials in the of City's municipal offices seemed to wake up to the realization that they had to act. It was announced early in the day that the newly elected Mayor would be appearing at the Park to speak to the citizens assembled there.

Watching through the front window of the bakery we saw the Mayor's carriage arrive. It appeared that his entourage encountered some difficulty making their way through the crowd but eventually he made it to a makeshift speaker's platform. Various assistants shouted for order and called for attention. After several minutes, the noise died down.

Madame Fournier and I stood just outside of the door of the bakery, so we might hear what was being said.

"Good people of Paris." He began. "I am speaking to you on behalf of all of your elected officials who are eager to initiate a plan of action that will restore order the order and dignity of your our city. We want you to know that your voices have been heard."

A loud cheer went up among the crowd.

The Mayor's Chief of Staff shouted for quiet so that his excellency could resume speaking.

"We have heard your concerns for your safety. We are aware of the heinous crimes that have been perpetrated here at our landmark Tower. We are taking action to calm your fears and solve the murders so you can all sleep at night. No one should be afraid to spend time outdoors in our beautiful City. The Eiffel Park belongs to us all."

Another cheer, this time louder and lasting well over two minutes.

"I am here to promise you the protection you deserve. From now on the Park will be patrolled day and night by a squadron of the Gendarme assigned solely to this section of the city. Never again will you have to worry about being safe. This is my promise to you."

The cheers that were sent up after these comments were almost deafening. This was what the people wanted to hear. The feeling of relief was almost tangible among those gathered in the Park. Their concerns had not only been heard but were handled in a way they could not have anticipated.

The Mayor could hardly get back to his waiting carriage as the crowd pressed toward him to shake his hand or kiss him on the cheek.

A promise had been made. The Eiffel Park would once again belong to the people of Paris. It was a promise that the Mayor would be held responsible for.

After weeks of congregating near the Tower carrying their banners and making noise, the crowd slowly dispersed. Several people stopped by the bakery for a loaf of bread on the way home from the demonstration. It was not long before our display case was almost empty. Madame turned the open sign over on the door and locked up for the day.

I lay on my bed wondering how the police presence would impact my father's hidden occupation at the Tower. Would he and his nemesis be able remain undetected if the Park were being constantly monitored?

Perhaps this was a blessing in disguise. Maybe this would be a chance for the Masked One to finally come to justice and face the punishment he deserved. I fell asleep praying that my father might finally be released from his role as protector and that I might once again be able to take care of him.

We observed, as we stocked our shelves each morning, that the constabulary arrived early to begin patrolling the Park and surrounding streets. They had to walk past the boulangerie on their rounds. Occasionally, members of the Gendarme stopped in for a croissant or a roll.

Madame cleared her throat when she spied them approaching if I was wiping off the counter or sweeping the floor. She made it clear to the officers that her shop was there to provide baked goods to the public and that it was not going to become a place where young police officers could get a free cup of coffee and then dawdle while they openly flirted with the local mademoiselles.

At first, a few people each day approached the Park to sit on benches or lay a blanket out on the grass. As the next few weeks passed, it became a more popular place to congregate. The weather was warming up and the local citizens welcomed the opportunity to enjoy the outdoors. The seasons were changing, and the summer months meant the time to welcome the tourists who would provide a certain boost to the city's economy.

Although we were still reminded that Paris was being protected by men in uniform, the local people seemed to be breathing easier and smiling more often.

It was then when everyone's defenses were down that the Masked One struck again.

It was as though he was acting to spite the police presence and to make the point that the authority of the city officials was no match for his ingenuity. Once again, the night was split apart by a blood curdling scream followed by his diabolical cackle. Another young victim lay on the ground at the bottom of the Tower.

The bakery was crowded in the morning and the voices were louder than before. Now rage was rekindled in the customers. A young officer walked by the window and I witnessed a passerby spit on his boots.

It was a scene that felt surreal.

Despite the growing intensity of the anger all around me, I kept thinking of my father. Once again, he had been unable to stop the force of his evil enemy. And I realized how this must have taken a toll on him.

Madame Fournier would ordinarily have been thrilled to have her sales case empty by noon, but during this time period, it did little to lift her spirits.

There was another quandary that disturbed my peace of mind.

I could not stop thinking about Jules. I had to find out how he had become the owner of Jeanette's locket. I was certain that it was the same piece of jewelry he had given to Celeste and I needed to ask him about it. It plagued me although it led me to a series of thoughts, I was afraid to entertain.

Jules had no knowledge of the photograph I had found so long ago and for that reason, did not think that another soul was aware of the origin of the locket.

Whenever I thought about his possible involvement in Janette's death, a cold chill ran up my back. Perhaps there was a logical explanation for his possession of the necklace. But, as I recalled his assurance that I no longer needed to worry about the woman, I wanted to know why he was so certain.

He said that Madame Marshand would never find out about her husband's romantic fling. How he could be so sure?

On the chance that I might find Jules at the courthouse, I took the afternoon off from the bakery and headed in that direction. I did not know how I would approach him if I found him there, I only knew it would be better this way than to see him at the Marshand home, where our conversation might be overheard.

I walked back and forth in the corridor of the courthouse and held my breath each time one of the courtroom doors opened. I listened for his voice and watched as people came and went. After about an hour of sitting on one of the benches in the hallway, I told myself that the entire enterprise was probably a foolhardy way to accomplish my goal.

And then, another courtroom opened and several people poured into the hallway. I saw him then, engrossed in conversation with two other young men who appeared to be lawyers as well.

Thankfully, they were moving in my direction down the corridor as they spoke to each other.

I moved away from the wall as they approached.

"Good afternoon, Jules."

I could tell he was momentarily shocked to see me there and he quickly excused himself from his colleagues.

"Natalie, what a surprise to see you. Is everything all right?"

"Yes. I just needed to speak with you and hoped I would find you here."

"Shall we go somewhere for a drink, or cup of tea or something? Are you sure that you are all right?"

"Yes, and if we could go somewhere quiet, it would be most appreciated."

We occupied a table at a small coffee house around the corner from the court.

"You seem to have something important on your mind." He said.

"I do and I hardly know how to begin to ask the questions that I must ask you."

"I would hope that you could just ask me. There is no reason for us to be less than honest with each other."

"I don't think you have been honest for quite some time, Jules. It is not your honesty that puts me on edge. I believe that you are involved with something sinister, and it is keeping me awake at night. I need to know what happened to Jeanette and what your involvement may have been with her potential death."

"Natalie, I think you are letting your imagination get the best of you. I told you not to worry about the girl's interference in our lives. I don't know how you jumped from my words of reassurance to thinking that I had something to do with her demise, if she is, in fact, dead."

"Celeste showed me the locket. It belonged to her. I saw a photograph of her when she was wearing that necklace. I know it was the one she wore and there was only one way you could have taken it from her. How could you make a gift of that locket to your innocent niece? Didn't you think it was possible that someone might recognize it?"

"You are quite the little investigator, aren't you Natalie? You know that it is possible I bought a locket for Celeste that resembles the one that girl wore."

"It may be possible, but I don't believe it. Your reassurance that we need not worry about that woman ever again was so adamant. I wondered from that moment on how you could be so sure unless you had a hand in her final disappearance."

Jules reached his hand across the table and pressed my hand down forcibly.

"Whatever I have done to protect my family, I had to do to spare them pain and social ostracism. You can't prove any of your theories or conjecture and my crime was covered up nicely by the sinister presence at the Tower of whom the entire city has been living in fear."

"So, you are admitting that you had a part in her demise. I hoped that my suspicions might prove to be incorrect and that you might have some other explanation for the locket."

"And what will you do now that your suspicions are confirmed? Will you be the one who reveals my brother's infidelity to his wife and daughter? Will you then add to their suffering by having me arrested and my crime disclosed? Monique is getting her life back in order. She is actively participating in society, after recovering from her husband's untimely death. If your sense of justice is stronger than your devotion to those you claim to love, then so be it. Do what you must."

He released his grip on my hand and stood up abruptly from the table, scraping the floor as he pushed his chair forward. In an instant he was out the door. I was left dumbfounded by his admission of guilt and the terrible burden of knowing the truth.

I had no proof that a crime was committed. The girl's body wasn't identified, and no one seemed to care that she was dead. I was glad that I had finally confronted Jules with my suspicions. Whatever I decided to do with the knowledge of his guilt, one thing was certain. I no longer wanted him in my life. I was grateful that I had not fallen for his romantic overtures in the past. I could have been deeply involved in the life of a murderer.

Quarante et un

The Scare

I was surprised to find the bakery closed when I returned from my encounter with Jules. Our neighbor, Madame Dubois, from the millenary shop approached me as I was unlocking the door.

"Mademoiselle Natalie." She said. "Madame Fournier passed out this afternoon in the boulangerie. She was taken to the hospital. I have been watching for your return. I thought you should know right away. My husband would be happy to take you to the hospital in our carriage, if you would like."

I nodded in agreement, unable to find the words to say.

Within minutes we were underway. I thanked Monsieur Dubois for the carriage ride as I rushed toward the building entrance. Madame Fournier was asleep when I arrived at her hospital room. I was relieved to find that Philippe was already there. We briefly hugged.

"Is she going to be all right?" I asked.

"The doctor said that they don't think it's anything serious. But they want to keep her here to watch over her for a day or two. For now, they have given her something to sleep, so she is resting well."

"I hope that she will be all right. I was so scared when I heard what happened. I don't believe she has complained of any symptoms lately, so this comes as a complete surprise."

"I don't believe my mother complains very much, even when she probably should. She is such a hard-working woman. I think it would be a good idea if she could ease up on the hours she puts in and take better care of herself. She has a hard time admitting that she is not as young as she used to be."

"I know you are speaking with the voice of a concerned son, Philippe, but you know your mother as well as I do, and easing up is most likely something she would find exceedingly difficult to do. Running a bakery goes hand in hand with long hours, as you are aware. I know how much you would like for her to get some rest, but Madame Fournier has been a baker too long to suddenly change her schedule and put in shorter days. Frankly, I believe she would get bored very quickly."

I told Philippe that I would be happy to stay with his mother overnight, so that he did not have to worry. He said that he thought it would be less traumatic for his mother to wake up in a hospital room if one of us were there by her side. It was decided that I would stay overnight, and he would check in with us first thing in the morning.

With an extra pillow and blanket that the room nurse was kind enough to provide, I made myself comfortable in a chair near the hospital bed. This might not have been the most comfortable of accommodations, but the day had been so full of stress that I was exhausted and fell promptly into a deep sleep.

Soon I was having the worst nightmares of Jules chasing Jeanette around the upper level of the Eiffel Tower. In the dream, as I approached the two of them, I saw him force her to the edge of the metalwork. As she turned toward me, she was no longer the woman who seduced Jules' brother. Instead, it was Madame Fournier that he pushed over the edge. I jolted upright in the chair and gasped for air. Madame Fournier woke up at the same time. She looked at me questioningly. I went to her side and stroked her hair.

"You are in the hospital, my dear friend." I told her. "We will talk more later. You are in particularly good hands and I am here with you. For now, just rest. Everything is going to be fine."

After being reassured, she went back to sleep, and I settled back in the chair.

I looked up at the doorway before I closed my eyes. For a brief second, I saw a shadowed figure leaning against the door frame. The vision disappeared before I was able to get to my feet, but I knew it was him.

Madame Fournier had been the most important figure in my life since my childhood. But there was another person who had known her longer than I had and who cared about her deeply. Although it was at a terrible risk, I surmised that he needed to see for himself that she was going to survive. I pictured him darting through the shadows, clinging to the sides of the walls so that to the observer, he was there and then he was not.

Though the vision had lasted only a few seconds, it took more than an hour for me to lean back comfortably into the pillow and fall back to sleep. Thankfully, there were no more dreams, probably because I knew that my father was safe.

Philippe arrived just as the nurse was leaving the hospital room in the morning.

Madame Fournier was awake and looked well-rested.

The room nurse took the time to speak with Madame and I about the medical event that had caused her to faint at the bakery.

Although she did her best to make light of what was said, I knew that Madame Fournier did not want to hear that she was probably overextended with the work that was required to run at bakery. She was particularly vexed when the young nurse pointed out that she was no longer a in her thirties and forties and probably needed to sit down to relax a couple of times each day. She left a bottle of vitamins for Madame to begin taking and then let us know that she would check with the doctor to see if the hospital stay needed to be extended.

Philippe's relief at seeing his mother sitting up and smiling was immediately evident.

He hugged her gently and kissed her cheek.

"Maman, I was worried about you. How do you feel today?"

"I am doing well, Philippe, I am sorry to have caused you such concern."

"That is all she has been saying all morning, Philippe, how sorry she is that we were worried about her. Oh, yes, and how embarrassed she is that she fainted in the bakery."

"Dearest Maman. That is so like you. I am just so pleased that you are doing well. But from today on, you must promise that you will take better care of yourself."

With her hand over her heart, Madame reassured her son that she would rest more and work less.

Her doctor looked in for a moment to report that there was nothing seriously wrong with her and that we would be allowed to take her home. Madame was dismayed as Phillipe insisted, she go right to bed when we arrived back at the boulangerie. He insisted that she delay opening the bakery until the weekend. He proved to be more stubborn than her and soon she was having the cup of broth that I made. Shortly afterwards she was resting comfortably.

Before leaving for work that afternoon, Philippe spoke to me in a soft voice.

"I want to see you soon, Natalie. I need to know if you have given any more thought to my proposal. I think of you every day and wonder if you have given me any further consideration. Perhaps, my mother's illness has presented a turning point in all our lives. At least it is an opportunity for discussion. I will be in touch with you soon."

I made up my mind that I would be up earlier than usual once the baking resumed on Saturday. I decided it would be a good idea to help to Madame Fournier during her early morning hours in the kitchen.

Though I was aware that the years were passing by for us all, I had not considered that Madame could no longer keep up the long hours and busy pace of a bakery owner. I was indebted to this woman who had sustained me all my life. I believed that I was now being called upon to pay a long overdue obligation. But as the early hours dawned on Saturday and while I was still wrapping an apron around my waist, I could hear the pans clattering in the kitchen. As I descended the stairs, I became aware of Madame's voice as she hummed a tune while needing the first batch of dough. I smiled. There was just no way to make her slow down.

I made a habit of this new pre-dawn ritual and learned more every day of the techniques and small touches that separated a professional baker from someone who only knew how to make a loaf of bread.

I learned the methods, timing and pinpoint accuracy of each recipe. She taught me that timing was everything to a baker. One could not forget when to check on a bowl of risen dough. She kept so many things in her head each morning and somehow knew exactly when the oven should be opened to reveal the crusty loaves, and how many layers of pastry and butter she had gently rolled out for her delectable croissants.

If I had to write it all down, the instructions would have filled volumes. Of course, Madame would not have tolerated that even if I had tried. Her years of experience translated to secrets she would only share with me.

I gave a lot of thought to Philippe's words as we worked in the kitchen.

I had always thought of Madame Fournier as my second mother and it would not be a stretch of the imagination for her to become my mother-in-law, should I marry Philippe.

My biggest problem was grappling with the idea of being married to anyone. I did not see myself in the role of a wife and doubted that I would be particularly good at it. I believe I was also petrified at the idea of becoming a mother. That role was something I felt totally unprepared for. I felt somewhat motherly toward Celeste as her au pair. I delighted in everything she did and took a certain amount of pride in being the person who tutored her during her formative years. But I knew during the entire time that I lived with the Marshands that that her parents had the final responsibility for her. That responsibility scared me to death.

Quarante-deux

An Invitation

*I*T seemed that while I was thinking of the Marshand family, they were also thinking of me. At least to the extent that my name was included on an invitation list. A courier appeared at the bakery with an engraved invitation delivered to me on behalf of Madame Marshand.

My presence was requested at a celebration for Celeste's sixteenth birthday. Madame Marshand wrote that it would be a small affair at their home on Saturday next. She added that the party would be attended by several of Celeste's friends and, of course, Jules.

How could I say no? I could not let Celeste down, but I wondered how I would be able to face Jules?

I did not have much time to ponder the dilemma as the party was only a few days away. I responded that I would attend. With her usual good taste and sense of decorum, Madame Marshand had turned the sitting room into a lovely and feminine space. Several small tables were covered with lace doilies and trays of inviting treats. Soft, colorful cushions were placed on the settees. Chairs were arranged around the room covered in matching fabric with pink grosgrain ribbons tied in pretty bows that fell elegantly to the side. A large punch bowl was displayed on the sideboard surrounded by glass cups and a silver ladle.

As I entered, Celeste greeted me warmly. Arm-in-arm she escorted me toward her waiting guests, introducing me to her friends as her dear au pair, whom she thought of more as her sister. I was deeply touched by this introduction.

Madame Marshand beamed as she looked at her daughter. It was obvious that she was proud of her attractive appearance. Madame mentioned several times during the afternoon that both she and Celeste were thrilled that I was able to accept their invitation. For my part, I found myself on edge as I anticipated the arrival of Celeste's uncle.

Thankfully, the guests were a lively source of conversation and the hours passed quickly.

It was obvious that Celeste was comfortable in this type of social setting. After years of training as a well-mannered young lady it was clear that she would fit well into the elite circle of Parisian society that now welcomed her mother.

Cook appeared to a round of applause as she presented a lovely, tiered cake on a rolling cart. She had fashioned pink bows out of frosting that delicately draped over the side of each layer artfully matching the decor of the room.

I was somewhat relieved at that moment, as I assumed that this might indicate an impending end to the party. Perhaps I might be able to depart gracefully before Jules made an appearance.

Madame served me a fresh cup of punch with my cake and commented that she could not imagine what had prevented her brother-in-law from attending the celebration. I merely nodded in reply and proceeded to expedite my own departure by eating a couple of bites of the cake.

I bid a good afternoon to several of the guests and kissed Celeste on her cheek, as I extended one more birthday wish to her.

It would be several days before I knew why Jules had been absent at Celeste's birthday party. I was glad that we did not know then.

Quarante-trois

Delusions

I worried what Jules might be up now that he had been made aware of my suspicions.

Had he perhaps entertained the thought that I would go to Madame Marshand to reveal the entire secret of her husband's affair? Or, worse, since he seemed to be capable of just about anything to preserve the Marshand name, and more importantly the Marshand fortune, I wondered if I was in danger of becoming a victim of his vile impetuousness.

It was amazing that I could get anything done during those days, worried as I was about Jules added to my constant concern for the safety of my father. My dear father, who had become the feared and ostracized Eiffel Spirit.

The only relief I had from all this stress was that the disturbances at the Park had come to halt of late. I suppose that I should have taken this as a good sign. But, instead, I worried that it was just the calm before the storm. What evil plans might the Masked One be making while the local citizens basked in a false sense of security?

The police protection that had been promised in the area of the Park had dwindled as peace prevailed. Was I the only person in Paris who still thought something terrible could happen at the Tower? Or was I the only one who carried this worry with her every day because it was my father, the Spirit of the Eiffel, who spent every long night and each day keeping an eye on his arch enemy?

I needed to see him. I had to have the reassurance that he was all right, despite the danger an encounter might present. When I was sure that Madame Fournier had settled down for the night, I removed her large key ring from the hook on the wall. After unlocking the door, I stood still and listened to see if I might have disturbed her.

Looking across at the park, I was tempted for a moment to abandon the plan altogether. I was not sure that I had the courage to go forward and risk the chance of encountering the evil force who inhabited the iconic structure.

The night was especially still, as if the entire city were holding its breath in anticipation.

My hope was that my father would be aware of my presence in the park and that he would approach me. Instead, my worst fears were realized as I heard a voice behind me in the dark.

It was a deep almost guttural sound, and I knew at once who it was.

"Ah, you are finally within my grasp."

I turned to face him, but as the moon darted behind the clouds, it was too dark to make out his features.

"What is it you want from me?"

"Justice. You ignorant girl. I want justice for what your mother did to me."

"What good will that do? You can't change the past."

"That may be true, but if I do away with you, I will eliminate all that she left behind."

Suddenly, the clouds parted, and I could see him clearly. And, more importantly, he could see me.

I heard him gasp.

"Claire. Claire." He was calling me by my mother's name. "My God, it is you."

He dropped to his knees and reached out a hand to me. For that moment, his entire demeanor took on a gentleness that was so foreign to him that he did not know what to say.

I swear that he honestly thought he had gone back in time and that he was in the presence of the young girl he had once loved and hoped to win at any price.

Out of the corner of my eye, I spied a figure approaching with lightning speed.

"You will not harm a hair on her head." He said. He held a knife in his upraised hand. I saw the glint of metal in the moonlight as he drew near.

The slight figure of the man that I knew to be my father was soon at my side. As we both turned to where the Masked One had been kneeling, we were aware that he had slipped into the shadows and disappeared.

He put his arms around me, assuring himself that I was all right.

Then, he stood back and studied my countenance.

"My enemy is growing old and less discerning about what is real and what is imagined. But, in this he is correct. You have become the image of your beautiful mother, and this puts you in even more danger than when you were I child.

I thought for sure this was the day he would fulfill his evil promise and that he would deal you a fatal blow."

"Father, I am sorry that I have caused you so much worry, but I came to the park tonight to reassure myself that you were still alive. My worry for your safety is ongoing and never ending."

Dearest, you must not put yourself at risk like that again, simply to ease your mind. It would make me incredibly happy if you would promise to stay away from the park completely. I would be even happier if you could move far from Paris altogether.

"Not unless you come with me, because I could never stop being concerned for your welfare."

"You know that is not possible. I must prevent the Masked One from fulfilling his evil plans. He will keep finding random surrogates on which to vent his unrequited love. He has no conscience and feels no guilt for ruining the lives of innocent victims in his unbridled wrath."

"Well, then I will avoid the park completely. But you must agree to send me word occasionally so that I know you are well."

"We both have a promise to keep then, Mon Ami. I believe we can do that."

I reached out to him for one more gentle hug. And then he was gone.

Quarante-quarte

Karma

 $\mathcal{F}$OR the next several weeks, I settled into a routine with Madame Fournier, helping her at the bakery with renewed energy. She was moving slower and it seemed that normal activities were becoming more difficult for her. Moreover, I was becoming concerned about something I considered as more significant, and which I found alarming.

I began to notice that she occasionally had lapses in memory that came as a complete surprise to me, and for which she was left wondering what was happening. Her usual banter with our regular customers was becoming less enthusiastic.

Madame Dubose came to our shop every Monday and Wednesday for a baguette, quite often holding the hand of her small son, Jacque.

Last week, Madame Fournier selected a cookie from the display case to present to the child. As she handed it to him, it was obvious that she had forgotten his name. She was embarrassed and for a moment, his mother reacted with surprise. I went to Madame Fournier's side and concluded Madame Dubose's purchase as I engaged her in a lively conversation about the weather.

I observed Madame Fournier out of the corner of my eye and saw her dismay at her lapse of recollection.

That night as I lay in bed pondering Philippe's proposal, and his innocent hopes for our future, I knew that I needed to inform him of the latest development where his mother was concerned.

He worried about his mother's dedication to the bakery and voiced his worry more than once. He wanted to take care of her now that she was getting older. I was trying to picture the three of us living together in a house outside of the City. I cared for Madame Fournier and would not consider it a burden to help take care of her.

Moving outside of the city would fulfill my promise to my father as well. Philippe was all I could ask for in a husband. I know that he loved me and that he was sincere in his plan to care for both his mother and me. I just did not know if I loved him with as much emotion as he deserved in a wife. Contemplating the proposal and this big change that my life would have to take was somewhat overwhelming.

But these concerns for my welfare were soon to take a back seat to the events that were about to unfold with the other family I was attached to and had become a part of.

Bernard arrived in the morning at the bakery with a note from Celeste. She asked that I come to see her and her mother as soon as I was able to get away. She asked that I tell Bernard when that might be, so they could send a carriage. I wanted to oblige Celeste's request as soon as I could, as there seemed to be an implied urgency to her message.

I asked Madame Fournier if she felt I she could handle things alone for a couple of hours and proceeded to accompany Bernard back to the Marshand's house.

Celeste ran into my arms as soon as I crossed the threshold.

"My mother will be so relieved that you are here." She said. "She has been worried about Jules these last few weeks and now there is a new development that she cannot handle on her own. I am not sure of the details. Maman asked that I send for you."

I waited in the study for Madame. She was holding onto her daughter's arm she entered the room and I rose from the settee to greet her. She looked rather pale and disheveled.

"Please be seated," She said. "This is the most unusual occurrence, and I don't know how to handle it."

She looked at her daughter as she continued. "At first, I was hesitant to tell Celeste what was happening, for fear she was too young to be exposed to this mystery concerning her Uncle Jules. But I realize that as a member of the family, she must be aware of the facts as I know them. It would be wrong to try to protect her from something which may be significant. I appreciate your prompt response, Mademoiselle Natalie, and will now bring you and my daughter into my confidence."

At this point, I was curious, as well as deeply concerned. I was certain that Jules was involved in the death of Monsieur Marshand's lover, but I had hoped that Madame and her daughter would never find out about Jeanette or about what was done to silence her. I was anxious that Madame may have discovered something, so I was quite on edge.

"Although you are not a blood relative of the family, Mademoiselle, I felt that I had to include you in this discussion. Celeste certainly considers you more than a hired member of the household staff.

"Jules has been missing for over a month now. We have not heard from him and he has not had contact with anyone in our circle of society. This is most unusual. I didn't know what to do, so I contacted the police to report his disappearance. One of the things they do in this type of case is to circulate a description among other police departments to compare the missing person to any unidentified bodies that have been discovered from recent accidents or crimes."

Once again, she looked at Celeste. It was hard for her to discuss details or mention such possibilities in front of her daughter. I felt her discomfort, as she proceeded. She cleared her throat and continued.

"Someone meeting Jules' description was among the passengers killed in a recent carriage accident in Arles. There were personal effects found on the body which are being forwarded to the local police department for us to inspect. Quite frankly, I don't think I can go to the police station alone and hoped I might ask you to accompany me."

"Of course, Madame. I will go with you. When do you expect the items to be available?"

"I was told to come in the first of next week. I hoped you could meet me there Monday morning."

"I'll be there Madame. In the meanwhile, I will be praying that the objects do not belong to Jules."

On the way back to the bakery, the developments played over in my mind. What if Jules were dead? What if he took the truth of Jeannette's violent death to his grave? Would the potential demise of Jules diminish my worries that Madame and Celeste would one day find out about Monsieur's infidelity?

I wanted Monday to come faster, so all of this could be in the past. I felt guilty as I realized I would welcome the end of the Jeannette dilemma even if it meant that Jules had been killed. It was not the way I had hoped he would pay for his crime, but if he were capable of murder, I no longer wanted him to be any part of my life or that of the remaining members of the Marshand family.

I could not bring myself to tell Madame Fournier that I was headed to the police station. I had already decided I would not tell her about the current drama with the Marshands.

I left on the pretext of shopping for shoes and arrived at the police station promptly at nine am. Madame was waiting on a bench in the hallway, impeccably dressed as always. She smiled and stood up when she saw me.

"I can't tell you how grateful I am that you came." She said.

"Of course." I replied. "Shall we take care of this right away?" I asked, as I led her to the inside office door.

The attending officer was truly kind to us and showed us to a small anteroom, while he went to gather the items for inspection. When he returned, he spread the few possessions on the table in front of us. There was a key chain, several sizes of currency, a shorthand-written note that appeared to be a shopping list and a tie clasp.

Madame inhaled sharply as she picked up the tie clasp and held it in her hand.

"This was my husband's." She said. "Jules asked if he could have it when Pierre died."

The police officer spoke up. "I'm so sorry, Madame. With the description you gave of your brother-in-law and now the positive identification of this piece of evidence, I am almost certain that the victim in the carriage accident was in fact your brother-in-law."

He looked down then and was silent for a moment.

"Let me give you a few moments alone with your friend. Perhaps then we can talk about what you might like to do about funeral arrangements for Monsieur Marshand."

I rested my hand on hers and offered her my handkerchief as the tears fell from her eyes.

"You have my deepest condolences, Madame. I know you were hoping that Jules was not the victim and that he was still alive and safe somewhere."

We sat there for several minutes while Madame composed herself.

When the officer rejoined us, she told him that she would take care of the funeral arrangements. She said that her butler would arrive at the station within the next few days to handle transporting the body so that it could be prepared for burial in the family plot.

She appeared to be in shock, although she was still handling herself with composure. After what she had been through with her husband's passing, I was sure she was familiar with what needed to be done regarding the arrangements for her brother-in-law.

It was a difficult few minute that were spent with Celeste upon our return to their house. The girl was quite upset about her Uncle's death. He was someone important to her, even more so after she lost her father. Although I hated to see her suffer, I alone was aware that coping with Jules' death might in fact be easier than finding out he was a murderer and that he had killed to hide his brother's affair.

Quarante-cinq

At Ease

I spent a restless night after dealing with the events of that day. The chapter of my life that included Jules from the time I met him, the unwanted advances; the family meals we shared; the court appearances; and more recently the secrets about Jeannette capped by my suspicions of his criminal behavior, were finally in the past.

My mind was free to focus strictly on what might be happening a short distance away at the Eiffel Tower. Those worries kept me awake until right before the sun came up.

Thankfully, it was a relatively quiet day in the bakery as well the surrounding area. I appreciated the calmness after all that had been happening lately. Madame Fournier was in the process of turning around the open sign in the window that evening when we were both amazed to see Philippe standing at the door.

"I should have told you ahead of time Mere, but I thought you would enjoy a surprise."

"My dear son, I am always happy to see you."

"Good evening Natalie." He said as he turned toward me. "You are as lovely as ever."

"It is so nice to see you Philippe. I'm not sure I feel very lovely after a day here at the bakery, wearing an apron covered with crumbs and flour."

"Well, I believe I am in the company of the loveliest women in Paris, and I look forward to a delightful evening with you both."

"I'll take the compliments for us both." Madame said, as she took her son by the hand. She led him toward the kitchen, and I followed behind.

"I can prepare a meal for the three of us. First, let us open a bottle of wine to share." Madame said, enthusiastically.

"I was going to suggest a restaurant meal, Mere, but honestly I eat out all the time and would welcome sitting down to something home cooked."

"I will go change then and be down to help in the kitchen shortly." I said.

What was about to be just an ordinary evening sitting by the fire with a book, had become something I was looking forward to. Madame and I put a quite simple meal together of broiled fish and rice. Philippe poured the wine and put the plates on the table, cheerfully entertaining us with some of the gossip about the people he worked with.

"One would not suspect an architectural office to be a place of drama, ladies, but you would not believe some of the things that take place. My boss was recently accused of taking advantage of the receptionist. The gossip reached a fever pitch, until someone disclosed that the girl had made similar accusations at her former place of employment and was in the habit of coercing money in this way."

During our meal, we heard about the havoc one of the young apprentices caused by failing to wear a tie to a meeting with some important clients. And there was another time that one of the firm's executives fired a secretary on the spot because she had kicked off her shoes while sitting at her desk.

Philippe enjoyed telling us these stories and seemed to take some pride in bringing tales of big city happenings to our small table in the back room of the shop.

"The main reason I wanted to see you both, was to announce my recent promotion to partner in the firm. They are very happy with my work and I am to be financially rewarded with a very nice bonus."

"That is wonderful news." Madame exclaimed.

I poured more wine and raised my glass in a toast.

"To your success, Philippe. I am so happy for you."

"I will be looking for a house of my own soon, and will begin a new phase of my life, now that I feel accomplished."

"That is wonderful news, son."

We cleared the table and cleaned up the kitchen in record time, thanks to the extra pair of hands.

Madame announced that she was tired and would-be turning in. She invited her son to stay overnight.

"The extra cot is not very comfortable Philippe, but it would be so nice to have you join us for breakfast in the morning."

I was surprised when he accepted the invitation. He asked if I might stay up a while longer after his mother went to bed.

I was happy to have some time alone with Philippe and welcomed the opportunity to speak with him about Madame's memory lapses and other signs of aging that I had noticed in her. More than once it seemed she struggled to regain her balance after reaching the upper pantry shelves.

As we settled on the small settee in Madame's living area, I mentioned that I had been wanting to tell him about my causes of concern for Madame Fournier.

"I don't think it is anything serious." I began. "But sometimes she seems to draw a blank. She becomes confused when this happens, as if she had left the room for a moment or two. I believe it would embarrass her to bring this up in her presence. I believe that she would probably consider this as a sign of getting older, something she would not want us to notice. I care for your mother deeply, Philippe and I wanted you to know what was happening because I am aware that she means the world to you."

"I'm glad you told me, Natalie. I will have to give some thought as to the proper way to handle this, without implying that I think she is aging rapidly. You are correct, this will have to be done gently.

I hoped I might have a minute with you tonight to ask if you have been giving any thought to marrying me. I believe that you and I would be very happy together and if my mother were living with us, we could both take care of her as she ages."

"I have considered your proposal. I think about it all the time Philippe. As you know, I have felt that I need to be near my father to be sure that he is not in danger. However, even he has pleaded with me to leave the city. He is worried that I need to remove the threat to my life that exists because of my proximity to the Tower."

"Then, marrying me would be the answer to everyone's prayers. I do love you, Natalie. I have for a long time. I will take good care of you and I will be a very caring husband."

"I am sure of that Philippe. Perhaps I have been over thinking this too much, and not giving myself a chance to be happy. I have no doubts that you would be good to me."

"Then, you are saying yes?"

"Yes. I accept your proposal Philippe. I will be your wife."

He rose and took my hands in his. I stood up and let him wrap me in an embrace. We kissed and caressed each other for several minutes while time seemed to stand still. I had made a commitment to this man who loved me; a lifelong commitment and I knew it was the right thing to do.

At breakfast we told Madame Fournier of our plans to marry. I had never seen her so happy. It was as if we had given her the best gift she had ever received. She looked back and forth at each of us as tears welled up in her eyes.

"The two people that I love the most will be together always." She said. "Nothing could make me happier."

"And we will take care of you, Mere, we will be a family together, my dearest mother."

"You know how much you have always meant to me." I added. "It will be my pleasure to have you in our home."

"I know this will mean an end to the bakery." Madame said. "And I must express that this will be a sad event for me. I have always enjoyed feeling useful, and I have treasured the company of my customers, some of whom are like family to me. It will take me a while to accustom myself to a change of this size."

"It will not be happening overnight." Philippe reassured her. "You will have time to get used to the idea, and perhaps work less hours each day as we get closer to our move. You need not be concerned that there is an urgency to closing the bakery and changing your entire way of living.

I promise that Natalie and I will be with you to support your needs as the transition takes place."

I saw the emotion in Madame's expression and in Philippe's loving concern for his mother. I knew we would surmount whatever situation arose as we moved forward with our lives. I wanted to reassure Madame that she would always be surrounded by love and that I was as devoted to her as her son was.

"Madame, please remember that we will be able to come back to visit the neighborhood often. I will be sure that you return to see your neighbors and friends whenever you want to. I will be happy to escort you on those visits, since your customers have become my friends as well over the years."

She hugged Philippe and I before returning to the kitchen to resume baking. I imagine that many thoughts must be occupying her mind as she pictured the drastic changes, we would all be facing. I knew that I would have to keep reassuring her that she would be cared for and loved and that the future would hold many happy days.

Now, I had to ponder what I must do about my father. I could not leave the city or marry Philippe without letting him know and yet I was aware that he did not want an encounter near the Tower that might put me in danger.

I decided that I could wait for a time before trying to arrange such a meeting. Philippe had already said, nothing was going to happen overnight. I decided to relax about the impending events and take a break from worrying for a while. At least that was my intention.

I was unaware that my vacation from worries would only last for a fortnight.

Quarante-six

Surprise

I sat down on a lovely, though somewhat chilly afternoon and penned a note to Celeste. I was sure that she would want to hear about my engagement and would be happy to know that I was in love and about to begin a new life. I wrote that I would apprise her of the wedding plans once they were made and would be thrilled to have her and her mother attend the ceremony. When I thought about family, they were the two people besides Madame Fournier, my father, and Philippe who I considered closest to me in the world.

I expected to receive a reply to my note after a few days, what I did not expect was a visit from the young woman with whom I had just shared my dreams for the future by my written correspondence.

Standing in the doorway of the bakery, Celeste looked like a younger version of her mother. She was becoming more and more of a beauty as time went by. I sprang from behind the counter to greet her at the door with a hug.

"My dearest, Natalie." She began. "I received your announcement and had to come in person to offer you my congratulations. I am so happy for you, and so sad for myself, if this will mean that you will be leaving Paris."

"It's true that Philippe and I will be making our home outside of the city, Celeste, but you must realize that I will still come to see you. I hope that you will be able to visit us as well, I simply cannot imagine a future where you and I drift apart."

"That is so reassuring to me. I told my mother that I don't want to be an intrusion on the life you are planning when you are married, but that I couldn't bear to think you would leave us behind without a thought."

"That will never happen. Come and have a cup of tea with me, and let us sit down for a visit, shall we?"

As we sat there in the bakery, I listened as Celeste described her busy social life and her own plans to travel during the upcoming summer break from school. As she spoke, I pictured the child I had so lovingly cared for and delighted in. So many precious memories drifted by me as I looked in her eyes. I was not just her au pair, but more like a big sister to this girl-woman and the connection we shared was something I never wanted to part with.

In spite of her somewhat girlish method of conversing, there seemed to be a seriousness to her demeanor that I had never before observed. During a moment of silence, I noticed her staring into the distance with a forlorn look on her face. I waited to see if she would resume her dialog.

"Mademoiselle." She said. "I must admit that I need to speak with you regarding another aspect of my life which I cannot confide to anyone else."

I leaned closer to her and reached my hand across the table.

As she lay her own hand on top of mine, she went on.

"There is a young man whom I have become fond of. He is in our social circle and he is very handsome."

"That sounds wonderful, my dear. I just cannot imagine why telling me this is so difficult, or why thinking about this young man seems to make you so sad. Is he in love with someone else, perhaps?"

"I simply don't know if I should disclose the details of this relationship to you. Or maybe I may have made a mistake coming here today."

"Give me a chance, Celeste. You know how much I care for you and have for so many years, tell me what's on your mind and at least afford me the opportunity to help you in some way."

"His name is Andre, and he is the brother of my best friend, Charlotte. Andre is four years older than me, but because we have known Charlotte's family for quite a while, mother allowed Andre to accompany me to a school dance last year. After that, he made sure that his sister included him in our plans to go to the theater or dinner quite often."

"It sounds as though he was interested in getting to know you better."

"If that was all that happened, it would be fine, but I was beginning to like him, perhaps more than a girl my age should have. I have never really been instructed in the ways of the world, Mademoiselle Natalie. I was not prepared for the type of affection that Andre soon began to shower on me. At the theater, he managed to sit next to me, and to take my hand in his when the lights were dimmed. I admit it made me happy, in fact I blushed when this first occurred. But I did not understand the new feelings that Andre awoke in me."

"Did you discuss any of these feelings, or these occasions with your mother?"

"Oh, no. I could never have done that, fearing that she would not permit me to be in any situation where the young man might be present."

"So, what of these occasions? I must say, Celeste dear that holding a young man's hand is not reproachable at all and is rather an innocent way to impart one's feelings of attraction."

"If only that was the extent of the relationship. My mother would think me too young for a romance of any kind, so when Andre suggested that we might be alone a time or two, I simply did not tell her. Instead, I employed Charlotte to help her brother and I plan clandestine meetings. At first, we met in the park. We spent hours on a bench just talking and holding hands.

Later he invited me for coffee or dinner in a secluded cafe. Charlotte would arrange to meet us afterward and walk me home, so that mother was never suspicious."

"Celeste, I am quite surprised at your behavior, but nonetheless, you are a young girl who has fallen for a young man, and you have apparently been letting your feelings guide your actions."

"All of that is true, my dear Mademoiselle. If only we had been content to just hold hands, I would not be here today pouring my heart out to you."

I could tell that Celeste was about to divulge more of this story than I might have desired to hear, but I felt as though I was obliged to listen. I might be the only person who possibly would.

"There was a night several months ago when Andre and I met in the park as we had before. Only this time, he told me we were going for a walk. A few blocks away, he entered a doorway and told me to follow him up a narrow stairway. After turning key in a lock, he entered a small apartment. Taking my hand in his, he led the way. The rooms were sparsely furnished and there was no one home. Andre told me the place belonged to a friend of his who had just begun classes at the University and who would be away for a while."

"So, you were there alone in this apartment?"

"Yes, and immediately I felt as though we should not be there without anyone else present. But, at the same time, there was a certain thrill that accompanied the moment and when Andre bent to kiss me, I did not resist. Soon, we were in each other's arms, and passion took over."

"I don't know if I am prepared to hear the rest of your story, Celeste. Perhaps, I should make another pot of tea, and give us both a moment to take a breath."

I needed the time to gather my thoughts and to tell myself not to overreact no matter what Celeste told me. After all, she was not a little girl anymore and her problems were not those of a child.

I calmed myself with an interior dialog that said I needed to be the adult in this situation. Celeste had come to me in a spirit of trust. She certainly did not want me to fall apart at the revelation she was putting before me, and she expected me to react in a mature fashion to whatever plea for help she was going to utter.

By the time I rejoined her at the table, I was quite composed. Holding the pot of freshly brewed tea, I reached for her cup and filled it with the sweet-smelling potion. Then, I sat back and nodded toward her indicating that she should go on.

"Mademoiselle, I know you will be disappointed in me for what I am about to say, but you are simply the only person I can confide in. I have always known since I was a small child how important my welfare is to you."

I remained silent but reached out toward her and gently laid my fingers on her hand, as a token of reassurance.

"Consumed as I was with feelings I had never felt before, I allowed that young man to take liberties with me that I am ashamed to say led to an act that should only be performed by those tied together in wedlock."

She looked up at that point, waiting I suppose for me to gasp or to become red in the face, or whatever reaction she anticipated her confessor to assume. I maintained a stoic composure and simply stroked her fingers gently, compassionately feeling the shame the girl was suffering.

"Mademoiselle, Natalie, are you terribly upset with me?"

"I don't believe there is any way that I can be more upset with you than you are with yourself, dear one. I will not add to your misery by bathing in my own disappointment or judgment. A moment of passion is one in which many things can happen. In fact, passion can be used in court of law as a defensive plea, that is how strong our emotions can be when they take over.

I believe there are times when a person can do things that would shock them in the light of day, and I believe it happens more often than we would care to admit."

"I could never confide in Maman about this. I would not even be able to find the words and I'm afraid that when she knows, she may never speak to me again."

"Perhaps you don't need to share the experience with her until much later, dearest."

"Would that be an option, my dear au pair. If only my shame were the only consequence of those few moments of passionate and reckless abandon."

"There is more?"

"I am afraid to say this out loud, but I cannot plea for your help without unveiling the rest of the story."

She paused here and spent a moment staring down into her lap. For a moment she appeared to be almost asleep, and it brought to mind that I was looking at the same face that used to look so innocent as she slept peacefully on her pillow during her childhood naps.

Finally, a tear escaped onto her cheek and she slowly lifted her head to look me in the eyes.

"There is a child." She said, and no more words could find their way to her lips.

She simply let loose a torrent of tears and slumped over the table, toppling the fragile teacup to the floor. Even as it shattered, she did not react, so deep was she in her reverie.

"My darling, Celeste." I said as my own tears began to gather behind my eyes. I was finding it difficult to maintain that hard won composure, for now I was being asked to help this girl that I cared for so deeply to come to grips with a challenge that was overwhelming to us both.

I rose and put my arms around her as she sat sobbing.

Several moments passed before she began to take in her surroundings, looking first at the broken china and the tea that was coating the floor beneath us.

"That is of no consequence." I said, pointing to the broken cup. "Come with me dearest, you must lie down for a short while, while I consider your dilemma and what advice is best to give you."

I led her upstairs to my meek chambers and pulled back the old duvet.

"Here, my sweetest." I said to her. "I will sit right here by you as you rest for a short time. Try to calm yourself and sleep, it will not do you or the babe any good, if you are overly distressed."

As I stroked her hair, I said. "You are not alone, my precious Celeste. I will be here in your need and we will work this out together." I added, "Everything will be all right."

Even though I spoke those words, I did not believe them.

Soon her breathing slowed down as I watched her relax.

"I don't know how to face my mother." She whispered as she drifted off.

"You will not have to face her alone, Celeste. I will be right by your side."

I sat there looking at her beautiful face and wondering how we had come to this moment. The girl was such an intricate part of my life. The love I felt for her was more than as her former au pair. I knew then that even if it meant putting my own plans aside for a while it would just have to be. I could not let her down now when she needed me the most. Over the years I had protected her and her mother from the truth about her father's affair.

I had also kept the deceit and duplicity of her uncle to myself, so that neither she nor her mother had to suffer the effects emotionally or socially of having a liar and an assumed murderer in their family.

Being pregnant out of wedlock was a scar on a young girl's reputation that would incur all kinds of implications that she and her family would never get over. My mind was spinning trying to come up with solutions to the dilemma that Celeste was facing.

I wanted to have a well thought out plan to present to Madame Marshand before Celeste and I approached her with the situation. I was so deep in thought I barely heard the knock on my apartment door.

Philippe was standing in the doorway with the most beautiful bouquet of tulips I had ever seen

"A surprise for my bride." He said with a grin that bared every tooth in his head.

"Shhhh." I replied as I gently closed the door behind me and stepped into the hall.

"Who is that?" He asked as caught a glimpse of the form on my cot.

"It's Celeste, Phillipe. She is not feeling well at the moment, so I encouraged her to rest a while. I'll order a carriage for her when she is ready to go home."

"Oh, I'm sorry that she is unwell." He said. "It has taken some of the enthusiasm out of the surprise I had for you."

"I am the one who is sorry, dearest Philippe. The flowers are gorgeous, and you are such a thoughtful fiancé, thank you so much."

"Can we go downstairs to put them in some water?" He asked.

"Of course, dear. Perhaps you can stay for some tea, while you are here."

"I would love a few minutes with my beautiful intended. I will have to go back to the office later, but they can miss me for an hour or so."

It was nice to have some time with this man who obviously loved sharing his time with me.

Philippe helped to gather the shards of china from the floor in the shop and wipe the area down. I placed the lovely tulips in a vase and placed it on the table where we soon sat together.

After the stress of Celeste's predicament, I enjoyed Philippe's light banter over a cup of tea. He regaled me once again with stories of the current office politics. My favorite being the most recent tale about the firm's newest receptionist.

"She brought in the most amazing cookies earlier this week. It turns out that Louise could put my mother to a baking challenge if she wanted to. Anyway, she stopped by my desk with a napkin folded around two of the treats and batted her eyelashes at me as she asked if I would like something sweet."

"Did you take the cookies from her?"

"As it turns out, I was pursuing the architectural plans laid out on my drawing board. I hardly looked up when she entered. When she asked if I wanted something sweet, I said that I already had something sweet, my fiancé. When I did look up, I saw her put the cookies on my desk and turn toward the door looking very dejected."

"Oh my, Philippe, the poor girl probably has a crush on you. Most likely she will cry into her pillow tonight."

"I won't flatter myself by believing that my Cheri. But I was proud of myself for bragging about you without even intending to."

I heard Celeste's footsteps on the stairs and rose to greet her. Taking her hand, I led her to the table where Philippe was sitting.

"Celeste, I'm sure you remember meeting Philippe that night at the restaurant."

"Yes, of course." She replied.

"It is nice to see you again." Philippe said. "I hope you are feeling better now that you have had a rest."

She glanced at me out of the corner of her eye, but I said nothing.

"I will leave you ladies to enjoy the remainder of the afternoon." Philippe said as he rose from the table. "I must return to the office."

He kissed me lightly on the cheek and bowed toward Celeste before heading to the front of the bakery where he bade his mother goodbye. I poured some tea for Celeste and sat down by her.

"I will order a carriage when you are ready, dear. Then, I will accompany you to your house. We will ask your mother for an audience, so that we might speak quietly with her. I have given some thought as to the type of arrangements that might be made, henceforth. We will have to consider your mother's standing in society because this certainly will have an impact on her reaction when we speak with her today. I believe I may have thought of something that might work to everyone's benefit. But we will have to see if my suggestions are acceptable to her. For now, I believe that you and I should proceed as soon as we can. Your mother would be more devastated if she thought we had kept this news as a secret from her."

"Thank you, Natalie. I could never have handled this on my own. I believe I would faint halfway through the details when conversing with Maman. I know she will have a lot of questions, and right now, I have very few answers."

"You must not think of her as the enemy, Celeste. Your mother will be shocked, that is certain, but she will only want the best for you and the child. This kind of thing has happened before, and solutions can be found. I can say without the slightest fear of being wrong, that someone that your mother knows has experienced a similar situation."

If we were going to the Marshand house to speak with her mother, I had to bolster Celeste's emotional state. We could not have an audience with Madame, that began with sobbing and was punctuated with desperation. It was imperative that our approach be positive and that we face the situation with a formidable plan that would allow everyone to avoid shame and disgrace. I smiled at Celeste and rose from the table.

"We will work this out. Now, finish your tea while I order the carriage."

Quarante-sept

The Plan

I must admit that I was anxious about the upcoming discussion with Madame Marshand. I would willingly forego the experience except for the fact that poor Celeste was an emotional wreck and could not handle this by herself. I worried not just for her but for the child.

Based on rumors that I'd overheard spoken in the past, I was aware that this situation occurred more often than those in society might care to admit to.

I was shocked into the reality of this situation and I was glad that Celeste trusted me enough to confide in me. But, emotionally, I was most definitely in uncharted territory.

Looking back, I have no idea how I put a plan together so quickly. I also do not know how I summoned up the courage to face Madame Marshand in spite of the fact that Celeste needed me so desperately.

During the short carriage ride, I realized that my own sheltered life had never allowed a situation like this to take place before with any of my friends or acquaintances.

Bernard opened the door and took a quick inventory of our expressions when we arrived. Holding tightly to Celeste's arm, I whispered to him that he needed to advise Madame that we needed to speak with her as soon as she could be available. I said we would be happy to wait in the study for her to join us.

Of course, Cook was right at my elbow as we approached the sitting area. I asked that she please bring some tea for the three of us.

I sat close to Celeste on the settee and looked around the room.

Had I really sat here waiting for an employment interview when I was younger than Celeste was now? If only, I was able to recreate my own innocence and that of my dear Celeste from that day and move forward knowing what I knew now.

It was easy to conjure up all the feelings of that day. I believe the current encounter was even more nerve wracking than what I went through then, even though I was just barely in my teens. Several other of my experiences, flashed through my mind as my nervousness built up. I had visions of Monsieur Marshand and his charming brother. I recalled how Jules swept me off my feet the first time I saw him, with his good looks and winning smile.

I pictured the young Celeste peeking into the room while Monsieur was dictating to me, hoping to have a minute of her busy father's time. As I permitted my thoughts to wonder, I lost touch for a moment with the reality of the situation and relaxed a little, letting go of some of the anxiety that had been churning in my stomach.

Cook brought a tray for tea, and remarkably set up the entire tea service without making any disturbing sounds. I believe the palpable tension in the air, scared her into making a quick exit.

I looked up as Madame stood in the doorway, tense with anticipation of whatever news we were going to impart and wondering why there appeared to be a sense of urgency.

Apprehensively, she approached the settee.

To my surprise, Celeste spoke first. She seemed to have grown up in the few minutes that she had been kept waiting for her mother to appear. Suddenly she was empowered to speak as a woman.

I wondered if the responsibility of carrying a child had just weighed in with her. But whatever it was, she took command of the moment.

"Mother, I believe you should sit down for this conversation. In fact, I would appreciate that as a gesture of neutrality during this discussion."

Madame appeared shocked as her daughter addressed her with such authority and she immediately sat in the opposing armchair. I had a feeling she was holding her breath.

"Madame." I spoke up. "I am here only to support your daughter at this time, but she will do the talking, since this is a family matter, and it needs to be handled at least initially by the two of you."

I turned toward Celeste and my expression said, it is your turn, I am going to be silent now.

"Mother, perhaps you remember Andre, my dear friend, and Charlotte's older brother. As you know we have been seeing each other socially for several months now."

Madame nodded but remained silent.

"We have gotten closer as time has passed and enjoyed many wonderful experiences together. Theater, parties and dances to name a few."

I saw her begin to falter and I increased my grip on her hand. It seemed to give her strength as she continued her story.

"Maman, as you are aware, my experience with men has been very limited, always accompanied by chaperones and under the watchful care of either you or the parents of friends who were also in attendance at the soirees where Andre and I made an appearance."

Again, Madame nodded, but I could see that she was becoming paler as Celeste differed from the actual reason for this conversation. I had a feeling that she may have already discerned the outcome.

"There was one evening when Andre arranged for us to leave a party that we had attended and to be alone, unseen by all. It was marvelous. For the first time, I felt I was becoming a woman, free to have feelings for a man and desiring more than a peck on the cheek as a token of devotion."

As Celeste expanded, I was beginning to worry that Madame might faint and wondered where the nearest smelling salts were, if they were needed. Would Bernard be able to help if Madame passed out?

"It is wrong, and unacceptable in society, but Andre and I engaged in acts that are reserved for the boudoir of married couples. I won't say I did not consent, nor that I was not an eager participant. I was really quite thrilled at being part of something so adult and so full of passion."

Here she paused again to gather her strength.

Although Madame Marshand grew paler and more seemed to be holding her breath, she uttered not a sound.

"What we hoped would not happen that fateful night, did occur Maman. I am now carrying your grandchild and I am more distressed than I have ever been, not knowing what the future holds and how you will react to my predicament. I approached Mademoiselle Natalie for advice and support and here we are, facing you with this news that changes all of our lives."

One tear trickled down Celeste's cheek as she spoke, but to my surprise she assumed a stoic stance as she waited for her mother's response. Madame was doing her best to hold herself together, as well. She did not faint as I had suspected she would. But she was unable to speak.

I rang for Bernard and when he appeared, I requested that he bring some water for the ladies and myself.

We sat there for what seemed like hours in total silence. Each of us were lost in our own thoughts. When Bernard returned, he carried a tray containing a water pitcher and some glasses. There was a very slight tinkling sound as he gently put the tray on the side table. Celeste jumped at the sound.

I had sat on the same settee many times as a member of this household sipping tea and engaging in various conversations. I would have welcomed the reincarnation of any of those times. None carried more significance than this meeting of a mother and daughter paused at a critical crossroads that would change their lives forever.

Finally, I rose. I handed Celeste a glass of water, which she gratefully accepted.

Then, I approached the tea service and poured us each a cup of tea, handing the first cup to Madame. Silently, I wondered if she would be able to hold the cup and saucer without spilling the tea or causing the set to become a collection of broken pieces on the drawing room carpet. Celeste held her hand up as I approached her, indicating that she did not want any tea.

I took the cup and saucer back to my place next to where she sat.

I didn't really crave the brew, but I thought I could restore an air of normalcy to the occasion if I sat there sipping tea. I cleared my throat to break the stifling silence of the room. Madame was lost in a reverie and her blank stare gave no indication of what was going on inside her head. I had a feeling that Celeste was unable to speak because after telling her story, there was nothing else to be said.

"I have been thinking about this for the last couple of hours, Madame. I would appreciate it if you and Celeste might consider a proposition that I would like to offer for your consideration. It is one that I believe you might take consolation in." I said.

It seemed that my voice was louder than usual, but I believe that was because it was the only sound in the entire house. Madame turned her head toward me. Celeste sat up straighter in her chair.

I could feel the sense of anticipation from both women and I hoped that I could articulate my thoughts with a self-confidence that would make my idea feasible to them both.

I lowered my voice to a near whisper in an attempt to settle the nerves of a mother who was clearly in a state of shock. I was also reluctant to speak louder, as I was sure that Cook, and possibly Bernard had their ears pressed to the door.

"My dear Madame." I began. "If I may presume to take the position of one who has been an adopted member of the Marshand family for several years, I will put my suggestion before you. I am hopeful that you realize I have always cared about the welfare of each member of this household."

I let Madame contemplate my opening comment for a moment before resuming. When neither she nor Celeste spoke a word of rebuke, I took the next cautious step.

"I am certain that you know how much your daughter has meant to me since the moment I first met her. As a widow, I am aware that the full responsibility of any decision that is made on Celeste's behalf is up to you. I have a proposal that might prove useful for the time being. I don't believe that either you or Celeste needs to contemplate the child's future destiny at this time. However, since Celeste's condition will become more apparent in the coming months, I would like to suggest that she be removed from your home, thereby preventing any disapproving glances or idle gossip.

I realize that Mademoiselle Celeste has a reputation to protect in society Madame, and I see no reason to share any knowledge of her present condition with the ladies you meet with regularly.

My proposition is this. Madame's sister in Spain has a large house and can certainly offer shelter to Celeste during the next few months. By confiding in her, Madame you would have an ally who could offer protection to Celeste and spare the family from any disgrace.

Celeste has a favorable relationship with her Aunt and her cousins in Spain. I am sure it would be no problem for her to become part of their family for the next several months. After that, you can join your daughter during her confinement. You might even choose to be present for the birth. That decision does not need to be made right now."

Madame looked at me as if I had just burst into flames. I had the feeling that she was surprised that I had the ability to take hold of the situation and come up with a logical and acceptable plan. Immediately she radiated a look of relief and the color returned to her cheeks.

"One more thing, Madame. I offer myself as Celeste's companion during the trip and while she gets settled in your sister's home. It will be easy for me to get away. I will simply say that sometime in the country with my former charge would be a lovely vacation. I will add that I would enjoy a retreat of sorts before my own upcoming nuptials."

Celeste remained silent while I had been speaking. She neither seemed nervous nor relieved. Her face looked so much older than it had been mere months before and I was concerned about how her emotional state might be affecting her unborn child. I held my breath as the silence in the room became more stifling. I waited for reply from Madame and though it seemed that I waited for hours, she finally spoke up.

"All of this is overwhelming right now, Mademoiselle Natalie. I am grateful to you for your concern and for your offer of help as my daughter and I face this unexpected situation. However, I will need some time to ponder the consequences of Celeste's actions and to consider your proposal."

"Of course."

"For the time being, I believe my daughter needs some rest. I am also in a state of exhaustion from shattered nerves. Would you be willing to return here on Wednesday next? We can sit down together again and discuss what specific plans should be made."

Celeste's detached demeanor had not changed. She neither smiled nor frowned and was looking straight ahead as if there was a spirit there captivating her glance. I was concerned by her dark and silent mood and prayed that by getting some much-needed rest, this would pass.

"Of course." I replied. "I will go back home for the time being to give you a chance to think and so that you can speak with each other."

I arose as Madame rang for Bernard.

"Mademoiselle will be leaving now Bernard." She said. "Please call for a carriage and escort her when it arrives."

I approached Celeste and ran my hand across her arm in a gesture of comfort as I whispered, "It will be all right."

And then I turned to leave.

Although the situation was delicate, I had to provide the details to Philippe in case I was called upon to be away with Celeste for a period. Trusting in his discretion, I told him why I was going with her and the importance of protecting her reputation.

On the Wednesday morning of our scheduled meeting, I rose early in anxious anticipation. I helped in the kitchen but looking back, I would be unable to describe anything I accomplished since my mind was miles away. Should I send a courier with a message to Madame? Had she already taken some other action to solve Celeste's dilemma? The moments dragged as I pondered these questions.

My main concern was for Celeste. I hoped her mother would be a gentle protector and not a heartless judge of a youthful mistake. This could have happened to anyone. Celeste was naive and had given her heart to the wrong man, certainly not the first such occurrence in the history of Paris.

I wiped the counter in the bakery so many times that Madame Fournier put her hand on mine saying, "I believe it is clean enough now, dear."

I looked at her strangely as she interrupted my thoughts.

"Are you well?" She asked.

"Yes, of course." I replied.

"You were daydreaming, Natalie. I suppose that is something a young woman on the verge of marriage might do."

"Yes, I suppose so."

"Have you and Philippe decided on a date? He is so vague when I ask him these things, so I don't have any information to give my friends."

Her words faded away as I saw Bernard enter the shop. He did not approach the counter until all the customers left.

He looked at me and then glanced over at Madame Fournier.

"Hello Bernard, may I be of service?"

"Madame said that I should ask if you might come by her home this morning."

Acting as though this had not already been planned, I simply said that I would like that very much. I asked if he would wait briefly as I retrieved my hat and gloves. Madame Fournier told me to enjoy my visit and to convey her best wishes to Celeste.

I endured another carriage ride anxiously anticipating a meeting of questionable outcome.

Madame was alone in the drawing room. Once again, a tea service was set up.

Bernard closed the door quietly.

"Natalie, I want you to know I am most grateful to you for offering to help us during this . . . situation." She began.

I could tell, Madame Marshand was never going to specifically address her daughter's pregnancy. This simply was not done by women of society. Matters of what went on in a woman's body were too sacred to be spoken of aloud. She proceeded to skirt the issue by addressing the solution without mentioning the problem.

"I care for Celeste, Madame. I have felt like a big sister to her for most of her life, I want you to know that I will do whatever is in my power to ease the stress that you both are under."

She sipped her tea and sighed deeply. A conversation that might have been brief if it were between people who could be open and honest was instead slow and stinted. Most of the time, Madame stared into her lap as she spoke.

"You know, of course, how difficult the last several years have been for me, Natalie. My dear husband died right there in our bed as I lay next to him. I don't know how I survived the months that followed. I thought I would be in mourning forever."

Now, it should be noted, that I sat there thinking how fortunate Madame was that she was unaware of her husband's affair. I had protected her and Celeste during that trying time.

A voice inside me cried out to tell her now. It was difficult to watch the tears well up in her eyes. There was no possibility that I would let her know that she was shedding her tears for a philanderer who openly met his mistress on the courthouse steps.

"And, then of course, we lost our dear Jules so tragically in that terrible accident. I really thought my world had collapsed."

Again, I had to fight the demon inside of me who wanted to reveal the Jules she did not know. I wanted to tell her how he had made advances on me years ago, when I was young and impressionable. And even worse, I wanted to tell her how her precious brother-in-law was most likely responsible for the death of her husband's lover.

Instead, I said, "I understand your grief Madame, having shared those times with you and with our darling Celeste."

"Have you given any thought to my proposition. I believe we could travel to Spain as if we were just going on a trip, while you stay here and maintain your home and your social activities."

"You are a smart girl, Natalie. After giving the matter much thought, I believe your plan is a good one. By staying here in Paris, I will be able to give off the air that all is well in our household. Then, after a month or so, you can return to the bakery or whatever else your life consists of. Celeste can stay with my sister until after the, um. Until after the delivery. Then, we will arrange for an adoption."

"Have you discussed this with Celeste? Is she in favor of the trip to her aunt's? Has she agreed to putting the child up for adoption?"

"Celeste is my daughter." Madame said, her voice more forceful now. "She will do what I tell her is best for her, and for the child."

Gently, I placed my cup and saucer on the side table and rose from the chair.

"May I speak to her before I leave?"

"Celeste is sleeping right now, my dear. She needs all the rest she can get before you leave for the long and somewhat uncomfortable train ride."

"Of course." I said as I smoothed my skirt and moved the chair back into position.

"When do you think we should undertake the journey?"

"Certainly before anything shows." She said. "I mean as soon as possible. Would you be able to leave as early as next week?"

"Yes, Madame, that would be fine. I will make my excuses to Madame Fournier and prepare immediately for the trip. If you would be kind enough to send a message with Bernard a day ahead of the determined departure time, I will be ready."

She bit her tongue finding it difficult to thank me for my help. She still thought of me as a servant, I could tell, and one simply does not say a heartfelt thank you to the hired help.

"I just can't bear the thought that scandal could spread a blight over the name Marshand." She said.

It took all I could do, not to roll my eyes at hearing her words. She had no idea of the scandals that had been averted. She had been dodging lightning bolts for years, unaware of their presence.

But I was not there to extend my protection over Madame, or even the family name as much as for Celeste. Her entire future rested on my being able to conceal the secrets regarding the contemptible actions of both her father and her uncle.

"I will take my leave, Madame, if it is convenient for Bernard to arrange a carriage."

She rang for the butler and did not address any more dialog to me that afternoon.

After giving him his orders, she reluctantly rose in slight deference to me, as I exited the parlor. I assume that she probably had to go lie down then, being completely exhausted, not only by the emotional distress of Celeste's "situation" but also by the exertion it took to be more than just civil to me.

Quarante-huit

Transition

OUR train ride through the countryside was peaceful and a welcome relief from the dramatic events of the previous weeks. I brought a book for Celeste since I believed that without distractions, she would most likely stare out the window for hours dwelling on her future.

There were elegant appointments throughout the train cars serving as a constant reminder that this was one of the most exclusive trains that traveled from France across the border to Spain.

The dining car had an excellent menu. I used this as another opportunity to entertain Celeste by pointing out the interesting choices that were offered. Neither she nor I had ever tasted some of the regional fare. I managed to invoke her curiosity more than once, by suggesting that we try something new.

She was more than anxious to share a decadent dessert or two during the trip, so I made sure that she made these selections. I don't believe that Celeste consulted the price list on the menu. However, I came to the realization early on, that I would not be eating such gourmet food if I were paying for our expenses.

In the evening, we readied ourselves to spend the night in the luxury train car that Madame Marshand reserved for us. We could have comfortably added two or three more people to the space allotted. I was overly impressed with the accommodations, although it seemed that Celeste hardly noticed her opulent surroundings.

During our second day of travel, I produced a map, and described the areas of France and Spain that we would be observing from the window. I read about the local customs and seasonal activities of the populace and I kept my young friend entertained with this information as we took in the view. Although we were just passing through, with occasional station stops, I was able to spark her curiosity and keep her occupied.

I wondered as we discussed the landscape and the cultural heritage of the locals, if our fellow train passengers might have thought I was Celeste's tutor, accompanying her on a geography excursion. More than once, I caught a knowing glance or a nod from others who were seated nearby. They seemed to be agreeing with my comments and opinions, perhaps learning something they didn't know before.

None of that mattered, however, because I was successful at capturing Celeste's interest and that was my sole objective. The further we were from Paris, the more I could see her relax.

When we reached the countryside of Salamanca there were only two stops before ours. The journey had taken a bigger toll on me that I envisioned. I had given little concern to my own comfort while taking care of Celeste and now that the excursion was ending, I realized how tired I was.

A carriage awaited us upon our arrival at the train station. We were greeted by a uniformed driver, who tipped his hat at us respectfully as we exited the train. I could not imagine a royal reception that would have excelled in the courtesy that was extended to us. The ornate carriage reflected the wealth of the family who owned it. I had a feeling that Celeste's Spanish relatives would make the Marshand's social standing pale by comparison.

We entered the estate through large wrought iron gates, passing the carriage house and several other small buildings as we ascended the driveway. My first glimpse of the Calderon House left me breathless. I could not have been more impressed if we had arrived at the Royal Palace. It was becoming clearer to me why Madame Marshand valued her place in society with such fervor. Without even venturing forth to the front door, I knew instinctively that she had probably been competing with her sister for years.

I had not given much thought when I worked for the Marshand family about Madame's life before she was married. I would soon be learning more details about the life of privilege which surrounded her as she grew up. I reflected that even before either of them chose their spouses, these two sisters were well established members of the elite class.

Celeste was welcomed with open arms upon our arrival. Her aunt and her cousin greeted her warmly with hugs and smiles that were sincere and warm. I noticed that her aunt took a long look at her, most likely in an effort to see if the pregnancy was discernible yet. I hoped that Celeste did not notice the look as she and her cousin hugged one more time.

Celeste turned toward me then and handled the introductions with grace and poise.

"I am honored to present my chaperone and dear friend, Mademoiselle Natalie. Mademoiselle, this is my mother's sister, my Aunt, Marie and my dear Cousin, Isabel.

"You are most welcome Mademoiselle. Her Aunt replied. "Let us all go inside; you must need to freshen up from your journey."

There was a welcoming feeling in this home that was obvious as soon as I stepped through the doorway. The parlor maid soon led me upstairs to show me the suite of rooms assigned for my use. My scant amount of luggage was soon delivered by one of the servants who laid the larger bag flat at the foot of the bed, so it would be easier to unpack. As I looked around at the space allotted to me, I was overwhelmed at the opulent surroundings. A large, canopied, four-poster bed commanded my attention immediately. The lovely bed coverings displayed a tasteful array of color and designs. At least ten sham covered pillows were artfully arranged at the head. Beautiful floral arrangements were displayed on the nightstand and the dresser. Lovely landscapes decorated the walls which were papered in a luxurious sculpted wallpaper that reminded me of the delft blue and white China stored in Madame Marshand's sideboard.

Most overwhelming of all was the personal bathroom space separated by a door from the bedroom. It contained a built-in vanity apparently designed for a lady's use when applying face creams or arranging her hair. The sink was made of a lustrous marble set into a lovely commode that again reflected the taste of royalty. I had never seen such colorful tiles as those used to decorate the commode and the sink. I blushed when I realized that the bathroom was equipped with a bidet. This was something I had only read about in a book and was not certain how to use.

After unpacking and freshening up, I changed into what I hoped would be a suitable outfit for dinner. I was afraid that I might feel out of place as a guest in this obviously wealthy home.

I stood looking out the window at the abundant grounds surrounding the house and hoped I would have an opportunity to explore my surroundings during the time I was there with Celeste.

Madame Marshand told me quietly before we left that she would join her daughter at her sister's estate as the time grew closer for the child's delivery. She asked that I stay long enough to ensure that Celeste was comfortable and feeling secure before returning to my own obligations in Paris.

Lost in my thoughts, I barely heard the slight knock on the door to my suite.

The door opened quietly as I turned toward it.

Celeste walked the short distance to the window and took me in her embrace.

"My dearest, Natalie." She said. "I most certainly would not have made it here to this safe environment, comforted by my aunt and my other family members without your help and consideration. I want you to know that I am in your debt for the rest of my life, and so is my child."

The lump in my throat prohibited me from speaking, but there really was no need for words.

Celeste had donned a lovely pink dress with ruffles at her throat and wrists. As I pulled back to look her over, I was amazed that she displayed the countenance of the sweet child I had always known and the beautiful woman she was rapidly becoming. Although, the first indication of her condition was slightly visible, it would have been difficult to discern without one's prior knowledge.

Together, we descended the stairs to join the family for what would be my first experience in the massive dining room. There were others seated at the table in addition to Celeste's Aunt Marie and her cousin, Isabel. Once again, Celeste took it upon herself to make sure that I was at ease. She hesitated as she stood alongside the table and said that she would like to make a brief announcement.

"Dear family, to those who have yet to be introduced, let me say that this is my beloved au pair, now friend and guardian, Mademoiselle Natalie. Please extend to her your kindest welcome as she is my dearest friend."

The gentleman at the head of table rose as he introduced himself as Celeste's Uncle

Alejandro Calderon. He then nodded toward a boy of about fourteen, introducing him as his son, Mateo. A young girl looked to be between seven or eight-years-old was squirming in her chair during the entire time, until her father focused on her.

"And this," He said. "Is my precious little lamb, Sofia, who is obviously anxious to meet you and is experiencing great difficulty finding her manners at the moment."

In spite of a reproving glance from her mother and her father's mention of her behavior, the child blurted out her own welcome, saying,

"You are very pretty Mademoiselle Natalie. Are you married?"

A small laugh rippled through all assembled which was curbed by a glance from Senior Calderon.

"Thank you, Sofia. I appreciate your complement." I replied. "In response to your question, no, I am not married, as yet."

The footman pulled out chairs for Celeste and me. As the meal commenced, I began to feel more and more comfortable amidst the conversation and the excellent food.

After dinner, we advanced to the drawing room for tea and patisseries.

Madame played a lovely sonata on the grand piano with an expert touch to the keys.

Isabelle was next to command our attention as she read aloud poetry putting the words into a cadence that the poet would have been delighted to hear.

I was further impressed by the fact that she read poems written in Spanish and French with the same amount of understanding of the words as well as the ability to convey the emotional content.

Afterwards, as she passed around a tray of sweets, Isabel spoke to her cousin.

"My dear, Celeste. I hope you can stay with us for a long time, I have missed you very much. I mentioned to Mama how wonderful it would be if you were able to join us in late December for the Nochevieja Universitaria. It is our annual festival here in Salamanca held at the end of the year. You would enjoy the performances in the Plaza Mayor, and the food is sensational."

"That would be lovely, Isabel." Celeste said. But as she glanced over at me, I had a feeling she was thinking that she would already be a mother by then and most likely occupied with a newborn baby.

As Celeste and I retired to our chambers, Madame assured me that I only need ring the bell on the nightstand if there was anything I might require at any time.

I was more than happy to have some time alone in the plush surroundings of my room. I enjoyed some reading of my own before my eyes started closing in the middle of a sentence. I leaned back into the pillows and fell asleep.

Although I had no reason to feel uncomfortable at the villa, I was anxious to return to Paris. I penned a note to Philippe every day and found that I missed him considerably. Despite his busy work schedule, he did write short notes a couple of times to me, as well.

I received a letter after my first week in Spain in which he pledged his undying love and told me how much he could not wait to hold me in his arms once again. As a postscript to his love note, Philippe wrote that there had been no suspicious activity at the Tower lately, and therefore no need to fear for my father's safety.

I was thankful for his reassurance and assured once again, that this kindhearted and thoughtful man was meant to be my husband.

The household seemed to absorb Celeste and I into its daily routine. We woke to a brisk walk in the garden before breakfast each day. The fresh air and delightful company of her cousin was awaking the teenager in Celeste again. Rarely did I see her stare off in her thoughts anymore. Isabel was a treasure, full of life and cheerfulness and she worked like medicine on Celeste's spirits.

I was comfortable in Señora Calderone's company. There were several afternoons when she invited me to tea, as Celeste and Isabel spent time together. I was made to feel at home with her, as we looked at family pictures, or the many art books that their library offered.

The Señora told me stories of her childhood with her younger sister. They grew up in the Loire Valley on an estate that housed one of the oldest vineyards in France. The family business was extremely successful, and their father was one of the wealthiest men in the district.

I was shown wedding photos from Madame Marshand's wedding as well as those of the Calderone's. Both were lavish affairs, with over twenty attendants and regally dressed guests.

It was interesting to hear some of the history of the family, and I was given a new perspective on the Marshand family, that I might never have known any other way.

Although I should have enjoyed the elegant surroundings and pleasant company of Celeste's relatives, my own life awaited me in Paris, and I want to get back to resume it.

I approached Celeste on a lovely fall afternoon as we sat together in the garden.

"There certainly is a growing chill in the air." I said. "One feels as though the seasons are changing and that winter is only a short time away."

"I agree. It is wonderful to sit out here and observe the autumn foliage on the trees and the blooms of Fall colors in the garden."

"As the calendar pages are being turned, how are you feeling about your approaching confinement?"

"Since we arrived here, I believe I have become more serene than ever. I am no longer anxious about the birth process. I have faith that everything will go well."

It did my heart good to hear those words.

"Are you getting cold out here?"

"I am fine for right now, Mademoiselle. This small blanket is the right weight for my lap and the shawl is doing the rest of the work to keep me warm. Are you comfortable?"

"Yes, but it will only be another half hour before the sun begins to descend and we will have to go indoors. What is your cousin doing this afternoon?"

"She is working with her French tutor and then she has a geography lesson before supper."

"I have noticed that she seems to take an endless list of classes. It is such a privilege to have the quality of education available to the Señor and Señora's children. I have been told that their instructors are the most prestigious in this part of Spain."

"I am sure that must be true. I don't believe that my Uncle would have it any other way."

"Madame mentioned that you turned down the offer of taking some classes yourself during the time you are here."

"I have so much on my mind with the impending birth and what I shall do afterwards. I'm afraid it would be difficult for me to concentrate on learning much of anything during this time."

"I know, dearest." I said. "I want you to stay busy with your reading and needlework as the time draws closer. Sometimes, when we ponder the same thoughts over and over without distraction, it is easy to become depressed."

"You are always concerned for me in some way, Natalie. And, for this I am so grateful."

"I hope that you will not be upset when I say that I will be returning to Paris in a couple of days. Your mother plans to join you in just a few weeks which I am sure will be a comfort to you. But in the meantime, I must return to some personal obligations that I cannot ignore."

"I have known this all along. I just hoped that if we didn't discuss it, it would not happen."

She looked at me, as if her pleading eyes would make me change my mind. I stared into my lap, not wanting to continue the conversation.

At last, Celeste reached for my hand.

"I can be a selfish child sometimes, Natalie. I seem to put myself first most of the time. I am being offered an opportunity to act in a mature fashion by not overreacting to your departure.

I believe that becoming a mother will be a big step in my maturity, and I must confess I am somewhat afraid of taking this step, which is being thrust upon me."

I smiled gently at her. "I think that it would be unnatural if you were not anxious about the impending changes to your life. From my conversations with other women who were expecting to give birth, there is always a certain trepidation of the unknown."

Again, she took my hand in hers.

"Of course, you need to return to Paris. I will be fine. You have a wedding to prepare for, and someone waiting for you there with open arms. I have family here who cares deeply for me, but that doesn't mean that I won't miss you."

We sat there in silence until we encountered the expected chill of the approaching evening. Somberly, we rose and walked toward the house. It was time to change for supper.

I sighed with relief now that the dreaded conversation had taken place. I could now begin to look forward to my train ride back home. As I prepared for the trip, I smiled to myself, thinking about Philippe. I pictured a loving reunion with him. I imagined Madame Fournier's welcoming hug. I was anxious to take a long look at the Eiffel Park and the rest of the City that I missed.

Quarante-neuf

A Blessing

I was swept up into a flurry of activity during the next few weeks that seemed to begin the moment I stepped off the train in Paris. I felt as if I were walking on air now that I could devote myself completely to Philippe and our wedding. The weight of the world fell from my shoulders knowing that Celeste was safe in Spain and soon to be in her mother's care.

I had done my part to ease her transition through the initial stages of her pregnancy and I felt as though I was leaving her in good hands with her aunt's family who cared deeply for her wellbeing. I prayed that Madame Marshand would be kind to her daughter and that she might be capable of some type of motherly compassion for her during this difficult time.

A routine had been established at the villa that accommodated Celeste's presence and I was assured that she felt supported. I hoped that Madame Marshand would respect the reassuring attitude of her sister and allow herself to be moved accordingly.

I was happy to have the opportunity to reflect on my own desires for the future. I only hoped that my dear Philippe did not feel as though I had neglected him. Not very many newly engaged young women, depart for another country within days of accepting their proposal.

Before I began the many preparations for our wedding day, there was something I needed to do. Shortly after I returned from Spain, I rose early one cold December morning. I bundled up in my large coat and gloves and wrapped my head in a scarf, so that only my eyes were uncovered. I sat on the same bench at the Eiffel Park where he had joined me in the past. I stared quietly ahead for several minutes wondering if he would appear.

"I am so happy to see you. This time it was I who was concerned for your safety."

"I needed to be away for a while to help a friend, but I am happy to be back now."

"And Madame Fournier, she is well, also?"

"Yes, Father, she is well. Her hospital visit served as a reminder that she needs to take better care of herself. Something I wish that you might learn."

I believe I saw him briefly smile.

"Did you come to the Eiffel Park for a reason today?"

"Yes. I needed to ask for your blessing."

I paused a moment as I glanced at him. No matter the state of his body, as thin and emaciated as he might appear, his eyes were crystal clear reflections of the purity of his soul.

"Philippe, Madame Fournier's son, has asked me to marry him. We have known each other our entire lives, and now we are more than just friends. I am concerned that once I become a wife, busy running my own household, that I will not have the opportunity to see you and check on your welfare as often. I don't know if I can handle both of those responsibilities."

"What if I promise to move into your home when you are settled, my dear. Would that be helpful? I believe I have come to the place where I am accepting my own mortality. Perhaps I might be content to be taken care of."

"Then, my life would be complete."

"So, one question then. Why do you continue to sit on a bench with an old man, when there is a young man somewhere in Paris who wants to give you his undying love?"

He put his hand on my knee and I grasped it tenderly with my own.

"Your mother will be so happy." He said before he disappeared.

Cinquante

Vows

𝒫HILIPPE and I were married in the small chapel at the Church of St. Francis Xavier. Mere blocks from the bakery, it was the church that Madame Fournier attended regularly. I believe both Philippe and I basked in the glow of her smile throughout the entire ceremony.

Madame invited her friends and neighbors, Monsieur and Madame Dubois and another longtime friend of hers from her school days. I extended an invitation to Chloe, who had been such a marvelous help in the bakery during the months that I was gone. Our only other guest was Edouard Lemaire, a good friend of Philippe's from the architectural firm.

Madame Fournier was eager to point out to those who attended that our marriage took place at the same church were Philippe had been baptized as a baby.

Of course, she baked us the most beautiful and flavorful wedding cake for our small reception at the bakery. We enjoyed a bottle of fine Champagne sent to us by Madame Marshand as a gift.

Her note was sweet. She expressed her heartiest congratulations, saying that although she and Celeste were not able to be present, we would see each other soon, for another celebration of a life that was about to occur.

I do not believe I was ever happier than on the day I made my vows to Philippe. As his gift to me, he made reservations at the prestigious Hotel Lutetia.

"I can't take you on the honeymoon trip that you deserve, my love. I can't afford to spend a significant length of time away from work." He told me. "So, I will spoil you with a stay at a premier hotel, where you will be treated like a queen for three glorious days."

From the moment our carriage arrived, the service was impeccable. It was hard for me to comprehend that I was going to spend the night in this elegant environment that I had heard whispers about all my life.

It was nice being "spoiled." The maid drew me a bubble bath when we arrived in our suite, and I almost burst out laughing, since this was an unexpected ritual that I would never have imagined. But I was happy. I told my new husband that my face hurt from smiling as much as I had that entire day.

We ventured onto the City sidewalks, looking like tourists, window shopping and whispering to each other. Passing pedestrians smiled at us, as if it was obvious, we were young lovers, let loose in a city designed for our personal pleasure. As we walked arm-in-arm, we hardly noticed our surroundings, lost as we were in our whispers of love and promises of more time to be spent by ourselves.

We talked incessantly, making plans, which we were sure would contain only the best of everything. We told each other about dreams we had never shared with anyone before. I believe we were already acknowledging that our vows insured that we could trust each other with all our secrets and hopes, without fear of judgment.

Without planning, we made last minute decisions about where we might stop for a meal or simple snack depending on our hunger now. Philippe consulted menus all along the Boulevard Raspail, making funny faces to indicate whether he approved of the fare.

As I cuddled up to Philippe on our last evening in the hotel, he said something I found remarkable.

"My darling Natalie, you must have been thrilled on our wedding day to see him in the back of the church."

"What? Who are you talking about?"

"Your father, of course. You mean you didn't see him as we were walking toward the door?"

"No. Who else saw him beside you, Philippe?"

"We were the last ones to exit the church door, darling. Remember, our friends were standing on the steps waiting for us to make an appearance. Perhaps the priest saw him but that would be all."

"I am so surprised by this news, Philippe." I said. I am thrilled that he shared that precious day with us, even though he was hidden in the shadows."

It was the final confirmation that this week was the happiest and most blessed of my whole life.

Philippe was still preparing our new house so it was decided that we would stay in my old apartment at the bakery for the time being.

Although he had shown me the plans for the house, I was not allowed to see the physical site. Philippe told me several times that he wanted me to be completely surprised on the day we moved in.

Madame Fournier saw this time as a chance to appreciate her last days in the bakery, since she would be moving also when the house was ready.

It was my dearest hope that my father would also share in our good fortune and rest for the first time in his life.

Philippe explained as he reviewed the architectural drawings with me, that the house was large enough for everyone to have their own space and that our suite of rooms was quite separate from where our parents would spend their time. I suppose that although I craved the privacy that living in our own home would provide, I could not ignore the importance of Philippe's desire for everything to be as perfect as possible. He simply would not cut corners to save time.

He told me that he had dreamed about our lives together for years. He said that he had always hoped that he would court and marry me; become a successful architect; create the perfect home and then take care of me for the rest of his life. How could anyone deny that type of passionate commitment. Besides, I loved him so much that his happiness was now my main concern.

Cinquante et un

Dark Days in the City of Light

PREPARATIONS were taking place for the holiday season. It seemed to me that the Christmas spirit was infectious because people smiled more often and displayed more kindness than usual to one another. Decorations festooned each lamppost and street sign in the city. There was a feeling of magic in the air. It was as though the festive ornaments took on a life of their own and multiplied overnight.

A temporary sculpture was erected on the corner near the bakery that appeared to be large, wrapped Christmas gifts stacked on top of each other. Each "box" was brightly colored and was adorned with ceramic ribbons festooning the works of art.

The City was famous for the Christmas markets that were sprouting up everywhere. There was no gift that could not be found among the offerings at the merchant stalls. Everything from paintings and ornaments to perfumes and Madagascar vanilla were set out on tables for the eager shoppers to peruse. Booths were set up selling mulled cider and hot chocolate to warm up the browsers as they strolled through the carnival-like atmosphere in the streets. Carolers positioned themselves every few blocks adding to the festive air.

Much laughter and gaiety pervaded the Parisian outlook during these days, and as a newly married woman, I relished the thought that the City mirrored my own uplifted spirits.

Philippe and I were crowded in my mother's old room of the upstairs apartment, but we hardly noticed, since we barely took up much space when we were together during those days.

I had not yet heard from Madame Marshand, but I was almost certain that Celeste's due date had come and gone. Of course, I had no personal knowledge of such things, but I did recall several ladies saying over the years that the baby would come when it was ready and going by a calendar date was usually a waste of time.

I was not prepared for the dark emotions that would soon rob us of the holiday joy we had been feeling.

There was a loud knock on the door of the bakery long after closing time.

Philippe responded to the knock since neither Madame nor I ever considered answering the door after dark to an uninvited caller. I sat on the edge of the bed as I waited for Philippe to return.

"Darling." He said, as he joined me again in our chamber. "You must come downstairs with me. It is a matter of some importance."

I had never seen Philippe so pale. He held himself perfectly still with a look of sheer intensity on his face. I put on my robe and followed him quietly as we descended to the shop level. I was certain that that I would soon hear news of my father's death.

Instead, I saw Bernard standing near the bakery counter. He held on the edge of the display case as if he needed it to hold him up.

"My dear Mademoiselle, Natalie." He said. "I am here with great reluctance to tell you of a tragedy that I can hardly speak of."

Philippe led me gently to the closest chair, and stood by me, holding firmly to my hand.

The silence was deafening.

"Mademoiselle, Celeste gave birth yesterday to a healthy baby girl who, I have been told is the mirror image of her mother's beauty."

Bernard sighed so deeply then, that I was startled into holding my breath.

"It is with sincere regret that I must tell you that our beloved Celeste did not survive the birth. I'm told that she was too weak after many hours of labor and that she simply did not have the strength to go on after the child was born. Madame Marshand sent me a telegram. She asked that I come see you in person. We are completely grief stricken."

I felt as if I had fallen through the floor of the bakcry and was now floating in another dimension, apart from the room I was sitting in. I was aware of Bernard's presence. I felt the press of Philippe's hand on mine, but the rest of my body was drifting off somewhere I had never been before. This simply was not possible. Celeste was only nineteen years old. She was healthy and well taken care of during her pregnancy. Bernard must have gotten the story wrong because this was unacceptable.

I didn't realize I had spoken those words aloud.

"No, this is unacceptable, Bernard. Go and get the correct story, and then I will listen to you. Philippe, let us go back to bed."

Philippe raised me up from the chair and held me tightly in his arms as I sobbed and moaned for my darling Celeste.

"They have called the child 'Madeline'" Bernard said, as he rose from the chair.

"Madame Marshand will bring the baby to Paris within the next few weeks. I must get back home, Mademoiselle. Again, my sincere apologies for having to deliver this terrible news and I beg your forgiveness for my harsh presentation telling you of this tragic event."

Philippe took charge. He escorted Bernard to the door, turned the key in the lock and came back to lead me gently up the stairs.

Somehow, we had not disturbed Madame Fournier during Bernard's visit. She remained sleeping in her apartment, which was probably for the best. Philippe whispered to me that he would talk to her in the morning.

I climbed into the bed and assumed the fetal position. I had never felt such sadness. It was as if someone had reached inside my chest and ripped my heart in half.

Philippe did not say a word. He simply wrapped himself around my body and held me as I sobbed all night.

Cinquante-deux

From the Ashes

I could not escape the feeling of overwhelming depression. Philippe and his mother tried to no avail to bring me back to the world of the living, but my thoughts kept returning to Celeste and the unfairness of the hand that had been dealt to her, and to her newborn babe. I was able to function in a normal capacity as far as physically carrying out whatever work I undertook. I participated in conversations, hardly knowing what was being said. I swept the floor and cleared the tables in the bakery, but these were just outward manifestations carved from habit.

My mind was far away, busy recreating memories of moments from the past. Scenes played over and over of a little girl holding my hand as we walked on the sidewalk; a child opening a box that contained the dog she had been longing to own; a young lady proudly displaying her decorated room, after pouring tea for an old friend. It was like living in a cinema audience all day long. The scenes from Celeste's life played out as clearly as if they had been a motion picture recorded for future viewing.

I was unable to release myself from the part of a grieving sister and I knew that the hole in my heart would never heal. Finally, when a courier delivered a note from Madame

Marshand, I knew that the moment of truth had come. She wanted me to come to see her granddaughter. If everything would have gone well, I would have flown to the Marshand home to see the baby, but now I held back in fear.

"Philippe, what if I can't stop crying when I see her? How can I contain myself for the benefit of Madame Marshand?"

"Darling, there is no need for you to contain yourself at all. Madame is aware that you loved her daughter. Why should you try to conceal your feelings?"

"Because I don't want to cause her more suffering by making her aware of mine."

"My darling, Natalie, you must be true to yourself. Madame Marshand knows you well after all these years. You have shared many experiences, most of which involved Celeste. If nothing else, my sweet, you must do this as a favor to the little girl you remember with love."

"Of course, you are right. I just need to summon the courage."

"Would you like me to accompany you?"

I fell into his embrace.

"Oh yes, my dearest Philippe, that would be wonderful. With your support, I know I will be strong. Just be prepared because I will need to lean on you quite heavily."

On Sunday afternoon, we dressed in our best clothes.

Philippe ordered a carriage. He told me it would be easier on my nerves to arrive this way rather than to walk to the Marshand's on what might be rather shaky legs. I gasped when I first saw the black wreath on the door. This was the third time that Madame Marshand had displayed this symbol of mourning. I had a feeling that this time was probably the most difficult of all.

Bernard opened the door for Philippe and me. It was obvious that he had aged during this terrible ordeal. He led the way into the parlor and signaled for us to be seated. Without a word, he closed the door behind him.

Momentarily, the door opened, and I was surprised to see Madame's sister, enter and approach me quietly. I rose and offered her my hand, but she gently took me in her arms.

"How is Madame Marshand?" I asked.

"My sister will be all right. She has been through many trials these last few years so I know she will somehow find the strength; however she is devastated. You might be alarmed when you witness the toll this has taken on her."

"And, the baby, Madeline, how is she?"

"Thank God, the child is easy to care for. She has a pleasant disposition. She cries when she is hungry, but otherwise sleeps quite peacefully."

"I am happy to hear that."

"Senora, allow me to present my husband, Philippe."

"I am so happy to make your acquaintance, Philippe. Natalie spoke of you often during the time she stayed at my villa."

"It is nice to meet you, as well." Philippe said. I could tell that he was uncomfortable. I never expected that his first visit to the Marshand's home would be under these sad conditions.

"Monique will join you shortly. Please sit down and make yourselves comfortable."

Philippe took my hand in his when we were alone again, and I realized how cold my hands had become.

The only sound was the ticking of the grandfather clock.

Philippe rose when the door to the parlor finally opened again.

Madame Marshand had lost a good deal of weight since I last saw her. The thought flashed through my mind that she probably was not eating very much in her grief-stricken state. I hoped that her own health was not suffering as a result.

She nodded toward Philippe and then embraced me in a gentle hug.

"Madame, may I present my husband, Philippe." I said.

"Madame, may I offer my most sincere condolences." He said.

"Thank you, Philippe. I have heard so much about you and wish we could have met under different circumstances. Please sit back down."

"Madame, I have no words to offer at this time of grief, except to say that I am thinking and praying for you."

"Thank you, Natalie. I have a message to impart to you today that is extremely difficult to convey. I would only ask that you let me say everything I need to say, before commenting."

"Of course." I said, as I tightened my fingers around Philippe's.

"When we realized that the birth process was going to be more difficult than planned, Celeste had a moment when she realized what the possible complications might be. The midwife told us that the baby needed to be turned, as it was presenting in the wrong position. Since my daughter was young and healthy, I was not concerned at first. I had heard of these breach presentations often over the years. It is the type of subject that comes up when ladies get together for tea. But my poor Celeste was working so hard to deliver the child and it seemed that her energy was abating. Although we continued wiping her forehead and giving her small sips of water, she was perspiring effusively, and holding on to the bed rail with an amazing amount of strength. And then I noticed the abundance of blood. You will excuse me, Philippe if this conversation seems indelicate. It is important to me that Natalie understands every detail."

Madame hesitated. For a moment, I thought that she had lost the courage to continue. At last, she sighed and looked at the two of us. Her eyes seemed to implore us for an answer as to why the somber events had occurred. After a little while, she went on.

"There was too much blood. I held my daughter's hand, and it was as though I was watching her life slip away. Celeste asked me to come closer. She managed to summon up the energy to whisper the few words that she had to say.

"I will quote her just about verbatim."

"She said, 'My dearest mere, I love you with all of my heart, though I have been so much trouble to you at times."

Tears escaped my eyes as Madame recited this testimony.

"Then she said, 'This baby is going to need a lot of time and attention. My darling mother, you have already played this part, but now the job should go to someone younger. Please ask Natalie and Philippe to raise the child.'"

"As I listened to Celeste, I was deeply hurt at first. How could she ask me to give up the only grandchild I would ever have? But the look on her face was so gentle and childlike, I knew that she was not doing this out of any resentment toward me but rather for the best interests of her baby."

"The midwife was successful at turning the baby in the birth canal, and asked Celeste to push just one more time. Again, there was an overwhelming amount of blood. It was obvious that the circumstances were dire. As Madeline took her first breath, her mother drew her last. The room was full of the sound of the newborn cries echoing in the void left behind by her mother's silence. I held my grandchild in my arms, as I finally let go of my daughter's hand."

Madame sat quietly after she had finished speaking. After a few moments passed, she rang the bell for the butler.

Neither Philippe nor I said a word.

Bernard entered with a tea tray and put it down quietly on the sideboard. He poured a cup for Madame and then one for Philippe and me.

No one had spoken yet.

When the butler left, Madame looked at me.

"I know this is not a decision that can be made in mere minutes, Natalie. If you and Philippe consent to my daughter's last wishes I want, you to be aware of some conditions that I must impose. I must insist on maintaining a presence in Madeline's life. I would like to be included at certain family occasions such as her birthday and perhaps family holiday celebrations. If you find this difficult to agree to, I would ask for some time alone with her during those seasons when I might fashion my own celebrations for, she and I to share."

"One more thing, I would like to mention is that I plan to contribute to her schooling and other financial needs. I don't want either of you to think that I am insulting you, but I am asking that you realize, this child is the only family I have left. It is important to me that I be allowed to share my wealth and social status with her."

"May I speak now?" I asked.

She nodded.

"Madame, of course I will have to discuss this with my husband, as it affects our entire future. I'm sure the deliberations will not take long. I will not want to keep you in the dark, however we have a lot to think about."

"I completely understand and would expect nothing less than your careful consideration. I will await your decision. While you are here, would you like to see Madeline?"

"I was hoping you would ask."

A lovely, canopied crib had been installed in Madame's bedroom, where the sleeping child was napping.

Philippe and I tiptoed to the side of the crib and peered over the side to see the most beautiful infant that I believe I had ever seen. She slept peacefully with her little fingers curled up in fists and a frown on her pretty face. She looked so tiny lying there among the ruffled crib decorations. Pink ribbons tied back the sides of the canopy at each corner and the baby was swaddled in the softest of pink blankets.

As we turned to leave, I took one more look over the side of the crib. I think Madeline knew that I was standing there. Perhaps her mother might have been whispering in her ear, because just then, she smiled at me.

Cinquante-trois

Family

$\mathcal{M}$Y husband and I now faced a decision of such great magnitude. But we faced it knowing that our love for each other was ample enough to share with the child we had been asked to care for. It broke my heart to think that Celeste would not know her daughter and see her grow up, but I believed it was my honor to comply with her dying wish to fulfill her role in Madeline's life.

I knew from the first time I held the child, that I would make sure she was told stories of her mother's childhood, and that I would make her familiar with the many aspects of what made Celeste such a special person. It would be a joy to share my own fond recollections.

So, the three of us became a family. All my fears of motherhood vanished during the first weeks of caring for my new daughter. There were the sleepless nights, and the long days of new parenthood, but I never felt that I was alone. Philippe took up his role of fatherhood with such ease, cradling the baby in his arms as if he had done this many times before.

Often, he would hold her and walk her around the apartment at night, humming a sweet tune and soothing her back to sleep.

If only the role that my own father played in my life would have followed such a smooth rhythm. For our time together was coming to an end.

Cinquante-quatre

Au Revoir

ALTHOUGH everything seemed to be falling into place in my life, the most important piece of the puzzle simply would not fit together. I was to be denied my greatest desire which was to care for the most selfless person I would ever know. And now I come to the most difficult part of the story that must be told. But I am the only one who can reveal the truth of a life surrounded by mystery.

My father still maintained his devotion to keeping an eye on his evil adversary.

I saw him very briefly one early morning at the Eiffel Park, soon after we adopted Madeline.

I told him how happy I was to be married to Philippe. I shared the news with him of Celeste's passing and told him that we would be raising her daughter. And then I said it was time to fulfill the promise that he made to me, allowing me to care for him, at last.

I said that Philippe and I would be moving to our new home and that he should no longer continue to feel responsible for staying at the Tower. It was time for him to come live with us and to let me care of him.

Then, I sat in silence as I waited for him to speak.

"There is not much left of the Eiffel Spirit." He said.

"Father, you have been through so much already. The Masked One is a formidable villain who seems to delight in your slow destruction."

"My energy has waned, Mon Ami. Four decades of being the watchdog of the Eiffel Park has left a mere shadow of a man."

"Then, let me take you with me and care for you."

"I wish that could be, but I must hold on until my last breath. There is no trusting the jealous creature who delights in the destruction of the happiness of others. I have prevented the demise of two young girls in just these past few weeks."

"Then, he must be eradicated, so you can be released."

He smiled and laid a hand on mine.

"If it were just that easy. No, he will wait until you and I are gone. We are the ones that he hates, and we will always be a target of his vengeance. Whenever he encounters us, he contemplates his lost love, and the anger and hatred flourishes."

My heart ached as I watched his shallow breathing and felt his cold hand on mine. How much longer could the Eiffel Spirit survive? He simply would not give in.

And then there was that fateful night shortly after I had spoken with him.

Madeline and I stayed overnight with Madame Fournier. I helped her to pack her belongings, mere days before we were to move into our new home. I don't know if I heard the sirens first . . . or was it that evil, cackling laugh that shocked my very soul.

But I knew immediately that the events of many other moments, years and decades had led to this night which would seal my father's fate.

Madame Fournier was wrapping her robe around her when I met her downstairs.

"Madeline is still asleep upstairs." I told her. "Please carry her to your apartment and wait for me there. I want to spare her the pain of what we might witness tonight."

Without a coat and without waiting for a response from Madame Fournier, I ran to the Eiffel Park.

I saw him slumped over on the bench we had recently occupied. I felt the icy cold breeze as the cape swept past me and then I heard the voice of Joaquin Picard.

"It looks as though fate will deal the final blow to this tired old specimen, called the Spirit. It is quite humorous. I have been robbed of the pleasure of taking his life, but as I look at him now, I see there wasn't much left of that for the taking."

He let out another hideous burst of laughter and then seemed to fly up the lattice work of the Tower.

I managed to put my father's arm around my neck and lift him gently from the bench. I knew that he was emaciated, but even so, I was shocked when I realized how little he weighed. It was like picking up a rag doll. He was barely holding on to me, yet I was able to get him back to the bakery and up the stairs without much exertion on my part.

The events of that night, as my father surrendered to his final destiny are ingrained in my heart. My only consolation was knowing that he and my mother were together again and that I was with him when he drew his last breath.

Although, the Eiffel Spirit was no more, I was certain that the Masked One was still nursing his evil desires and I awaited news of his next barrage of destruction on more innocent victims.

Cinquante-cinq

The Red Mask

$\mathcal{M}$ADELINE is a carefree and happy soul. She laughs and dances with such instinctive joie de vie and has blessed our lives every day. She is almost five years old now and reminds me so much of her mother sometimes that it hurts. She has the same sweet disposition and takes so much joy in making Philippe and I smile. We have already bought her a small dog, who we named, 'Ami.' Madeline cannot get to sleep at night without her precious puppy next to her.

Her mind is sharp, and she learns quickly, so much like Celeste. Madame Marshand visits us occasionally, and I bring Madeline to the Marshand residence over the holidays. Last Christmas, I allowed her to stay overnight. Madame must have thanked me four or five times, saying it made her so happy to share the holiday with her granddaughter.

Madame sends gifts quite often. Recently, I asked Philippe if he thought we should speak to her about the overabundance of presents, but he said that I should just accept them graciously.

"As long as we teach our daughter to be appreciative, there is no reason to put a halt to her grandmother's generosity." He told me. He said that it was her only way to express her love.

Madame Fournier also dotes on Madeline with nothing short of devotion. Our daughter is blessed with two loving grandmothers and parents who adore her.

Chloe became Madame's young apprentice working all day beginning when I was in Spain and continuing when I returned and was preparing for my wedding. Chloe was eager to learn the secrets of the bakery's success and was already familiar with most of the clientele.

Philippe convinced his mother to sell the bakery and move in with us when our new home was finally ready. The timing was perfect because Chloe was about to be married and she and her new husband expressed an interest in buying the bakery. They live upstairs in my old apartment. Downstairs they converted the space that used to be Madame Fournier's private apartment extending the seating area for the bakery customers.

I kept my promise to my mother-in-law to escort her back to her neighborhood periodically. Madeline has always enjoyed taking her grandmother's hand while she visited with her old friends and neighbors.

Madame enjoys a special delight in having the child with her. She seems delighted to show her off. I believe that Madeline gives her life meaning during her older years.

When we lived upstairs and Madeline was a baby, she woke to the scent of fresh baked bread. I think that she may have retained a sensory memory of that time which is familiar and comforting.

On this afternoon, I sat with my cappuccino waiting for Madame and my daughter to return from their visits with the neighbors. Surrounded by the familiar sounds of customers coming and going and the delightful scents of fresh baked pastries, I found the familiar setting to be quite soothing. So many memories were centered here in this boulangerie, I was caught up in a daydream as scenes from the past played back.

Philippe worked late at the office some evenings when a deadline loomed. His ambitions and talents had been rewarded with success and recognition in his field. As his wife, I was pleased at his satisfaction when he told me about a completed project. I enjoyed the delight in his eyes when a new and challenging assignment came his way.

He was aware that I accompanied his mother and Madeline to the old neighborhood for the afternoon. It was to be a day for recollection and pleasant visits. No one expected anything eventful to occur.

The bakery was extremely busy which was a tribute to the talents of Chloe and her husband. Both were willing to work hard for its success. Chloe had paid close attention to Madame Fournier when learning how to bake the delicacies for which she was famous.

Her young husband, Etienne, was quite handsome with an ingratiating smile and demeanor. I was certain that some of the ladies from the outlying areas went to the extra effort of patronizing this boulangerie, just so they could be blessed by one of Etienne's smiles.

Philippe planned to come by the bakery in the afternoon to escort his family home in time for dinner. I looked forward to seeing him as the time for our rendezvous approached.

I hoped for a quiet moment with him to tell him about Madeline's new brother or sister, who had just barely become a presence within me. I anticipated a surprised and excited reaction.

I looked up from my book as Madame Fournier arrived and walked toward the table where I was sitting. I could tell that the day had been a success as far as the time she had spent with friends. She appeared to be happy and refreshed.

As she drew near, she acquired a quizzical expression.

"Where is Madeline going, Natalie?" She asked. "Is someone going outside with her?"

"Where did you see her?" I asked.

"A moment ago, she was wearing a cape of some sort. She passed me as she ran through the bakery door."

Only moments before, Chloe had asked if it would be all right if she took Madeline upstairs to read her a story.

"Chloe." I yelled, as I jumped up from my seat. "Did you tell my daughter that she could run outside?"

"Ladies, I hope you didn't mind." Chloe said, looking at me and Madame Fournier. "I said that I would meet her at the Eiffel Park as soon as I found my scarf."

"What is Madeline wearing?" Madame Fournier asked.

"I found that red cape upstairs, when we moved into the apartment." Chloe answered.

"It appears to be the one I had as a child." I said.

And then, I stood very still. As if in a trance, I pictured my daughter, spinning there before the Tower . . . I was aware that she was feeling like a bird with its red wings spread, taking flight in sheer abandonment.

I rushed from the bakery with Madame Fournier and Chloe at my heels.

Cinquante-six

Resurgence

*H*IS laugh was louder than ever. For blocks in each direction people were mesmerized by the sound. The evil cackle rang through the streets, while a child expressed her sheer happiness in a carefree dance.

"At last, I will have my revenge." A loud voice echoed through the stillness of the twilight.

I was consumed with fear and my blood ran cold. The meaning of his message pierced my heart, as I moved frantically toward the tower. At that moment, the essence of the Eiffel Spirit was resurrected! It pervaded the atmosphere around the entire park, and several blocks in all directions.

The door to an architectural firm was flung open with a great amount of strength. And then, a man was seen running through the streets of Paris, approaching the Eiffel Park at lightning speed.

Although breathing heavily, he continued to run. He was determined to save someone he loved. It was now his turn to assume my father's identity, eliminating the evil desires of the Masked One.

Joaquin Picard's lifelong hatred and profound disrespect for life was finally on the line.

As he neared the Tower, the young man caught a glimpse of what looked to be a bright red figure moving to its own rhythm on the expansive lawn of the Eiffel Park.

Then he heard the high-pitched giggle of child-like laughter and recognized the sound, at once. The dancing figure was the child of his heart.

At that moment, the evil cackle filled the air once again with dread.

With a rush of adrenaline, fueled by the lingering inspiration of the Eiffel Spirit, the man ran again until he reached the foot of the Tower.

Drawing on a source of inner strength, he inserted one foot into the latticework on the filigreed leg of the iconic structure. Each opening in the elegant design became another rung in his rapid climb until at last he spied the source of the evil laugh. Unafraid, he remained steady until he reached the first level of the Tower and stood face to face with the masked villain.

In one swift glance he looked down to see his precious child, still gleefully dancing to a song only she could hear. What looked to him to be widespread red wings encircle her movements as she stayed enraptured in the joy of the moment. In that same split second, he scanned the lawn to see someone running toward the child. He knew at once that it was the woman he loves.

I ran out of breath, and lost momentum as I approached Madeline. I was only living for the moment I could encircle her in my arms. Now, the man turned his attention to the villain who is poised to swoop down and deliver a deadly blow.

With a spurt of energy that he called up from a source deep inside his soul, Philippe yelled, "This is no longer your Tower. You will not rule henceforth fueled by your raw and untamed jealousy. No longer will you inflict fear on this city, and you will not harm those I love."

Lunging forward, he delivered one enormous push, strengthened by his devotion to his family. On the lawn below, we were mesmerized awaiting the outcome.

In the same moment that I anticipated the demise of the Masked One, I prayed for the safety of our protector.

Finally, I encircled Madeline in an embrace and we both hold our breath.

As the reign of terror ended in that split second, it seemed that the entire world sighed with relief.

And then, Philippe, joined us on the lawn beneath the linden trees.

Breathing heavily and looking very pale, he embraced my daughter and me, turning us away from a view of the shattered remains staining the lawn of the park.

Love and devotion finally conquered tyranny and fear. The Eiffel Spirit was vindicated.

Thoughts of my father sometimes fill me with sadness. I wish I could erase the years of mistrust and doubt that were spread though the gossip of what was purported to be his exploits.

I will go forth defending him to those I love because it is important that they know the truth.

I want to be sure they understood why he lived the life that he did.

I will love him until the day I die.

Rest in Peace Eiffel Spirit. You will never be forgotten.

FIN

About the Author

An avid reader since her childhood in New York, Anita Robertson has always cherished the delight of a well-told story. Raised in a home where poetry was read at the Sunday dinner table, she wrote stories and poetry at a young age and has published prize winning poems over the years. Ms. Robertson is a life-long devoted fan of the Los Angeles Dodgers. She considers traveling as one of the most rewarding experiences of her life, having been to London, Dublin, Glasgow, Lisbon and most notably Paris, which she has visited several times. The Eiffel Tower became the inspiration for the Eiffel Spirit as its imposing presence worked on the author's imagination. Ms. Robertson has four children and seven grandchildren and currently lives in Eastvale, California.

www.ingramcontent.com/pod-product-compliance
Lightning Source LLC
Chambersburg PA
CBHW051230260626
47162CB00002B/350